Praise for
Nancy Naigle

"*The Shell Collector* is a beautiful story full of love, loss, and second chances. A collection of vivid characters, an inspiring setting, and heart-held hope for a better tomorrow."
—DEBBIE MACOMBER,
#1 *New York Times* bestselling author

"As an avid shell seeker, I enjoyed *The Shell Collector*—a tale of surprises deposited among the tides, with its underlying message of finding just the shells we are meant to discover. A tender story of faith, love, and friendship that will warm the hearts of beachgoers and lovers of the sea."
—LISA WINGATE, #1 *New York Times* bestselling author
of *Before We Were Yours* and *The Book of Lost Friends*

"A touching story about love, loss, and healing, *The Shell Collector* gives you all the feels. I enjoyed spending time at the beach collecting seashells—and pondering the encouraging messages inside them—right along with the characters. Don't miss this uplifting, faith-affirming read!"
—BRENDA NOVAK, *New York Times* bestselling author

"*The Shell Collector* is a beautiful, emotional story about the glorious sunrise that can come after a dark night, about surviving loss and finding hope and joy again. Amanda, Maeve, and the entire cast   then
heal it all over again. I loved
—RAEANNE THAYNE, *New*

"Set in a scenic beach town, *The Shell Collector* has the quaint feel of small-town living that brings with it both nostalgia and appreciation of nature and the sea. . . . A pleasant story of friendship, family, and life after loss that will be appreciated by fans of the Christian overtones of Karen Kingsbury and the beachy settings of Mary Kay Andrews."

—*Booklist*

"Readers looking for a heartwarming holiday story will enjoy *A Heartfelt Christmas Promise*, set in a vibrant small town populated by lovable people, gorgeous horses, and a very cute puppy."

—*Booklist*

"Libraries looking for holiday romances that are sweet rather than passionate will want to snag *Christmas Angels* for their collections."

—*Library Journal*

"Another superbly crafted and thoroughly entertaining novel by a master of narrative-driven storytelling, Nancy Naigle's *Christmas Angels* is certain to be an immediate and enduringly popular addition to community library collections."

—*Midwest Book Review*

"Naigle's wonderfully heartwarming *Hope at Christmas* will appeal to romance and women's fiction readers alike."

—*Library Journal*

"Bright with abundant holiday cheer and good-hearted community members, and, like a dash of HGTV with a large dose of Hallmark, *Christmas Angels* is delightfully entertaining."

—Booklist

"*The Shell Collector* gives voice to the profound truth of grieving and learning to come alive again. Nancy Naigle beautifully shows how love can come in so many different forms, as long as you're open to the unexpected miracles life has to offer. In her own words, "Life is rarely predictable if we're doing it right."

—ERIN CAHILL, actress

Books by Nancy Naigle

Adams Grove Novels

Sweet Tea and Secrets

Out of Focus

Wedding Cake and Big Mistakes

Pecan Pie and Deadly Lies

Mint Juleps and Justice

Barbecue and Bad News

Boot Creek Series

Life After Perfect

Every Yesterday

Until Tomorrow

Seasoned Southern Sleuths Cozy Mystery

In for a Penny

Collard Greens and Catfishing

Deviled Eggs and Deception

Fried Pickles and a Funeral

Wedding Mints and Witnesses

Christmas Cookies and a Confession

Sweet Tea and Second Chances

Stand-Alone Titles

Sand Dollar Cove

inkBLOT

Recipe for Romance

The Secret Ingredient

The Shell Collector

Christmas Novels

Christmas Joy

Hope at Christmas

The Christmas Shop

Christmas in Evergreen

Christmas in Evergreen: Letters to Santa

Christmas in Evergreen: Tidings of Joy

Christmas Angels

Mission: Merry Christmas

A Heartfelt Christmas Promise

What Remains True

What Remains True

A Novel

NANCY NAIGLE

WATERBROOK

WHAT REMAINS TRUE

This is a work of fiction. Names, characters, places, and
incidents are the products of the author's imagination
or are used fictitiously. Any resemblance to actual events, locales,
or persons, living or dead, is entirely coincidental.

Published in the United States by WaterBrook,
an imprint of Random House,
a division of Penguin Random House LLC.

WATERBROOK® and its deer colophon are registered trademarks
of Penguin Random House LLC.

LIBRARY OF CONGRESS CATALOGING-IN-PUBLICATION DATA
Names: Naigle, Nancy, author.
Title: What remains true: a novel / Nancy Naigle.
Description: First edition. | [Colorado Springs] : WaterBrook, 2022.
Identifiers: LCCN 2021032861 | ISBN 9780593193617 (paperback) |
ISBN 9780593193624 (ebook)
Classification: LCC PS3614.A545 W53 2022 | DDC 813/.6—dc23
LC record available at https://lccn.loc.gov/2021032861

Printed in the United States of America on acid-free paper

waterbrookmultnomah.com

1st Printing

First Edition

Interior book design by Virginia Norey.

Title page art from an original photograph by
FreeImages.com / Custom0305

It's easy to get caught up in this fast-paced world, juggling priorities and multitasking, only to wake up one day and realize you've forgotten to allow time to think, rest, respond, and renew.

Embrace this day, and make it your goal to make each one memorable. Say yes to new opportunities.

What Remains True

1

Merry Anna Foster loved spring for its promise of new beginnings, and this year she needed one desperately. She inhaled the fresh mountain air. Where else, aside from Antler Creek, could you work in a store that had a screen door for taking advantage of beautiful days like this? It was just one more reason she loved living and working in this small town. It had turned out to be a good first step in her new beginning.

Across the way, a woman held two sets of sheets and an embroidered kitchen towel in one arm. In the other, she cradled two candles, while three quilt-block ornaments hung from her widespread fingertips as if she dared the porcelain tiles to clink together.

"Let me help you with that." Merry Anna raced to her side.

"I've got it. I should've picked up a basket, but honestly, I had no intention of buying anything." She piled her treasures on the counter. "I could absolutely live in this store."

Merry Anna had felt the same way the first day she'd happened upon Hardy House Fine Linens and Gifts. She rounded the counter and pulled the generous stack of items toward the register. "I know what you mean. A couple of months ago, I was passing through town, just like you, only that day there was a Help Wanted sign in the window." The antique register clicked and dinged with each manual entry. It was beautiful but a real beast on her nails. "And here I am."

"You just stayed?" The woman's eyes widened with a look that easily translated to *Are you crazy?* even without the finger twirl at the side of her head.

"I did." And maybe it had been crazy, but the happiness in her heart meant more to her than a stranger's opinion. "I'd just meant to stop for gas and a quick lunch," Merry Anna explained. "Then I saw this place and peeked in. The rest is history. I'd never done something like that. No plan whatsoever, but I'll tell you . . ." She leaned in. "I've never been happier in my entire life."

"Then it wasn't crazy at all. Good for you. Some things are just meant to be."

"I suppose so." Merry Anna folded each item in patterned tissue paper, then tucked the bundle gingerly into a bag with the Hardy House logo on the front. She held up one of the hand-painted tile ornaments on display at the register. "I didn't even know what a barn quilt was when I stopped in. Aren't these great?"

"Yes. I bought a different one for each of my girlfriends. They are so unique and beautiful in their own way, and I love the personal story about the location of each one that's written on the cards. I didn't have time to take the barn-quilt tour today, but I plan to bring a few friends and make a day of it soon. I figure I'll use those ornaments as the invitations."

"That's a fantastic idea." Merry Anna picked up a stack of shiny brochures. "I'll tuck these in your bag too. They have all the information you need about the tour." Often she dreamed of moving out of her rental and into a home with her own barn quilt, but she kept that to herself. There was a lot she kept to herself these days. It was necessary to do so when she'd first arrived, but now that she'd been here a while and gotten to know folks, it was harder.

The customer handed over her credit card. Merry Anna finished the transaction and walked around the counter with the pretty bags. "Here you go." Leading the customer to the front door, she said, "If you haven't eaten, the Creekside Café is a real treat. Tell Maizey we sent you over, and she'll give you the locals discount."

"Well, thank you." The woman's smile warmed all the way to her twinkling blue eyes. "I love this place."

Me too. "You have a wonderful day. I hope you'll come back and see us." And she wasn't just saying that. Sure, after years of retail, she knew what to do, but doing it and meaning it were two different things.

"Count on it," the woman said. "My friends are going to love this store too."

Merry Anna waved, holding the white screen door so that it wouldn't slap against the frame. Just as the woman stepped off the curb and loaded her loot into the trunk of her car, Merry Anna's boss, Krissy, walked out of the coffee shop next door with a cup in each hand.

She raced over with a grin on her face, leaned in toward Merry Anna, and whispered, "You are very good for my business." After handing her one of the cups, she slipped by Merry Anna and walked inside. "I don't know what I did to deserve to have you show up out of the blue, but I sure am thankful for it."

Merry Anna made her way to the long white glass counter. "Works both ways."

"I bought you a tea."

Merry Anna twisted the blue cup in her hand. "Thank you.

You didn't have to do that." She lifted the hot tea to her lips. "Oh, it's my favorite."

"Which is why I *did* have to do it."

"Thanks." From the moment they met right there in that store, it had been as though they'd known each other forever. Krissy had just left her teaching job back in Hilton Head to try to make her dream come true of having an upscale shop on that Main Street in the town where she grew up. Merry Anna was on her own new journey. Entirely different circumstances, but they were both sort of settling in at the same time, which drew them closer.

Merry Anna sipped her tea as she straightened and restocked the hand-painted replica tiles of the barn quilts associated with the county's barn-quilt tour.

Krissy was sort of a celebrity in this region for all the full-size barn quilts she'd been commissioned to paint. She'd done the small porcelain tiles on a whim one afternoon, and they'd brought in steady revenue for the store ever since.

"Are Matt and Liz coming tonight to help paint more of these?" Merry Anna asked. She'd met Krissy's brother, Matt, the first week she moved here. He and Liz were the perfect couple. She wouldn't be surprised if there'd be wedding bells in their future.

"Oh, I meant to tell you. They're preparing for the Spring Fling. It's a huge deal, and they host it every year. They're going to help, but we're taking all the supplies to their place to work on them. Matt's going to cook. I hope you don't mind."

"Mind? For a home-cooked meal, you couldn't keep me away. Besides, I've been dying to see Angels Rest." The inn on the hill was the talk of the town, and Merry Anna hadn't come up with a good way, short of paying to stay a night or two, to get up there to check it out. She had been gushing over the handiwork Matt did around the store when Krissy told her about his house and all the things he'd done for Angels Rest. Plus, Matt and Liz were such a sweet couple that it was enough to keep a gal's hopes up that there might be everlasting love out there for real someday.

Krissy helped the next customer who walked in pick out a wedding gift. Hardy House wasn't huge; it was just one of the narrow brick two-story buildings nestled in the middle of the main block between Java Nice Day Coffee Shop and Hoppers Fly Fishing Outfitters. Every building on the street had its own personality. Hardy House, all white with gold accents, stood out from the other buildings, which dressed their awnings and shutters in shades of red, green, and blue that looked just right against the mountain backdrop.

The trees were so green with new growth that it looked as though someone had tossed fake Easter-basket grass in the branches, and flowers spilled out over the edges of the planters that lined Main Street. Everything was in full bloom, and it was the prettiest thing she'd ever seen in her life. Sometimes she couldn't believe she'd been so lucky to have come across this town, where she could soak up the peaceful beauty every single day.

For so many years all she'd done was work. She'd missed this kind of stuff, and for what?

The mailman, an older, white-haired man, came in and placed a stack of envelopes on the counter. "Having a good day?"

"Yes sir, I am. I hope you are too."

"Always a delight to see your smile." He turned and waved his hand in the air as he departed.

He was always saying something charming. Sweet old man.

She tucked the mail in the slot next to the register, then walked over to greet the next customer at the door.

"Welcome to Hardy House." Merry Anna handed her a small white basket. "Let me know if I can help you with anything."

She clutched the basket. "It won't fit in here, but that beautiful barn quilt caught my eye." She pointed to a large, colorful square board painted to look like a quilt square. Krissy had hung that one there just yesterday. "How much is it?"

"That's a thirty-six-inch. The artist only does one-of-a-kind barn quilts. That one is two hundred dollars. She does custom work too." One customer told Merry Anna that they'd paid more than three hundred for the one they'd ordered online, and it wasn't even custom. These were a bargain. "It's the same price if you order a custom one. Might as well get exactly what you want, right?"

"I've got to have one, but I wouldn't know where to begin on a custom design. And this one is just like the quilt my grandmother had on the bed when I was growing up."

"The Carpenter's Wheel," Merry Anna said with confidence, although until yesterday she'd never heard the term. "The colors on this one, turquoise and taupe, are so eye-catching and up to date. Let me introduce you to the artist." Merry Anna lifted her hand to get Krissy's attention, but she was already headed their way.

"Someone mention me?" She stuck her hand out. "Hi, I'm Krissy. So, you think you might want a barn quilt of your own? That's so exciting!"

Merry Anna left the two of them to talk and create. It had been a four-foot yellow barn quilt that had initially caught her eye in the Hardy House display window the day she'd happened into town. Only, truth be told, she'd thought it was a carrom board at the time. She wondered if her grandmother still had that old thing in her attic. It was quite obviously not a carrom board when she saw it up close, but she was thankful for the memory. Plus, when she'd admitted the faux pas to Krissy, they'd gotten a good laugh out of it—and her first lesson in barn-quilt history.

And from there, things just kept falling into place. Merry Anna had talked herself right out of heading to South Carolina. It wasn't until after her divorce from Kevin and then being here in this town that she'd realized that all she ever did was focus on work. It had always been her priority. Being part of a family business, she'd been pulled in as a teenager, and it had taken over her whole life. When Kevin asked her who she was without that job, she didn't have an answer.

It had been six months after the papers were signed when he'd called complaining about the "pittance," as he'd referred to it, that she'd agreed to for alimony. She'd been right across the street filling up her gas tank when he called. She'd made a deal with him on the spot that for three months, she'd try to live on the exact same amount she was giving him. If she could do it, then he needed to leave her alone and never call her again. If she struggled, however, then she'd go back and adjust the amount. Fair was fair. And so she was living on what seemed like a reasonable amount of money, and if he wanted more, then he could get a real job for once.

And that's how she'd ended up in Antler Creek that day, taken the job at Hardy House, and accidentally found a whole new rhythm to her life.

She'd been planning to use the leave of absence from the family business, the Supply Cabinet, to figure out what she really wanted out of her life besides work. The national office-supply chain had taken over her life somewhere along the way, and she hadn't even noticed.

Antler Creek, where she didn't know a soul, had turned out to be the perfect place. No one knew anything about her financial status, her career, or *her*—and that was liberating. No one had any expectations of her for the first time in her life.

At the end of the day, Merry Anna counted out the cash drawer and balanced the sales tickets. The task would take way less time if they used a new register that automatically summed the daily sales, but the antique one was such a conversation piece. The machine drove her absolutely nuts in the beginning, but now using it was a great way to wind down the day. She especially loved it when they beat their forecasted sales, as they had today. *Sometimes the old-fashioned way is good enough.*

She snickered at that thought. Being COO of the Supply Cabinet chain had been something her family had groomed her for from a very young age, and she'd loved it—or at least she thought she had. Merry Anna was known for automation and streamlining processes, so keeping quiet with suggestions for the Hardy House hadn't been easy. *"Time is money,"* she'd been known to say. She rolled her eyes, embarrassed at some of her behavior now that she'd been away a little while. She'd rarely listened to pushback from team members on new processes, accusing them of just not wanting to adapt to change. How many of those complaints might have been legit feedback? If she ever went back to headquarters, she would do things differently.

She put everything away and dropped the deposit in the safe. Krissy would take it to the bank at the end of the week.

Time to get home to the bunkhouse. Her mom and dad would die if they saw where she was living, and Kevin would accuse her of lying about living there, because it was a far cry from the home they'd lived in together. As modest as it was, though, she found it quite charming. The little house on the hill used to be owned by the guy who lived on the horse farm next to it. It was where his guests and ranch hands would stay. He sold it to Krissy, and when she heard that Merry Anna needed a place to stay, she decided to let her rent the place rather than renovating and flipping it as she'd planned.

She stepped outside and locked the front door of Hardy House to leave, then pressed the screen door tight until it latched.

Looking back at the window displays they'd worked on today, she found delight in how crisp and lush they looked. They'd look even prettier once the sun went down and you could see the twinkle lights. That wouldn't be for a while yet. The days were starting to noticeably last longer.

Traffic on Main Street still slowed after five, though.

She walked down the sidewalk, enjoying the softer sounds as the town quieted and families finished their days. She could picture parents preparing meals while kids did their homework and wished away those last couple of weeks before school was out for the summer.

Her cell phone jingled, something she was beginning to really enjoy. She'd left her business phone on her desk when she started her leave and picked up a new one. Only a few close friends and her parents had this number. "Hello?"

"Hi, honey. It's Mom. I've got you-know-who here with me."

Mom was clearly on speaker, a habit that drove Merry Anna nuts. "You can say his name, Mom. Hi, Kevin."

"Hi, Merry Anna. I'm already out of money for the month. How about you?"

"It's barely the middle of the month, and by my budget, I should still have forty-eight dollars left over at the end," Merry Anna said.

"Don't spend it all in one place," Kevin said with that snarky laugh of his.

"Look, I don't mind helping you get on your feet, but, Kevin, you have to work if you want to live the lifestyle we used to have together." The wager wasn't over yet, but she didn't see any problem with living modestly. "I have to tell you, living on this much money isn't half bad." She smiled as she walked. "In fact, it's pretty darn good. It's going to be very hard to leave this place."

"Seriously?" Kevin's voice rose, the way it did when she said something he didn't agree with.

"Yes. I really mean it."

"You're insane," he sputtered.

Mom said, "Be nice, Kevin." She reprimanded him as though he were one of her own kids, and probably it seemed that way, since he and Merry Anna had met in the first grade.

"Living on twelve hundred fifty dollars a month can be done." *And I've never been happier.* She placed her hand against her heart. *I really am.*

"A deal is a deal, and it's not over. I'm also not convinced, although you do sound different. Calmer. I don't know, just different."

"I *feel* different, Kevin." She waved to George, the owner of the hardware store. He'd been in just the other day to buy his wife a new apron for her birthday. Such a sweet man. "I'm trying new things. Listening. Discovering."

"That doesn't sound like you." Kevin cleared his throat. "I've got to ask. Is there someone else?"

Did he really just ask that? Even if there were, at least she'd waited until after the divorce, unlike him, who'd broken the cardinal rule while married. But she wasn't going to go there. What had needed to be said had already been said about a hundred times. Can't change it. "No, just me, but that's okay too."

"I guess we'll see how next month goes. You wouldn't lie to me about your spending to make your point, would you?"

"No, I wouldn't. Thanks for being the mediator, Mom."

"Anything for you, my darling. Don't be a stranger. I miss you, and the business needs you."

"The business is fine, but I miss you too." Merry Anna strolled down Main Street. Going home was so much easier since most of it was downhill. But the driveway to her house was a steep uphill climb. Too bad she hadn't been able to rent the big old manor house at the foot of the hill. Someone had bought it just a few weeks ago. It needed some TLC, but it could be a stunning home again with some work.

I feel as though a little TLC could transform me too. But the thought of another man in her life left her a little numb. *Maybe I should get a puppy.*

The hike up the hill was a better workout than a run on the treadmill she'd so faithfully used every morning back at home. She was even a little winded. When she entered the bunkhouse, she noticed that the room air conditioner had kept the place comfortable despite the pounding sun today, but this evening it was nice enough to open a few windows. She flipped the switch, and the unit rumbled to a stop.

She opened a window on each side of the bunkhouse to get

a cross breeze. When Krissy had said she owned a bunkhouse she could let her rent, Merry Anna had no idea that it was a real, cowboys-had-been-hanging-their-hats-there bunkhouse. Chaps with long leather fringes, some in bright colors, still hung across the wall about ten feet in the air. Rodeo numbers had been stapled to one wall. Lots of them, from all over— Texas, Wyoming, Oklahoma, Arizona, and the East Coast too. She wondered how many people had contributed them.

It was a man's world, with the galvanized roofing panels as wainscoting and the big woodstove, but she'd girlied it up a little over the past few weeks. The feminine stuff in Krissy's store was so hard to resist. Merry Anna had added soft pinks, yellows, and oranges, with flowers, throw pillows, towels, and an awesome barn quilt that Krissy had surprised her with just last week.

She grabbed a bottle of water from the fridge and walked outside to sit on the porch swing. The patinaed chain creaked, but she didn't mind. It was just one more item to add to her list of things she'd never done before. Who knew saying yes to new opportunities could bring so much unexpected joy?

I wish this could last forever.

2

Adam Locklear pushed a hand truck loaded with cattle feed out to the loading dock and dropped it with a thud. Every Thursday, like clockwork, Old Man Jones showed up to pick up feed. Adam owned Locklear Feed & Seed, yet he usually left the details to the manager he hired and the staff, but Jones had been a friend of his grandfather's, and that meant he deserved special treatment. So whenever Adam was in town on a Thursday, he made sure he was there on the dock when Old Man Jones arrived.

The two-tone-brown 1984 Ford truck swung into the lot and backed up to the loading dock. Every time Adam saw that truck, it reminded him of Grandpa, only his had been the F250 XLT in tan and maroon. He missed that old truck . . . and Grandpa.

"How are you this morning?" Adam called out.

Jones slid out of the cab, his right leg dragging a bit as he walked around the side of the truck. He laid his arm against the bed rail. "Doing okay. Can't complain. No one'll listen."

"I'll listen. Got your order right here. Start talking while I load." Adam stepped from the dock into the bed of the pickup, lofting the fifty-pound sacks into a stack.

"There was a day when I could sling those around like they

were a sack of burgers too," Jones said, nudging his ball cap back as he watched.

"Well, you just keep selling me that good homegrown beef, and I'll keep slinging these sacks for you."

Jones tugged his hat back down and shrugged. "That I can still do. How's it going around here?"

Adam shrugged. "Good. Keeping the lights on."

Jones nodded, but that was not what he was really asking about, and Adam knew it.

"Heard you placed first out in Texas a few weeks ago," Jones said.

"Yes sir." Adam stacked another bag of feed. Jones knew that Adam's folks didn't like him rodeoing. They'd much rather he settle down and just run the store, get married, and have a family, but Jones lived it. He understood. "I'm having the best year of my life." Adam jumped out of the truck to the ground. "If I keep my head right, I'll make the finals this year."

"Your dream." Jones looked him level in the eye. "You be careful." Jones patted his leg and grimaced. "You're going to feel every one of those buckoffs when you're old and gray like me. It ain't for sissies."

"No sir. I know it, but finally everything is really going my way. The rides. Heading for the finals in Vegas." He crossed his fingers. "And I've sold off the bunkhouse and the manor house to buy in with a stock contractor. If I can win this thing, my name will mean something, and I can shift to the livestock side of things."

"Where it don't hurt so bad," Jones added, finishing his sentence.

"Got that right. Won't be as much fun either, but if I can go out on a high note, it would be good timing."

"Yeah, well, you and I can say that. Most folks just think we're crazy." He twisted his wrist, rubbing it with his other hand. Probably an old rodeo injury. "Don't end up old and alone like me, boy. When I was your age, I had more women than I could nod to. Now no one wants to take care of a broke-up, wore-out, cranky cowboy."

"But I'm not cranky."

"You will be. You hurt like this, you'll be cranky." He pointed his finger to heaven. "Even that guy can't fix these battle scars. He keeps us alive, thank goodness, but if you're gonna rodeo, you gotta pay the price at some point. Now or later. Used to think later was the goal. Now I'm not so sure."

Adam walked over to the truck to shake Jones's hand. "How many miles are on this old thing now?"

Jones got in and slammed the door. "As many miles as *I* have, I presume. I just put in the third motor and fourth transmission."

"Keep on truckin', old man."

"You know it. Are you riding here locally this weekend?"

"Yes sir. Can't miss out on points rides when they are this close to home."

"I hear ya. Good luck. Maybe I'll see you out there."

"I'd like that." Since Grandpa couldn't be there, Jones would be the next best thing.

Just as Jones revved up the truck, the new woman in town walked by. Adam had seen her around often enough, but she hadn't even noticed him. Probably didn't even know that bunkhouse she was living in used to be his. Her wavy brown hair swung across her shoulders. He imagined his fingers tangled in it for a moment, then caught himself.

"Who is that?" The comment came from behind him.

"Oh, nobody." Adam blew off the musing and focused his attention back on Jones.

"Mm-hmm." Jones snickered. "'Nobody' got your attention. Careful, boy. Get your heart all tied up in knots, and it'll throw off your balance. Can't ride a bull with no balance."

"You don't have to tell me. There'll be none of that. I'm not going to take a single chance of blowing this dream year."

"Good luck. See you around." Jones took off with the window rolled down and country music blaring from the radio.

Adam went back to the loading ramp and handed his gloves to the kid standing there. "Here you go. All yours, man." He couldn't have been more than seventeen, tall and lanky. Adam probably looked like that when he was that age.

"Thanks, Adam!" The kid slid his hand into one of the gloves and knocked his other knuckles into the leather.

Adam went inside to his office, sat down at his desk, and worked through the inventory reports and last week's sales numbers. The store was still holding its own, even though he'd spent less time here this year than any other.

He glanced up at the picture of Grandpa on the wall in front of him. "I've got to get this right, Grandpa." Adam's medical degree hung on the wall, too, half-hidden by a stack of farm-equipment catalogs. He'd completed the education part to please his father, but rodeo was what he'd always known he'd do. His schooling wasn't a complete waste. He'd used a lot of those skills on himself, and buddies, after ride wrecks. He knew more than some of the EMTs who hung around behind the chutes. Dad never saw it that way, though. He was an utter disappointment in his father's eyes. Adam could see it every time the man looked his way.

He got on the phone and placed the special orders that had

come in that week, then got the new kid working on cleaning up the shelves. One thing about this old building was it got dusty quickly, and Grandpa didn't like a dirty store.

"It might be a farm store, and the people that come in here might have dirt on their boots, but this place will always be clean to show our appreciation for their business." Grandpa's words were as clear now as if he'd been standing here saying them himself.

At the end of the day, Adam walked through the store and checked behind the kid. "You did a fine job."

"Thank you." The kid grinned, straightening with pride. "Only I got to ask. Why do we have to sweep all the time? Everyone just tracks in more dirt."

"Because we appreciate our customers, and they deserve a nice store to come spend their money in." Adam's heart warmed as he heard Grandpa's words come from his mouth. "Make sense?"

"Yes, it does."

"Then I think we'll get along very well around here." Adam started to walk away, when the kid called out his name.

"Adam? I just wanted you to know that I want to be just like you. Riding bulls and living in Antler Creek. You're the man."

"Thank you for that, but I think it'd be best if you be you. You don't need to live anyone's dream but your own. Trust me. I've made my share of mistakes." He turned and walked away, wondering whether if Dad hadn't given him the ultimatum, he might not have tied himself so tightly to this life.

The store was empty of customers now.

"Hey, guys," Adam called out to the employees. "I'll finish here and lock up if y'all want to take off early." Since he'd be gone most of the weekend riding again, it was the least he could do.

Everyone whooped and called out a happy chorus of good-byes.

Adam rolled the last stack of feed from the loading-dock display inside, then watered all the vegetable plants before calling it a night.

It wasn't even a mile to home, but he always drove his truck in case he needed to deliver something for a customer. He pressed the accelerator on his diesel Ford F450 and eased out of the lot. Before he turned onto the street, he got out of his truck to pull the pole gate across the entrance driveway. He pushed the latch into place, then turned and almost walked right smack into the pretty brown-haired woman. He stumbled back. "Sorry. I didn't hear you coming."

"Probably because that truck of yours is so loud."

It sounded like a gripe, but she was laughing. She had the straightest teeth of anyone he'd ever met, and up close like this he could see a little dent right there at her left cheek when she smiled.

"I'm Merry Anna."

"Hi. Adam." He extended his hand, and she reached for it and shook it. She had a nice grip. "I've seen you around recently."

"Yeah. I'm still kind of new to town."

"I know. I mean, it's a small town. No one can move into town without all of us hearing about it. Plus, I've seen you going to work at Hardy House." He gestured to the bag she was carrying. "Wait a minute. You're not frilling up the old bunkhouse, are you?"

She lifted her chin. "You might not even recognize the place."

He bent forward as though she'd kicked him in the gut.

"Oh no! I love that old bunkhouse. There are a lot of good memories in that place."

She nodded. "You must be the guy Krissy bought it from."

"That's me. What've you heard?"

"Not much."

He doubted that.

She must have read the look on his face, because she quickly and apologetically added, "No, really. Krissy just mentioned she'd recently bought it, which was perfect timing for me, being new in town and all. She's letting me rent it until I figure out what I'm going to do long-term. Oh, I know you don't even care about any of that."

"Maybe I do. We're neighbors, after all."

"True. I'll let you know if I need to borrow a cup of sugar." She stood there fidgeting.

Maybe he was supposed to laugh. "I'm not really a borrow-a-cup-of-sugar kind of neighbor."

"I was kidding," she said.

"Me too. Well, not really. I'm out of town a lot, so if you came over to borrow . . . well, I probably wouldn't be there."

"For work?"

"Yeah. But not for work. I rodeo."

"Well, it's been nice meeting you."

Not one single blink or eyebrow raise. That was unusual. She'd already started to walk away. "Hey, I sold the manor house just below you too. A woman named Tara is moving in next week. I think you'll like her. She's all fired up and ready to renovate that place."

"That's great. It's a beautiful house."

"It was my grandfather's house. It was hard to let it go, but I've got an opportunity that requires a lot of cash, and that was the only way I could do it."

"I'm sure that was a difficult decision."

"It was, but it'll be better off in someone's hands that will take care of it. I'm excited to see what she does with the place."

"I'll be sure to introduce myself. Thanks for letting me know." She took a slow step forward, as if she predicted he might call after her again.

Why am I acting like a smitten teenager? Yeah, she was pretty, but he wasn't interested. It was perfectly clear she sure wasn't interested in him either, and that never happened. And that wasn't sitting well.

"All right, then. Hey, can I give you a lift to the house?" Now he'd done it. An act of desperation. "I mean, it's a lot hotter this evening than it has been, and you're on my way. I'd feel bad to just drive on past you."

She looked apprehensive.

Rather than wait for an answer, he jogged around to the passenger door and opened it for her. "Hop on in. I'll have you home in no time."

She sucked in a breath, pushing her hair behind her ear. "Okay, thank you. That's thoughtful."

He slammed the door behind her and got in the driver's seat. He was so anxious to get her home that he didn't even look before he pulled forward. A driver in a red car laid on his horn, causing Adam to slam on the brakes so hard that Merry Anna bumped her head and was now rubbing it.

"I'm sorry. I swear I'm not usually a reckless driver." He drove her on home without further incident, except to his ego. "Sorry about the almost wreck. Is your head okay?" Adam asked.

"I'm fine."

"Are you sure?" He grabbed a penlight from the console. "Look at me."

"What's this? Playing doctor?" She dodged the beam of light.

You wish. "No, but I do have a medical degree. If you get a bad headache or start feeling off, give me a call. I can run you to the hospital."

He scribbled his number on a piece of paper and handed it to her.

"I really don't think that's going to be necessary." But she did take the phone number. She climbed out of the truck and started for the front porch. As he'd been taught, he waited there until the lady got into her house.

But rather than walk up the steps, she veered back around and walked up to his side of the car. He pressed the button to lower the window. "Yes ma'am?"

"Are you really a doctor?"

"No, I do have a sports medicine degree, though. I own the Feed & Seed, and I ride bulls. Rodeo is my life."

"So you spent all those years studying sports medicine and *don't* practice medicine." She cocked her head. "Is that right?"

"Yes. It's a long story. Maybe one day I'll tell you all about it."

"Thanks for the ride. You're very interesting."

He dropped the truck into reverse and hauled out of the driveway, feeling better knowing that she wasn't immune to his charm after all. Not that it mattered. He had one thing on his mind this year, and it was in the shape of a gold belt buckle and the biggest payday of his life.

3

The Spring Fling at Angels Rest had been the talk of the town all week, and finally Saturday was here. Merry Anna helped her boss box up all the miniature quilt tiles they'd painted with the Angels Rest logo on them. Krissy left to take them over to the party as keepsakes for all who attended and to help Matt and Liz set up for the celebration.

The store closed at two today, giving Merry Anna plenty of time to get ready for the party tonight. She had the rest of the afternoon to do whatever she wanted.

She'd never considered herself crafty, but helping Krissy paint barn-quilt tiles had been so much fun that she was itching to try a few things on her own, so much so that she'd splurged on some paint and was attempting a full-size barn quilt at home in her spare time. She'd only painted the background and penciled the design so far, but she hoped it would turn out as nice as the little plaque she'd painted that read, "Say yes to new opportunities," which she'd already hung in her bathroom so she'd remember the phrase every day.

Once Merry Anna started painting, she just couldn't stop. An old bookshelf and a couple of old ceramic pots that were in the shed now wore a fresh coat of color. An old johnboat resting on its side next to the bunkhouse caught her eye. She guesstimated she had just enough paint left to cover the outside of it.

Surprisingly, when she finished, the little boat looked almost seaworthy again. Not that she'd put it to the test.

"Hello."

Merry Anna spun around at the sound of the woman's voice. Stepping out from behind the boat, she saw an older woman dressed in denim capri pants and a shirt with birds appliquéd on the front. Her big white sunglasses and bright lipstick made her look like a Hollywood celebrity despite the casual attire.

"Hello. I didn't hear you come up." Merry Anna balanced her paintbrush across the top of the can and walked over to her.

"I'm Tara." Her chin was set proudly, and the little woman couldn't be more than five feet tall and a hundred pounds soaking wet while holding a sack of potatoes.

"Adam told me you bought the big house down the hill." Merry Anna checked her hand for paint, then extended it to the woman. "I just moved in recently too. It's so nice to meet you."

"And you as well. I see you've put a lovely coat of paint on that old boat." Tara grinned. Her lipstick had bled into the wrinkles around her mouth, and her white hair looked as soft as a cotton swab. "What are you going to do with it?"

"I have no idea." Merry Anna let out a nervous laugh. "I'm really not all that creative, or maybe I am, but my life before I moved here didn't allow me the free time to express myself that way. I'm kind of winging it."

"It's a lovely color," Tara said. "You have a good eye. I live for fun projects and home decor. That shade of blue is quite trendy right now."

"Really? Beginner's luck, I suppose." The boat did look pretty now that it had some color. No one would ever guess it had looked like something to throw on the burn pile an hour ago.

"Oh, I don't think luck had anything to do with that. I believe one has an eye for design or they don't. Can't really teach that." Tara stepped closer to the boat. "You know, some folks might turn that thing up on its side and add shelves for a bookcase, which is cute if you live on the lake, but we don't. A better idea would be to put it up on something so it's counter height and fill it with potted plants. It would make the most whimsical raised bed. A nice way to present the plants in a way that does not require weeding . . . which I hate because it's a complete waste of time. Plus, it wouldn't matter if it leaks."

"I don't really know if I like weeding or not. I've never done it."

"Then let me save you the trouble," Tara offered. "You won't like it."

"I've never been good with plants, but now that I'm not working sixty hours a week, maybe they'll stand a fighting chance. I could put in some tomatoes and herbs. What do you think?"

"That's a wonderful idea. Plant some of those cherry tomatoes too. I do love those." Tara smacked her lips playfully. "I'll help you eat them, because that's one thing about veggies people forget. They seem to come ripe all at one time. Feast or famine."

"Well, neighbor, I'd love to feast with you. Hopefully, it'll be successful."

"I can help you. I'm great with plants. I'm crafty too. In fact, this is going to sound quite braggy, but I'm pretty good at most things." Tara paused. "With the exception of computers."

"Ah! Now, computers—that's something I can help *you* with."

"Wonderful. Maybe you can help me figure out how to get Wi-Fi set up in that old house so I can order stuff." Tara looked hopeful. "I've got huge plans for that place, but to bring it back to its former glory, I need more than what I can get locally. I've got supply-house connections online if I can just *get* online." Tara hugged her arms to herself. "It's going to be a beauty."

"I can't wait to hear all about it." Merry Anna looked past Tara toward the house. "It had to have been a gorgeous home at one time."

"Yes. Stately, even. It still has good bones." Tara gazed at it like a lovesick teenager. "The moldings are exquisite. It's a shame it's been empty so long. Deferred maintenance is bad enough, but a home without a heartbeat living in it . . . well, that is surely the death of a house."

The sorrow in the old woman's voice tugged at Merry Anna's heart. "That sounds horrible."

"Nah. I'll save her. It would have been much more fun to work on this one with my husband, but at least I won't have to compromise on anything."

"I'm really sorry for your loss."

"Don't worry yourself over it. I've got heart enough to bring that one back to life." Tara winked and went on. "I'm ready to resuscitate that thing. I even found some wonderful pieces down in the basement I might be able to do something with. Nary a light down there. Good thing I had a flashlight with me."

"You need to be careful in the basement, especially in the

dark. We should exchange cell phone numbers. That way if you get into any trouble, you can call me for help."

"And vice versa. Probably should tell you that I'm a bit hard of hearing, though. Sometimes I don't hear my phone. So if I don't answer, don't worry."

Merry Anna somehow doubted she'd be the one needing assistance, but if it made Tara feel better to think so, who was she to argue? "Of course. And you let me know how I can be of service. I work at Hardy House, but other than that, I have plenty of free time. Actually, I think I can help you with one thing right now. I've got internet up here. Paid a crazy price to get decent speed, but I'm pretty sure you can pick up a connection from your place. If so, you can just use mine. I've got unlimited, so it's not costing me a thing extra to share."

"How generous. Thank you, Merry Anna. I have a feeling we will be very good for each other."

"I hope so." Merry Anna looked at the paint on her hands. "I better get the brush clean before the paint dries on it. Are you going to the Spring Fling at Angels Rest tonight?"

"Is that tonight?" Tara's eyebrows disappeared under her bangs. "Adam mentioned it when I moved in, but honestly I haven't given it a second thought."

"I'm going to walk up in a little while. Would you like to join me?"

She hesitated, but only a moment. "You know, that sounds wonderful. I could use a good walk. Yes, I'd love to join you. Do you want to just swing by on your way?"

"I'll do that. I thought I'd leave my place at about seven forty-five, but I'll come down a little early and see if I can get you connected to my internet before we go."

"That would be great. I'm so excited. I've got a list a page long of things to buy. I'll bake you some of my famous oatmeal-raisin cookies if we get it going."

"Deal!" Merry Anna said with enthusiasm. The truth was, she wasn't a fan of oatmeal or raisins, but she was happy to help a neighbor.

"What's the attire for this Spring Fling tonight?" Tara asked.

"Casual. I'm going to bring a sweater. Sometimes the nights get cool up here."

"I'll be ready. See you then." She turned and started heading down the driveway.

"Thank you for coming up. I'm really glad to have you as a neighbor." Merry Anna watched Tara head back down the steep incline to her house. It was hard to say how old she was, but she sure didn't lack energy.

Merry Anna cleaned her paintbrush and put away all her things before going inside to take a shower. With a towel on her head, she grabbed a book from her to-be-read pile next to the bed, then picked a bunch of grapes from the refrigerator to nibble on while she read, tucked in the chair by the big window in the front room.

She tugged the bookmark from where she'd left off, and it didn't take but two sentences to sweep her away into the lives of Kellie and Andrew, a sweet couple who had their whole lives planned out right from high school, only to end up apart. She could identify with the heroine. She'd thought she and Kevin had everything all figured out too.

What might have happened if something had stalled her dream wedding to Kevin for a few years? Maybe she never would have married him at all, or perhaps he'd have found a career he could stick with and they'd have entered matrimony on even footing. It was hard to imagine their marriage any other way than what it was. And lately his cheating was all she could think about.

Being here, away from him, was freeing. She hadn't felt this stress-free in longer than she could remember, which only confirmed that her spur-of-the-moment decision to stay in Antler Creek was a good one.

Angels Rest was straight up the mountain road from the bunkhouse. It wasn't all that far, but Doe Run Road was a steep climb. She put on her tennis shoes and grabbed a light sweater, then walked down to Tara's house.

She rapped twice on the door and called through the screen, "Hello, Tara. It's Merry Anna."

"Hi! Come on in." Tara popped her head around the corner. "I was just putting a couple things away. I'm almost ready."

"No rush. Where's your computer?"

"On the table there by the hearth."

Merry Anna walked over to the laptop. Tara might claim technology ignorance, but she knew how to pick out good equipment. With a touch of the keyboard, the screen lit up. It took only a few clicks to get to the network settings. "Just as I thought. You can use my internet connection. It popped right up."

"Really? I can just connect to your internet from here?" Tara came bustling into the room. "You're kidding me. No wires or anything?"

"Not a one. My Wi-Fi signal showed up on your connection. All I had to do was put in the password, which by the way is the word *happiness,* but the *i* is a *1* and the two *s*'s are dollar signs."

"I'm going to have to write it down. I can barely remember my name these days." Tara grabbed a pen and wrote the password on a sticky note and stuck it right on the laptop.

"I set it up so it'll connect automatically. Hopefully, you'll never need the password."

"Well, I've got it just in case, and I'll split the bill with you."

"Don't be ridiculous. As long as I'm here, you're covered. If I decide to move, I'll transfer it over to you. Fair enough?"

"More than fair." Tara clapped her hands. "I really appreciate your help. I've got so many things that I want to find for this place."

She wasn't kidding. A spiral notebook was filled with items from switch plates and replacement bulbs to pot racks and a stepladder. "Wow, you're going to be in front of that computer for a while."

"Well, the shopping online helps me pace myself. I get so absorbed in the projects that sometimes I overdo it and end up in bed achy for two days."

"Well, that's not good."

"No, it's not, but I do know my limits." Tara pulled a jacket out of the closet. "Are you ready to go to the party?"

"I am." Merry Anna walked to the front door, and Tara tied the sleeves of her jacket around her waist for the walk.

The hike wasn't as long or steep as Merry Anna thought it might be, and Tara did fine. She jabbered on about her late husband. Life wasn't the same without him, but now she got everything her way, and that was pretty nice too.

Finally, they saw the ornate carved wooden sign posted at the edge of the Angels Rest property.

"I've heard about this place," she said. Tara sounded starstruck.

"I've been dying to see it in the daylight myself." Merry Anna noticed the detailed artistry on the sign as they got closer, and then just past the mailbox, where the trees parted, they could see the house.

"What a beauty," Tara said in almost a whisper.

"It sure is." Merry Anna noticed the barn quilt on the side of the building. Krissy's handiwork. She knew the design by heart after painting the tile ornaments with her. The story behind it was that when Liz came to town, she found a quilt at the antique store that reminded her of one that she had when she was a little girl. Matt had asked Krissy to replicate it into a barn quilt and register it on the tour—to help entice Liz to stay and open the inn. The romantic gesture warmed Merry Anna's heart. *Must be nice to be loved so much.* Kevin had never been the type to do something like that.

There were cars parked three wide on the long winding driveway in front of the house.

"Glad we walked," Tara remarked.

"Everyone in town must be here."

Merry Anna and Tara moved through the crowd. Lemonade was flowing, both pink and the old-fashioned yellow kind, and someone had a blender going to make the frozen variety, which they waited in line for.

After they had their drinks in hand, Krissy came toward them, waving her arms. "I'm so glad y'all came."

"Wouldn't have missed it," Merry Anna said.

"I've been wanting to see this place," Tara added. "I've heard stories about it, but it's even more beautiful than I'd imagined. And believe you me, I have an imagination!"

Matt came up to Krissy and settled his arm around her

shoulder. "Welcome. Krissy said you'd be here. So glad you both could come. Make yourselves at home."

"This place is so great." Merry Anna was impressed by the architecture of the grand log structure. The wood gleamed, rich with texture.

"You should come join us for some fly fishing," Matt said. "Liz can outfish me, but I think I have her beat on tying flies." He leaned forward and whispered, "But don't tell her I told you that."

Tying flies? Anything with flies didn't sound like fun to Merry Anna.

A man with a hardy build walked over and clapped Matt on the shoulder. "You hogging all the beautiful women in this town, Matt?"

"No sir. I'm just lucky like that. Have you not met our newest neighbors? Merry Anna is working with Krissy and living in the bunkhouse, and Tara here bought the old manor house."

"Well, I've seen them both around. Ladies, I'm always at your service." The man tipped his hat. "George Goodwin is the name. I own the hardware store," he said to Tara.

"You and I will be on a first-name basis. Your staff has been so helpful. I've got so much I want to do."

"Perfect! So glad to hear it. I can't wait to learn all about your projects, but right now I need to go catch up with my beautiful bride. Come say hello to Dottie if you can. She'll be so excited to meet you." George meandered off, gripping and grinning as if it were a county meeting and he was running for mayor.

Merry Anna realized she recognized many of the locals from the store and the Creekside Café.

Maizey waved from the buffet table. She must've had a hand in the food being served tonight. It smelled delicious.

"I'm starving," Krissy said.

"Me too." Merry Anna was dying to get her hands on some of those hors d'oeuvres that had been filling the room with a mix of sweet and savory aromas since they got there.

"You two go," Tara said. "I'm going to see if I can't get a tour of all the rooms."

Krissy and Merry Anna went and filled their plates.

"What do you know about Adam?" Merry Anna put her napkin under the plate.

Krissy leaned back, looking surprised by the question. "Adam Locklear. You met him?"

"Yeah. The other day, on my way home. He almost ran into me, then offered me a ride."

"He's kind of Antler Creek's version of a famous sports hero."

"How so?"

"You mean besides the fact that he's drop-dead hand-some?"

She pictured the dark-haired rugged man with the light scruff of a beard. She wondered if that had been a five-o'clock shadow or if it took him weeks to baby it. "Yeah, besides that," Merry Anna said. It had been his charming confidence that had first caught her attention.

"Nice guy," Krissy said. "Used to spend summers here at his grandfather's ranch. He left Adam the Feed & Seed, but Adam spends most of his time on the road. He's a rodeo star. He rides bulls for a living, and he's the most eligible bachelor in this town. Every woman for two counties has dreamed about that guy at some point."

Krissy may have once been one of those dreamers from the look in her eyes.

Her boss smiled and shrugged. "I guess eligible isn't really the best way to describe him. Maybe more like unattainably eligible."

They both laughed as they noshed on the finger foods. "He seems nice. Different. I can't explain it."

"There's something about him that women can't resist." Krissy raised an eyebrow. "Maybe it's the whole cowboy thing, or maybe just that he's not available."

"I'm not either, so no worries there. But it was nice to meet him."

"He's gone a lot. His folks wrote him off over the rodeo thing, but he and his grandfather were really close." Krissy filled her in on some of the trivia about other people at the party. "See the lady over there next to the fireplace? She runs the candle factory. Smart gal. They say she's a marketing genius. And over there, the two young guys. They're George and Dottie Goodwin's boys. If you ever need something hauled or small jobs done, they are really helpful." Krissy excused herself to catch Liz to see if they needed help.

Merry Anna hadn't planned to stay very long, but she'd spotted Tara with Matt and Liz, and it looked like she was getting the tour she wanted. Merry Anna wished she'd tagged along now, as she was getting antsy standing there alone. She tried to relax, reminding herself that her new mantra was "Say yes to new opportunities," and that meant giving things like this a fair chance.

Tara came over, all smiles. "George says he and Dottie will give us a ride. You ready?"

"Absolutely."

George herded Merry Anna, Tara, Dottie, and their sons to his Suburban. He revved up the engine and drove them back down the mountain and pulled right into Tara's driveway. "This place used to be the prettiest house in town. We're really happy you've got big plans for it," he said.

"I look forward to you helping me along the way," Tara said. "This truly was a pleasure. Thank you for the ride back."

"You're my new best customer. I have to keep you happy, and any friend of Krissy's is a friend of mine."

"You can drop me here, too, George. I can walk the rest of the way." Merry Anna slid out of the back seat. "Thanks. See you soon, Dottie."

Merry Anna and Tara both waved as he backed out of the driveway.

"What a delightful evening. This really is a neat town." Tara took a deep breath, a smile playing on her lips. "Thank you so much for inviting me to join you tonight."

"I enjoyed it too. I'll see you around."

"You sure will!" Tara said as she climbed the stairs to her porch. "I think we're going to be wonderful neighbors."

Merry Anna waited until Tara walked inside. She thought of all the drop cloths and scaffolding filling Tara's house. It was a huge renovation undertaking for just one person. *I thought painting an old boat was a big deal. That's nothing compared to what Tara is doing at more than twice my age.*

Merry Anna walked up the hill to her house. The gentle sounds of the night cloaked her in comforting peace. There were so many things about living in this small town that she'd never have experienced had she not stopped for gas that day.

She sat on her stoop, looking down the hill toward the manor house. The lights shone through the glass. Was Tara still working on something? All Merry Anna had the energy left for was going to bed. She looked to the sky, hoping for a shooting star, until the chill chased her inside.

It didn't take her long to change into her pajamas and crawl into bed.

Noise woke her from a deep slumber. Since she was disoriented, it took her a moment to realize that the commotion was coming from outside. She jumped up and raced to the window. Pickup trucks filed onto Adam's property. The whooping and hollering got louder and louder, and the celebrating went on into the wee hours. She watched from the bunkhouse, passing judgment and making assumptions about Adam and his friends.

Just my luck to have a rowdy neighbor.

It was all she could do not to call the police.

She loved Garth Brooks as much as the next girl, but if she heard them belt out "To the oasis" one more time, she was going to march right down there and tell them to stop or she'd knock them to that oasis—and not in a friendly sort of way.

She went back to bed but just lay there staring at the ceiling. She had shut the windows an hour ago, and she hated missing out on the fresh country air and frogs' banjo sounds bouncing off the mountain, but enough was enough.

She got up again and peered out the window. In the middle of the field, a man danced on top of a round bale in the horse pasture, probably about ready to break a leg. Then again, those rodeo types probably weren't afraid of that. Hopefully, it wasn't Adam acting a fool up on that hay. That would be even more disappointing.

And he seemed so nice.

4

Monday morning rolled around, and Merry Anna didn't have to work until noon, so she drove down to the Feed & Seed to see what kind of plants they had. It was the first time she'd started her car in two weeks. It was just so easy to walk or ride the bicycle Krissy had given her to use while she was in town.

Tara had called yesterday to see if Merry Anna wanted a couple of old barstools that she found in one of her storage closets. They'd seen better days, but Tara suggested taking the backs off them and setting the boat up on the stools. They seemed like the perfect height, and with just a little effort, she was able to remove the backs, just as Tara had recommended.

Merry Anna wished she had that kind of vision. Who looks at a couple of dusty, rusty, broken barstools and imagines that transition? She swept a quick coat of paint on them to give them a little makeover. They looked great, and she couldn't wait to get her little garden growing in the make-shift planter.

She'd known Tara only two days, but they seemed like old pals.

Merry Anna wheeled her cart through the Feed & Seed. A huge stack of birdseed filled one endcap. She'd noticed that

Tara's bird feeders were low on feed when she was there, so she put a five-pound bag in the cart to give her as a thank-you for the barstools. In the garden area, staggered bleacher-like shelves were filled with all kinds of herbs, flowers, and vegetables. Tomatoes were at the top of her list. She read the tags, but she wasn't sure what the difference was between a Better Boy and a beefsteak tomato, even after reading the little sticks in each container. She was practically cross-eyed, when Adam walked up and asked if he could help.

"I sure hope so. I don't know anything about growing vegetables or herbs, but I thought it would be fun to give it a try. Fair warning—these plants may die in the process."

"I'm not sure if it's in my best interest as the owner of this establishment to tell you that we guarantee our plants. If they die, you can bring them back and we'll replace them. But murder—that's another story."

"I plan to do my best."

"I'd suggest cherry tomatoes. They are the easiest to grow, and they'll serve up a load of fruit."

"Perfect. Tara said she loves cherry tomatoes. Definitely one of those."

"Glad y'all are hitting it off. She's a nice lady." He turned the pots, scanning them for the best one, she presumed, but they all looked the same to her. He placed a sturdy-looking short plant on her cart. "And here's a good regular-sized tomato that is pretty disease resistant. I sell a ton of these." He placed one of those in her cart too.

"What about herbs?" she asked. "Any suggestions?"

"What are you going to cook?"

"I don't cook," she admitted sheepishly.

"You don't cook? Then why do you want to grow your own herbs?"

"I don't know. They smell good? Maybe I'll learn to cook something with them or dry them maybe? I could infuse them with olive oil and use them on salads. I do know how to make salad." Truth was, she usually bought the bagged kind and just tossed in a few other ingredients to fancy it up, but that counted for something, didn't it?

"Nothing wrong with that. Herbs are over there."

"Great. I'll pick some out."

"When you're ready to check out, come see me. I'll give you some fresh strawberries. Just got them from the local farmer up the road." He pointed down the street, not that it helped her with knowing where this farmer lived. "Peak of the season is usually Mother's Day. These are the biggest red berries you've ever seen and so sweet you'll swear they were sugared."

"Sounds delicious. Thanks."

She made her way to the shelves of herbs. Looking through them, she realized there were some she'd never even heard of. Sticking to what she knew, she grabbed small containers of mint, basil, rosemary, and lavender. All those were used in aromatherapy. You could never have too much of that. She rubbed the leaves between her fingers on a few of the other plants and sniffed, trying to imagine how she might possibly use them. Feeling particularly ambitious, she put some cilantro in her cart, then went back over to where the vegetables were to get a jalapeño-pepper plant. She loved salsa. Never made it before, but how hard could it be? It didn't really require anything but chopping. She could totally do that.

She pushed her cart to the register.

"Plant marigolds near your vegetables to attract beneficial insects that attack and kill aphids, and the scent keeps some harmful ones away," the guy at the counter said without even looking up, as if he'd said it a million times.

"It's true," Adam said, coming over from across the aisle. He lifted two marigolds from the shelf and placed them on the counter. "She needs all the help she can get. First-time grower."

The guy at the register laughed as he punched in the numbers at the register.

"Thanks, I think." Merry Anna stood there as her items were rung up, feeling uncomfortable with the way Adam was hanging around, especially after all the racket he and those guys made the other night. It was like living next to a frat house, and it was hard to keep that thought to herself.

She paid for her purchase and started to wheel her things out to her car.

"Hey, wait a second. I almost forgot." Adam disappeared inside.

She quickly loaded all the plants into her trunk and shoved a beach towel up next to them to hopefully keep them from toppling over on the short ride home.

Adam returned and put a big cardboard flat of strawberries in the trunk. The smell rose from them, making her mouth moisten.

"I can't eat that many strawberries. I'll just take a few."

"Freeze them. You can bake with them."

"I told you I don't cook."

He looked at her, incredulous. "Seriously? Like at all?"

"Barely."

"What do you eat, then?"

"I pick up takeout from the Creekside Café."

"Well, that is the best food around. Can't hardly blame you for that. So, you've never even baked a pie in your life?"

"Never."

"You don't know what you're missing out on." A look of

something that couldn't really be explained as anything other than delight filled his expression. "I'm going to teach you."

"No, you don't have to do that. I've gone this long without knowing how to bake a pie. I think I'll be just fine."

"I don't mind. Here, you take these strawberries home. Hull them and slice them, and then tuck them in the freezer. I'm on the road this week, rodeoing in Texas and Virginia. It'll be a long week, so how about we bake a pie as soon as I get back. Monday? Wait, better make it Tuesday. Are you working Tuesday?"

She stood there speechless for a moment.

"Are you working Tuesday morning? If not, we can start around eight in the morning. Then we'll be done in time to have warm pie for dessert with lunch. Otherwise, how about six in the evening? That'll give me time to feed my horses and then get cleaned up before we get started." He raised his hand as if to stop her from remarking. "So, pie for dessert either way."

"I don't know."

"What's to know? Tuesday morning or afternoon?"

This was beginning to sound too much like a date, and that was the last thing she was interested in. But that little voice in her head screamed, *What about saying yes to opportunities?*

I hope I'm not going to regret this. "Tuesday morning," she said. A rush of nervous excitement zinged through her. She hoped her cheeks and chest weren't flushed, as they were known to be sometimes. "Sure. Yes. But if we could do it around ten or ten thirty, that'll work better for me."

"Great. I'll see you then. Want to do it at the bunkhouse or at my place? And don't worry. This is just a neighborly act. I'm totally committed."

"Oh? And she doesn't mind?" Merry Anna wasn't quite sure why that bothered her. Sure, it was flattering that he was choosing her, but she wasn't looking for a relationship.

"Not like that. My commitment is to rodeo. I've got my eye on that title this year, and there's no time for anything distracting."

I'm a distraction? "I see. Well, we'd better bake at your house, because I'm pretty sure I don't have everything we need."

"Sounds like a plan. Tuesday at ten thirty. We're all set."

"Except for one thing." Embarrassed to have to ask, she hunched her shoulders and her voice dropped to a whisper. "How do you hull a strawberry?"

"You need the whole 101 lesson, I guess." He chuckled playfully. "No problem." He took a big strawberry from the top of the box and leaned in. "That just means that the little green leaves at the top of each strawberry need to be removed." He tugged his knife from his hip. "Simplest way is to just slice off the top, but I'll show you a little trick about that next week." He held the strawberry between two fingers, then sliced it down the middle. "Open up."

She leaned back, unsure of how she felt about him trying to feed her an unwashed strawberry.

"Come on. They're good. See." He popped half into his mouth.

She could smell the sugary sweetness from there. She reached for the berry, then bit into it. He was right. It was the best strawberry she'd ever tasted. "Oh my gosh. These are good."

"Fresh from the field."

"Okay, I'm going to hull these and freeze them this afternoon."

He closed the trunk and handed her the receipt from her purchases.

"I look forward to making my first fresh strawberry pie with you next week," she said as she slid behind the wheel.

"Me too."

She pulled away from the loading dock, trying to quit looking in her rearview mirror. She drove back to the bunkhouse. *How did that even happen?* She carried everything up to the house with no answer. *It's just a pie,* she reminded herself.

Trying to keep her mind off Adam, she turned her attention to her new little garden. She heaved the boat up onto the two stools that Tara had given her, then tested to be sure it wouldn't easily tip. Satisfied it was sturdy enough, she placed the plants inside and watered each one.

"Well, little garden, I'm going to do my best. I hope you enjoy your new home and reward me for my efforts by giving me lots of fruit and herbs. I owe my new friend Tara at least one tomato sandwich." She crossed her fingers. "Please."

She poured a bag of potting soil into a bigger pot and moved the tomato plant to where it would have room to grow. She had high hopes and a strange sense of confidence, when really she had no idea what she was doing. It felt good to push her fingers down into the damp soil. The herbs and vegetables practically filled the boat, creating a reasonably respectable garden.

It was more than an hour later when she finished tucking the last one tenderly into the dirt. She swooped her hair from her face with the back of her hand. "I did it." After that little win, even hulling strawberries didn't seem as ominous.

She brushed her hands off and went inside to get started. Looking around at all the cowboy gear still in the building, it was hard to imagine Adam ever hanging out in this place, but it sounded like at some point he may have lived here. She wondered how many of his things he'd left behind. Were those rodeo numbers once pinned to his shirts? She'd seen a rodeo on television, but she hadn't paid that much attention. All she remembered was that it looked dangerous and dirty—two things she never was on purpose.

But she was getting used to a new set of normal. The homeowners association in her previous neighborhood would never stand for a loud party in the middle of the night. Cops would have been called in an instant. Then again, she didn't know any of her former neighbors. It was a lot easier to call the law on people you didn't know.

Maybe she lost a few hours of sleep, but what was the harm, really?

She found a small knife in one of the kitchen drawers and worked on the strawberries. It wasn't quite as easy as Adam had made it look, but she managed to get through the whole box and filled several freezer bags full of them.

She had to admit the berries looked pretty stacked in her freezer, which was usually void of anything besides a couple of random frozen dinners and the occasional pint of ice cream.

5

Merry Anna was quite pleased with all she'd accomplished during the week. She'd successfully hulled and sliced all those strawberries and put them in the freezer with nary a cut. And so far, every single one of her new plants seemed to be thriving in the old boat. Since the garden was on the back porch, there was just enough sunshine balanced with shade throughout the day.

It might be her optimism, but it sure did seem as though the cherry-tomato plant had grown at least an inch! Was that even possible?

Things at Hardy House had been busier than ever. She loved interacting with the locals as much as with the tourists who breezed through town. Closing time was five o'clock on Friday, but there'd been a steady stream of customers, so she'd let them browse and waited to close until everyone got what they came for.

Merry Anna pulled the door shut behind her and locked it just after six thirty. Hungry after the long day, she walked over to the Creekside Café for dinner.

Maizey spotted her as soon as she went in. "Good to see you. I've got a table right over there for you."

"Thanks. I'm starving."

"If y'all were as busy over at the store as we were here, I bet you didn't even get lunch."

"Come to think of it, I'm not sure I even had a sip of water all day."

Maizey held up a finger. "That's easy to fix." She whisked behind the counter, then came back with a tall glass of ice water. "You having the special again?"

"As always." In all the time she'd been in Antler Creek, Merry Anna hadn't had a single bad meal. Even the liver and onions, which she'd about had a heart attack over when Maizey had set the plate down in front of her, had been delicious. It was that day that she decided to quit being so picky and let Maizey feed her whatever the special of the day was. She hadn't been disappointed yet.

Maizey put the order in, and Merry Anna watched her busy her way through the crowded restaurant. Three waitresses couldn't handle this place as well as she did single-handedly. Maizey stood talking to a young woman at the door, and then the two of them walked over.

"Have you met Ginger?" Maizey asked.

"No, I don't think so. Hi, I'm Merry Anna. I work over at Hardy House."

"Yes, Krissy and Liz were talking about you at the Spring Fling. I can't believe we haven't crossed paths. Do you mind if I crash your table? The kids are at ball practice. I just need a little grown-up time."

"Sure. Join me."

Looking a little frazzled, Ginger slid into the booth. "Thank you. I swear my life is always in high gear. Sometimes I just need to catch a breath. Do you have kids?"

"No, I don't."

She sighed. "I love 'em. I do. But sometimes between them and my husband, I am just worn out."

Merry Anna really didn't know what to say to that. Not only didn't she have kids, but she'd never spent much time around them. Yet she did know how much stress a husband could be. Kids were probably at least three times that.

"I bet you love working with Krissy. She's so great."

"She is." Merry Anna chuckled. "And just being around all that pretty stuff is hardly like work at all."

"I bet." Ginger smiled and took a big glass of sweet tea from Maizey. "Thanks, Maizey."

"You probably need some kind of caffeine-free tea with no sugar to relax," Maizey said. "But who can drink that stuff?"

"I know, right? No, I need this to get through the night. We'll be out late." Ginger turned to Merry Anna as if she needed to explain. "As soon as the kids get done at practice, we're driving over to James County for the rodeo. The little ones love doing that mutton bustin'."

"Mutton busting?" Sometimes it was as if these people spoke another language.

"Oh, they probably don't do that where you're from. It's when the kids try to ride a big ol' fat woolly sheep out of the bucking chutes."

Merry Anna must have looked horrified, because Ginger immediately began to defend it.

"It's not dangerous. They plop a helmet on their head. Basically, the kids cling to the back until they slide off. It's harmless for them and the sheep. It does mean extra laundry for me, but they come home tired. That's a plus."

It sounded crazy to Merry Anna. "You're not terrified they'll get hurt?"

"No. Kids are rugged. It's all in good fun."

Maizey walked over and slid two specials in front of them. "How's that for fast?"

"You're the best," Merry Anna said.

"Got that right," Maizey said with a laugh.

"So, you've never been to a rodeo?" Ginger took a bite of her food.

"No, but I saw it once on television." She hadn't really understood the entertainment factor of men trying to hang on to a wild horse or mad bull the size of a pickup truck.

"It's not the same. Oh, you should come. If you've never been, you'll probably have lots of fun. I didn't mean to make it sound like a headache. Come with us."

"It's your family time. I don't want to intru—" But before Merry Anna could spit out an excuse, Ginger reeled her in with her excitement.

"No, you wouldn't be. I'd love it if you'd come. Lots of times, Krissy and Liz are there too. Really, you don't want to miss out. You can ride with me. There's plenty of room for one more."

"I'd need to change." This whole saying yes to new opportunities was taking more time than she'd expected.

"That's fine. There's time. You're staying at the bunkhouse, right?"

"Yes." Was there anyone in this town that didn't already know her business?

"I'll pick you up there."

Merry Anna had changed into jeans and a long-sleeved blouse. This was becoming her more-than-often look. She was going to have to break down and buy some more appropriate clothes. She felt like she was in costume with the blingy western belt she'd bought last week. It had been an impulse purchase and a little bright for her normal taste, but then this whole rodeo scene wasn't her normal either.

The ride over to the arena was mind numbing. Ginger's kids were still hyped up from sports practice and probably a sugary drink, too, by the sounds of it. If Merry Anna hadn't been so nosy, she probably could've just zoned out, but it fascinated her how animated the children were about every little thing.

When they got to the arena, all worry about her snazzy new belt fell away. She was about as underdone as a girl could be. All the other women were decked out in western wear, from the hats on their heads to the boots on their feet, and the amount of rhinestones, conchos, and fringe had to exceed some kind of limit.

Ginger's husband, Roger, explained that it was bull riding tonight and mutton busting for the kids but that sometimes they had other rodeo events too.

Merry Anna spotted Adam across the way, wearing a royal blue western shirt and chaps with shiny silver conchos and long fringe. It was strange to see him dressed in all that gear. It was like watching an actor play a part.

The noise level rose the closer it got to starting time. Merry Anna, Ginger, and the kids found their seats in the bleachers just before the announcer got things rolling.

The rodeo started with a prayer and the national anthem. She'd never felt so proud to be an American as she did at that moment. All eyes were on the flag, all hands were on hearts, and every single cowboy hat was lowered in honor until the very last note.

It didn't take but a minute for the first bull rider to be announced and the first chute gate to clang open. Music filled the arena as a cowboy flopped like a rag doll astride a two-thousand-pound huffing beast. The bull spun and jumped, and with every move, the cowboy threw his arm in the air as if he were reaching for something.

Would those bulls be quite so mean if they heard some soothing classical music instead of that loud, headbanging rock and roll? That would be an interesting study.

Her experiment would have to happen on another bull, because in less than five seconds, the cowboy had been tossed in the air and had landed in a puff of dirt. The bullfighters dodged the animal, trying to distract it until the cowboy could scramble to the side of the arena and out of harm's way.

Merry Anna sucked in air, thankful the young man had escaped injury. Her heart pounded as hard as if she'd been out there running alongside them.

"No score, and this cowboy is going home with nothing but your applause tonight," came the announcement over the loudspeaker, "so give him all you got." The crowd clapped and shouted for him.

She stood there clapping, when Ginger leaned over. "If they stay on for the whole eight seconds, they get a score. That's what every cowboy is holding on for. Otherwise, they get nothing but this." She exaggerated her clapping. "Kind of all or nothing."

Merry Anna noticed the spurs on the rider's boots. "They wear spurs? I thought that was just an Old West thing and mostly for the jingling effect as the cowboy entered the quiet saloon in a one-horse town."

"Oh, they use them too," Ginger said with a nod.

The announcer introduced the next rider. "In chute number two, poised to take the whole PBR championship if things keep going his way, local rodeo star Adam Locklear."

Everyone cheered, and she scanned the crowd. They were serious fans. Some even wore shirts with Adam's face on them.

He was wearing a heavy vest over his blue shirt now. He stepped over the chute, and a group of bull riders helped him get set on his bull. He wiggled down with his hand in front of him, and one of the other guys pulled the rope so tight that Merry Anna wondered how he'd ever get loose from the back of that bull.

She held her breath. The music playing was more like a jaunty countdown. Her nerves tingled, making her scooch to the edge of her seat, although part of her didn't even want to watch.

The announcer's booming drawl filled the arena. "While Adam gets set, show him his big hometown following tonight!"

The arena erupted, cheers rolling through the air.

It was like watching in slow motion as Adam pulled his chin to his chest and gave a nod. With that, the chute flew open, and he came out on top of that huge bull. He had to be a good five or six feet off the ground.

"He's riding Shotgun Shiloh," the announcer said. "One huge Brahma."

Merry Anna winced as the bull, as black as gunpowder, jetted out the gate and veered back toward it, whipping Adam around with him.

She screamed, even though she didn't mean to. In fact, everyone else had been just as jolted as she by the sheer power of that exit. The braided, thick rope that connected Adam to the bull swung as Adam jerked to and fro.

Merry Anna was on pins and needles throughout the longest eight seconds ever. Adam spurred and held on by one hand tied to the rope, bobbling atop that huge animal until finally the buzzer sounded.

She realized just then that she'd grabbed Ginger's arm, clutching it as if that would somehow keep Adam from flinging off Shotgun Shiloh and landing in their laps.

"I'm sorry." Merry Anna rubbed her friend's arm. "I didn't mean to."

"I didn't even feel it." Ginger screamed and clapped. "Wasn't that something?"

"Something. Yes, for sure."

The pickup men raced their horses alongside the bull, and Adam reached toward one of the horses and used it to dismount from the bull and then scrambled for the gate. He climbed quickly to the top and shook his hat in the air.

The crowd went absolutely wild!

The bull snorted and faced off with one of the bullfighters for a hot second but then finally trotted down the arena alley. Those bullfighters might look like clowns with their baggy clothes and face paint, but there was no goofing around in that job. Fearless is what they were.

Over the loudspeaker, the announcer exclaimed, "And our local favorite, Adam Locklear, has done it again—the first cowboy to ever ride Shotgun Shiloh in this arena! Give a big round of applause to him and his score of 92.5."

Adam climbed over the rail, and the other cowboys pounded his back with enthusiasm. He grabbed his flank strap from the ground where the bull had kicked it off, and then he headed behind the chutes.

"He's flat-out crazy." Merry Anna hadn't meant to say it out loud.

But Ginger laughed. "I don't know about that, but he's darn-sure fearless."

"My heart is racing like I just finished a boxing class."

"It's exciting. Didn't I tell you?" Ginger nudged her. "Glad you came, right?"

"It was something, all right. It's scary enough, but when it's someone you know, it's terrifying."

She only half paid attention as the next bull riders took their turns. They barely made it out of the gate before they hit the dirt. Adam had made it look effortless.

It went so fast. One . . . two . . . three more cowboys with no score. And yet those eight seconds she had watched Adam felt like forever.

The scores were announced, and Adam was the big winner for the night.

Merry Anna saw Roger and Adam talking on the other side of the arena.

Ginger leaned in and whispered, "Look at the way all those cowgirl wannabes come on to him. They treat him like he's some kind of movie star."

She'd noticed. It even irritated her a little, and that bothered her more than they did. It took almost twenty minutes for the two men to make their way through all those cowboy-hungry women to where she and Ginger sat waiting with the kids.

Roger lifted Ginger straight into the air, spun her around, and set her back down. "Great night. Yeah!"

"That was a fantastic ride, Adam. Congratulations!" Ginger flung both hands in the air and high-fived him. "I hope your luck never runs out."

"I hope it lasts long enough to get me to the finals," Adam said.

"Ain't that right," Roger said.

"Hey." Adam had been standing right next to Merry Anna that whole time, but he acted as if he hadn't really noticed that it was her until that moment. "Good to see you. I didn't know you were a rodeo fan."

She didn't want him to think she'd come to see him. "I'm not. Ginger invited me to join them tonight."

His eyes narrowed. "What'd you think?"

"Well, it was terrifying," she said. "Exciting. Scary. Frankly, I'm glad it's over."

"Me too," Adam said.

"Then why do you do it?"

"I didn't say I didn't like it." His smile was broad. "That's a topic for when we have time for a much longer explanation."

She could only imagine what the story would be.

"Hey, Adam, we need you over here," one of the bullfighters called from inside the arena. "There's a reporter who wants to talk to you."

"Thanks, man." Adam turned back to them. "Sorry, I gotta run. I'm glad y'all were here. Thanks for coming, and, Merry Anna, I'm glad you came too." He waved as he trotted off, knocking the dust from his black cowboy hat and rounding the panels.

Ginger smiled as she watched Roger jog over to Adam, and then she turned back to Merry Anna. "I'm going to go over and grab a few T-shirts for the kids. You want to wait here or come along?"

"I'll wait here with all your stuff so you don't have to drag it around."

"That would be awesome. Thanks." Ginger had one kid on

her hip and a train of three others like little ducklings behind her as they wove through the crowd in the opposite direction of everyone else.

"Hey there," an attractive blond woman wearing a cowboy hat said from nearby.

Merry Anna hadn't even noticed her walk up. "Hi. Oh, did you need to get by?"

She smiled. "No, I'm not in a hurry. I saw you talking to that guy a minute ago." She pointed straight toward Adam. "The one who rode Shotgun Shiloh. You know him?"

"Yeah. Sort of."

"He looks like someone I used to know from back home in Indiana."

"Must be someone else. He's from Antler Creek."

"Oh, well I guess all cowboys look pretty much the same under those big hats." The woman walked off without another word.

Ginger came back over. "Who was that?"

"I don't know. She didn't say. She thought Adam was someone else."

"Sure she did. She was probably feeling you out to see if y'all were an item."

"I doubt that." But for a brief moment, she wondered what it might be like to be the one who had his attention.

"I've got a million stories from when Roger used to rodeo." Ginger thumbed toward where her husband was standing. "I'd never say it to him, but I'm so thankful he had to give it up. They wouldn't allow him to ride anymore after his last wreck. It was bad, but now I have my husband back. I'm so grateful for that." Ginger gathered the cushions and all the things they'd toted from the car.

"That sounds like a long story." Merry Anna grabbed a canvas bag and slung it over her arm. "Load me up."

"It is too long to tell. Want to carry the tote bag or this little guy?" Ginger bounced the baby on her hip.

"No, I'll let you do that. If I drop a blanket, at least it won't cry."

"You're not scared of a little baby, now, are you?"

Merry Anna wasn't teasing when she said, "I might rather try that mutton busting."

6

Merry Anna steadied her watering can over her growing plants. Tender green shoots had to be a good sign. The sound of a car coming up her gravel driveway made her hurry up the last trickling drops and walk out to the front of the house.

Krissy got out of her car. Dressed all in white with a straw belt around her waist, she looked as though she were stepping out of a travel magazine.

"Why aren't you at work?" Merry Anna asked. "Oh no, I wasn't supposed to open this morning, was I?"

"No, I just went to the bank. Matt is putting up more shelves for me, so I thought I'd drop by and see how you were settling in over here."

"Fine. I've added a few feminine touches."

"Oh gosh. I told Matt he might have to do some upgrades for you. I feel bad with you living here in this place the way it is."

"Don't be silly. I'm quite comfortable, and the air-conditioning works fine. It's great." If nothing else, it made her humble. She hadn't really realized it before, but she needed that. She appreciated the bunkhouse and what it represented right now. "I even painted that old boat and put it on the back porch. I have a little garden started. With any luck, I'll have tomatoes to share."

"Look at you. I never would have taken you as the type to grow her own groceries."

"Oh, I'm not. Those plants are probably on borrowed time, but I'm giving it the old college try. Then again, I was a business major, which doesn't really help me with this."

"Well, you feel free to paint or do whatever you want in here to make it seem like home while you're in town. If you feel the least bit like it's just not going to work, please let me know. I want you to be happy here." Krissy tucked her keys into her purse. "I know all this was supposed to be temporary, but, Merry Anna, I love having you working with me in the store."

"I love working there. It's been a breath of fresh air, and you have such an eye for beautiful things."

"You do too. You've been good for business."

"Helloooo." Tara walked up the driveway, her hand raised over her head in an animated wave. "Am I interrupting?"

"Not at all. You remember my boss, Krissy, from the party?"

Tara cocked her head. "I do. Hello again."

"Don't call me boss. It sounds ruthless." Krissy elbowed her. "I'm her friend too."

"I remember. Good to see you again so soon."

"You know, your house used to be the most beautiful home in Antler Creek." Krissy stepped over next to Tara. "I used to fantasize about walking down those stairs in my wedding gown. When I was a little girl, it seemed like a castle. I bet I sketched a hundred pictures of it over the years."

"Well, it's more like a dungeon right now, but I aim to get

it back in shape. And, Krissy, as long as you aren't in a hurry for that wedding, you are more than welcome to say your vows on that staircase. In fact, I'd love it!"

"Be careful. I'll take you up on that."

"Good. It'll motivate me to work faster."

"Don't let her fool you," Merry Anna chimed in. "She's already doing hard-core demolition, and you should see her project plan. She's got a handle on it."

"I've yet to get into your store, but I did do a little window shopping over there last Sunday. Once I get this place in shape, you'll see a lot of me. Local is the best way to furnish a home."

"I couldn't agree more," Krissy said. "And Flossie over at the antique shop may actually have some original furniture from this house. I know when Liz was searching for pieces for Angels Rest, Flossie hooked her up with some of the original bedroom sets."

"Oh my goodness. I won't wait to ask her about that." Tara's eyes danced with excitement. "Wouldn't that be wonderful?"

"Decor is as important as the construction, if you ask me," Krissy said. "Who's doing your contract work?"

"I am." Tara lifted her chin. "My late husband was a general contractor. He taught me everything he knew, only I read the directions too."

All three women laughed. "Then you are unstoppable," Krissy said.

"I'll do as much of it myself as I can, but I am smart enough to know when to call in the big guns, which starts with the electrical update. That's one fire hazard I don't want to delay correcting."

"Can't blame you there," said Krissy.

"Well, I do have my limits. I don't mean to bother you two, but I hoped Merry Anna could help me search the internet for light fixtures. I've got pictures of what I'm looking for, but it's quite the treasure hunt."

"I'd love to help," Merry Anna said.

"Can I see the pictures?" Krissy asked.

Tara handed her a folder full of them.

"Wow!" Krissy said as she flipped through them. "These are beautiful."

"I really want the front lights to make a statement but stay in check with the era that it was designed."

"You gals are going to have fun without me. I hate to leave, but I have to get to the store," Krissy lamented. "I can't wait to see what you pick out."

"We'll keep you posted," Merry Anna said.

Krissy walked back to her car.

"I probably should've called first," Tara said.

"No, she just dropped in too." Tara and Merry Anna walked around back. "No problem. I was just finishing up out here." She tucked her gardening tools under the seat in the boat. "Come on inside. Let's see what we can find."

Merry Anna walked inside. The air-conditioning was a relief.

Tara took one step inside and stopped. "Oh my goodness." Tara stood in the living room and turned in a circle. "I know you called this place the bunkhouse, but this really was a bunkhouse."

"I told you. It was completely furnished, but I've softened things a bit with curtains, linens, and pillows. It's helped."

"I had no idea." Tara's mouth dropped wide as she looked

around. "It's actually sort of fun with all the saddles and reins. There's a lot of rodeo stuff in here. I can see which feminine touches you added. It works."

"I'm trying, but since I don't know how long I'll be here, I've been trying to resist spending too much money on things I'll just leave behind," Merry Anna explained.

"Now, wait a minute. Don't tell me you're not going to stick around." Tara's brows twitched with disappointment. "You seem so happy here."

"I was actually just passing through one day and stopped to get gas. This town is so charming that I ended up staying." Merry Anna knew that sounded crazy. "It was on a whim, but it was the best decision I've made in a long time. Honestly, I'm happier than I've ever been. I never intended to stay more than a month. It's already been three."

"Sometimes those who wander are not lost," Tara said. "Ever heard that saying? Have no idea who said it, but it's true. Sometimes you just land where you're supposed to. I figure that's how I came to this place. I was led here by something, and I just accepted it."

Merry Anna pulled up the website for Tara and let her start scrolling through the large inventory of light fixtures. "Help yourself," Merry Anna said, heading toward the kitchen. "I'm starving. I'm going to grab us a little snack."

Working at the tiny counter, she made three sandwiches: one pimento cheese, one chicken salad, and a third with cucumber and cream cheese. She cut them in triangles and stacked them intermingled on a plate. It almost looked as though she knew what she was doing. Pleased, she put two glasses of ice on the tray and grabbed the tea pitcher, carrying it all back out to where Tara was busy on the computer.

While pouring the tea, she thought about what Tara had

said about everything falling into place the way it was supposed to. Merry Anna had always been a planner. Figure out what you want and make it happen, even if you had to shimmy the edges off the circle to get it to go into the square hole. That had always been her approach. Except for the situation with Kevin, and really she'd been just too beat down to fight that.

The first person who was kind, the first place that was pretty—bam, she dropped anchor. Maybe it wasn't serendipity but just dumb luck.

She set a glass down next to Tara. "Here you go."

"Aren't you the little hostess. Thank you, dear."

Before they knew it, two hours had passed and Tara must've added forty fixtures to her wish list. "How will I ever narrow it down?"

"There are so many to choose from. It's overwhelming." Merry Anna looked at the sketches Tara had brought along.

"You're such a great helper." Tara rubbed her hands together. "I'm excited to have another opinion."

"I'm enjoying it. I've never done anything like this," Merry Anna admitted. Her and Kevin's house had been brand-new when they moved in, but the builder had already made all the preliminary decisions. It was fun listening to Tara talk in contractor terms—hanging lights versus suspended fixtures, carriage style versus lanterns, and so many subtle differences that she would have never known to look for.

Merry Anna's phone rang, and she knew that ringtone. It was Kevin. "Tara, can you excuse me? I need to take that call."

"Sure. Go on."

Merry Anna grabbed her phone and stepped out on the porch. "Hi, Kevin. What is it now?"

"That's not a very welcoming greeting."

"Because lately any call from you ends in an argument, and I'm kind of over that."

"Well, I just wanted to check in on this wager. Have you realized yet I can't live on this amount of money?"

Even his voice bothered her now. "Quit your bellyaching. I'm just fine, and I'm only working part-time. Get a job, Kevin, because what I'm realizing is the money is not the issue. In fact, I'm happier on less. Give it a try."

"There is no way you are living on that," Kevin snarled. "I don't believe it for one minute."

"Well, you're just going to have to, because it's true." Merry Anna was tired of the ongoing argument.

"You're not using any credit cards?" he challenged.

"Not a single one," she said in a confident tone. "I can show you the bills."

"Fine."

"So, you'll leave it be? Accept the alimony and never bring it up again?"

"I don't think this wager has been fair. I think we need to extend it through the summer. Anyone can skimp for a month or two," Kevin whined. "We're talking forever here."

His words stabbed her. He seriously planned to live forever off her money? *Jerk.* "You know what? This has been so easy that I will extend it just so you don't think I haven't been fair, but might I remind you that you cheated on me? You haven't pulled your weight in years, and the last thing you deserve is this fair shake that I'm giving you. So I will prove my point, and in September we will shut the door on this conversation for good. Understood?"

"You don't have to be so bitter." His words were spat with anger, and then he hung up without a goodbye.

She dropped her phone from her ear and stared at it. Her hand shook. *I have every right to be bitter.*

Merry Anna turned off the ringer on her phone and stepped back inside. "Sorry about that." She watched Tara scroll through another website. "How's it going?"

"Great. I just found the perfect hardware for the bathroom cabinetry. By the way, I heard they're having a potluck lunch at the church on Tuesday. Want to go with me?"

"Oh, I'd love that, but I have plans. Adam is going to teach me how to bake a strawberry pie on Tuesday."

Tara turned and faced Merry Anna. "Would that be the Adam from the horse ranch? The cowboy?"

"Yes." Merry Anna could see the assumptions boiling over in Tara's mind. "No, no. It's nothing like that. Neither one of us is interested in anything more."

"How long has it been since you dated? I'm practically a hundred, and I know men lie to get that first chance."

"I was married to my high school sweetheart. We just got divorced. I never dated anyone but him," Merry Anna said. "We were always together . . . until now."

"Oh goodness. You need me around here."

She imagined Tara in a big fairy-godmother dress with a magic wand and wings. She politely kept that thought to herself.

"Adam is handsome and very well-spoken," Tara said. "I really enjoyed negotiating the deal on the house with him. He's quite smart."

"I wouldn't know."

"Well, I've been around the block a time or two with house projects. I'm no spring chicken," she said with a laugh. "I sold real estate for years, and my husband and I flipped houses before it was trendy. We completed lots of projects over the years, and we met all kinds."

"Are you flipping this house?" Tara could probably make a huge profit once she finished all those projects.

"No way," Tara said without hesitation. "I want that beauty for myself. We always talked about a stately old home in the mountains. I never thought I'd be doing it without him, but here I am. Still living our dreams."

"I hope when I'm your age I'm as confident and able as you," she said.

Tara was quiet for a moment, and Merry Anna wondered what she wasn't saying.

"You know, I heard you're kind of down on your luck right now," Tara said. "Don't let that keep you from staying focused on where you want to be in your life. It's easy to get sucked into things that don't matter."

Down on my luck? That wasn't true, but she had kind of let people assume that, and if Tara had heard any of Merry Anna's conversation with Kevin on the phone earlier, she could see where she might have gotten that idea. It had been easier than admitting she'd recently gotten divorced. And what would people think if she started telling them she was trying to live on a budget just to keep from having to pay her ex-husband more alimony?

"I appreciate the advice," Merry Anna said. "I know folks in a small town love to talk, but I'm not as down on my luck as you seem to think. I've got a roof over my head, a job I'm really enjoying, and a lovely new neighbor who just moved in. I think we'll be friends."

Tara's eyes danced. "I believe you're always going to be just fine."

7

After a long week of back-to-back rides, Adam was glad to wake up at home in his own bed. His last ride on Sunday had landed him in the mobile sports-medicine center, and he felt it in every muscle and joint in his body today. He'd made that precious eight-second buzzer, covering Shenandoah Shotgun, but that bull wasn't about to stop for some whistling noisemaker. The bull twisted just as Adam tried to release, and instead of dismounting, Adam was dragged nearly halfway across that hard dirt arena before the bullfighter got him loose. Then that doggone creature turned and gored him right in the hip.

Thank goodness it was his longtime friend Drew Minton working. Most riders called him Doc. A retired pro bull rider himself, he gave straight talk when it came to injuries, and it wasn't the first time he'd given Adam the speech about considering another line of work. It wouldn't have been a welcome discussion coming from anyone else.

Drew did the best on-site stitching of any of them. Rather than drive back Sunday night, Adam had crashed at Doc's place and then driven on home last night.

Adam rolled over in bed. He curled his toes. Even *they* hurt. He eased himself closer to the edge of the bed, then set his feet on the floor. He'd had some good rides, but a couple of them had been brutal. The gore would at least give him a new story to tell, but being dragged around had left him more bruised up than he'd been in a while. He'd almost rather pull a shoulder out of socket or break a bone than be banged up like this. He got out of bed and limped into the bathroom.

One glance at himself was all it took for him to see he looked as bad as he felt.

He twisted the handle in the shower to as hot as it would go, then popped a couple of pain-reliever tablets into his mouth and swallowed them while he waited for the water to warm up.

With his hands on the countertop, he leaned forward and took in a breath. Riding bulls was no easy way to make a living, and he wasn't as young as he once was, which was why he was so determined to make a change, albeit not too far from the business he loved so much.

He stepped into the shower and let the water run over him. His muscles eased, but the bruises, which were just starting to color, stung to the touch.

He got out of the shower and taped a fat wad of gauze over his hip, where the new stitches pulled tight now that the area had swollen. He tugged on a clean pair of Wrangler jeans and walked back into his bedroom. From there, he could see both the bunkhouse and Grandpa's old place. It had been a hard decision to sell them, but he finally had the money put aside to partner with a livestock contractor and move to the more sedentary side of the sport.

He knew it was a necessary change. He was ready, but he still had a hard time picturing himself on the sidelines and not in the chute. The excitement of stepping over the rail to sit down on that untamed animal. The rope in his leather-gloved hand, binding him in to help him withstand any leap, jump, or toss. The smell of fear. The threat of injury. The sheer strength of the animal. The thump of the music. The slam of the gate. The roar of the crowd. And nothing better than the sound of the buzzer while still sitting on that beast. Victory!

He slid a fresh shirt off the pile on his dresser and pulled it down over his head, wincing as he pushed his arms through the holes. *Whew.* He blew out a breath. Tomorrow would likely be even worse.

But today he had plans to teach Merry Anna how to bake a pie. It had seemed like a great idea then, but now he wasn't so sure he was in any shape to spend time with anyone.

Suck it up, Cowboy. He'd made hundreds of pies over the years—so many that he didn't even need a recipe anymore. *I'll make it work.* Besides, baking always made him feel close to his mom, and he missed spending time with her.

Mom's apron hung just inside the pantry, as if she might show up and help him out. That wouldn't happen, though. Ever since his dad had given him the ultimatum about giving up rodeo, there'd been nothing but silence between him and his parents. They'd only come to see him ride that one time.

He'd quit talking about it with them, as if ignoring it might make everything okay again, and it did for a while. But then there was that accident at the PBR finals in Vegas. His injuries were plastered on every sports page, and the footage running on the news clearly showed the bull had won that round. Adam was lucky he came out of those injuries at all.

He stretched his arms over his head and straightened his back. *It never will be right again.* Unfortunately, that went for his back and his parents, because when he wouldn't—couldn't—give up rodeo, they'd distanced themselves from him and this town.

He went downstairs to the kitchen and gathered the things he'd need for baking with Merry Anna. He rewashed three pie plates that had gathered dust in the drawer.

Adam glanced at the clock on the oven. Merry Anna should be there soon if she were the punctual type.

He took a glass pitcher out of the hutch and made some lemonade. He tried to stay away from sugar, but Mom had taught him how to be a good host, and he didn't have much else to offer aside from water.

Merry Anna was walking down the driveway when he looked up. Wearing a sundress and flats, she looked casual yet beautiful, with her dark hair moving across her shoulders in the light breeze. The way the sun hit it, her hair had a reddish cast to it he hadn't noticed before.

Right on time, she knocked on the front door.

After a two-count, he went to the door, hoping not to look too anxious for the casual get-together. "Hey there. Come on in."

"Thanks." Merry Anna looked behind her. "I think your dog smells the strawberries. Can we give him one?"

"Shorty loves them. Toss it in the air. He'll catch it."

"Here, hold this." She handed Adam a purple cloth tote bag and then took out the baggies of berries. "I think we may have enough strawberries to make pies for everyone on the street, but I wasn't sure how many to bring." She took a couple of berries out and one by one tossed them in the air. The black-and-white corgi caught each one. "He *is* good." She reached down and patted him on the head.

"He's a good dog." He lifted the bag easily. "This had to be heavy on the walk over." He led the way to the kitchen and set the bag on the island.

"Your kitchen is fabulous." She'd followed him. Standing there wide-eyed, she looked at him with a crooked smile. "Sorry, I just hadn't pegged you as the chef's-kitchen type."

"Told you I was a good cook."

"I'm beginning to see evidence of that. I'm impressed."

He smiled at that comment. "I'm a pretty good host too. Can I get you something to drink? I've got coffee, water, or lemonade."

"Lemonade sounds good. I never think about making that."

He clicked his fingers and scooped a handful of strawberries into a glass. "How about a fresh strawberry lemonade?"

"Seems fitting for the theme of the day."

"Yeah, glad I thought of it." He tossed a couple of ice cubes into the blender, along with the frozen strawberries and lemonade. Just a few short bursts, and everything was an inviting sunset red. He poured two glasses.

"Thank you." She took a small sip. "That's very good."

"And that, my new friend, is your first recipe with frozen strawberries."

"I think there's hope for me after all. Even *I* could do that."

"Just don't forget to put the top on the blender tightly. I made that mistake when I was about twelve."

She laughed out loud. "Oh no! You didn't."

"I sure did. My mom cleaned up strawberry seeds from the walls and tile for a year. She was so mad at me." He cocked his head. "She might still be mad about that."

"I'll be careful not to let that happen, although it sounds exactly like something that would happen to me."

"So, here's the good news. The recipe is pretty much the same whether you are making the pie from the fresh strawberries or the frozen ones, because they hold a lot of moisture either way." He picked up a frozen strawberry. "The trick is to cook them down until they are completely thawed before you bake the pie."

"Okay." She rubbed her hands together. "I'm ready."

"I don't really use a recipe, so we'll just have to pay close attention to what the measurements seem to be, and I'll teach you how to know when enough is enough."

"What can I do?"

"Get the sugar canister from the counter over there, and there's cornstarch in the cabinet just above it."

She gathered the items and carried them to the island. "Good to know I *can* come over if I need a cup of sugar," she joked.

"I already warned you that I'm really not that kind of neighbor."

She looked offended.

"I'm so rarely here," he said, stumbling over the explanation. "You know what I mean."

"Well, I won't have any, so I guess that makes me not that kind of neighbor too."

"Poor Tara is in a bad way, then, isn't she?"

"You're right, and she's so nice." Merry Anna folded her hands in front of her. "I might have to buy sugar just to improve our neighborhood rating."

"That would be easier than getting me to stick close to home."

"So I hear."

"Yeah?"

"I mean, it came up at the Spring Fling. They said you were

on the road all the time, which is pretty much what you just told me, so it's no secret."

"Nope. Not a secret. It's what I do."

"How'd it go the rest of the weekend?" she asked.

"Well, I'd planned to come straight home Sunday, but things didn't go according to plan." He placed a hand over his injury.

"What happened? Did you get bucked off?"

"No, I rode to the buzzer, but the bull got the last word."

"That doesn't sound good." She took a step back.

"It wasn't," he admitted. "He dragged me around a bit. Gored me at the end."

"Gored you?" She stood there with her mouth open for a second. "Are you okay? Should you be in bed or something?"

"No, I'm fine. Believe me, it's been worse. Just banged up and bruised." He could see the terror in her eyes. The same *You're crazy* look he got often but with that softer lowering of the eyelid like Mom gave him.

"Enough about that. We've got pies to bake." He lined up the pie plates. "I figured we'll make the first one together, and then we'll make two more. I'll just be your spotter on those. This is easy. Just about anyone can do it, but you'll get props because there isn't much better than fresh strawberry pie. Ready?"

"Yep."

"We'll make the pie crust first."

"Oh my gosh. You even make the crust?" She flipped her hands in the air. "I'm totally in over my head here."

"A good crust is critical. Trust me. You can do this."

"You've never seen me in the kitchen, but I do appreciate your confidence in me."

"No offense, but it's the recipe I'm confident in." He'd been making these pies since he could barely reach the counter, so certainly she could handle it.

"Which you've already told me you don't follow." She let out a slow disbelieving breath.

"Would you please get the butter and flour from the fridge?"

"Sure." She opened the door, then turned to him. "You keep your flour in the refrigerator?"

"Yes. The key to good crust is keeping the ingredients chilled."

She bobbed her head as she grabbed both and toted them to the island. "How does someone even learn that?"

"I learned from my mom."

She sucked in a deep breath, and he walked her through every teeny step.

She measured out the salt and then tossed it into the bowl.

He grabbed some salt and tossed it over his shoulder. "For good luck."

"Here." She took a pinch and tossed it toward him, most of it landing on her sleeve. "I'll give you my share. You need it in your line of work."

"Real funny." He finally formed the dough into a ball, wrapped it in plastic, and tucked it in the fridge. "We'll let it chill while we make the pie filling. That way it'll be easier to roll out."

"Sounds good. So what next?"

"The pie filling." He picked up one of her bags of berries. "You did a good job hulling and slicing them."

"Thank you. This guy up at the feedstore gave me some tips." She tossed her hair back, playing up the compliment.

Is she flirting? "Must've been a really great guy," he teased, hoping that she was. When she didn't follow up with anything else, he got back to business. "You know, there's a little hack you can try at home too. You can use a straw. Place it at the bottom of the strawberry, then push it straight up through the middle. It will take out that whole core and the hull all at once."

They measured all the dry ingredients, then cooked down the berries on the stove, until they were finally ready to mix everything together.

"There are a lot of strawberries to stir. I might need an oar." She stirred and stirred. "You didn't warn me this would be aerobic."

"You look like you'll be able to keep up." He reached past her to preheat the oven to 350, then got the dough out of the refrigerator.

They rolled out the dough, making a mess with the flour on the island, but the crust turned out perfect.

"Looks great," Adam said.

She beamed, and that natural smile made him smile too.

"I like to bake my pie crust about fifteen minutes before filling it so it stays crispy and flaky, but you don't have to," he said. "What would you like to do?"

"Let's do it your way."

"I've lived my whole life to hear a woman say that." He laughed. "Okay, the oven is preheated. Just butter the underneath side of this pan. It's a little smaller, so you can set it inside the pie plate and it'll keep the crust from bubbling up."

"You really do know all the tricks."

I'd like to show you a few. His thoughts betrayed him. *Stop. No time for that. Stay focused on baking. One goal this year.*

He set the timer for fifteen minutes. "We can cut the other

dough round into strips so we can make lattice on top of the pie. It looks so impressive. No one will ever believe this was your first time baking."

"*I* can't believe it. If it tastes even half as good as it looks, I'll be thrilled."

"Even the likes of *you* can't ruin this pie."

"Ha!" She grabbed for the dish towel, laughing, but he grabbed the other end, and for a split second, there was a moment when he wanted to tug that towel and her right into his arms.

She picked up a tiny wad of dough, balled it up, and threw it at him, only the throw went wild.

She threw just like a girl, way too high, but instinct kicked in and he leaped into the air to catch it. He landed and the fresh stitches at his hip pulled, causing him to groan like a bloated cow.

"Your injury." She pointed just above his waistband. "It's bleeding through the gauze."

He looked, then tugged his shirt straight. "Just a little. It'll be fine. There are a lot of stitches holding it together."

"It looks like it hurts."

"I got hung up. It happens in this sport. That bull outweighed me by more than ten times. I guess that is sort of a fight. Wish I could say, *You should see the other guy,* but the truth of it is, that bull went home without a scratch. I won the gold buckle for riding him."

"The gold buckle. I'm guessing that's the best?"

"Yes. First place, and the most points for that night despite the ending."

"I'm not sure I call *that* winning." She pointed at him with concern in her green eyes.

"All in a day's work. Looks worse than it is this time." He winced.

"I can't imagine it being worse." She pressed her hand across her mouth.

"I'm fine." He applied pressure to that area.

"I'm sorry. I was just playing around. What can I do?"

"Don't apologize. It was all in good fun. It's nothing."

"We didn't have to do this today. I'm so sorry. Really, this can wait."

"No, I'm not one to lay around. Helping you make pies is way easier on me than working the horses, and that's what I'd be doing if you weren't here."

He could tell she was holding back a lecture. Women were like that—thought they knew what was good for him. But he was a cowboy, and that put him in a whole other category that some would never understand.

After several more minutes of lively banter between them, the timer went off. "Let me get that," she said as she walked over to the oven to take out the pie.

He watched her remove the smaller pie pan and move it to the side, surprised she'd held whatever it was that was on her mind to herself so long.

"So, now we just pour the filling in?" she asked.

"That's it."

She dumped the gooey rich-red mixture into the crust.

He grabbed a spatula and gave the bowl a quick sweep to get the rest while she held it. "Now put your lattice on top and then back in the oven," he said.

She lifted each soft piece of dough one by one, trying to line them up just right, then crossing the other way. Finally, she pinched the criss-crossed slices to the bottom crust, like he'd shown her. With a pot holder in each hand, she slowly moved the pie back into the oven. "For how long?"

"About forty minutes. When the lattice is golden brown and the pie has bubbled up nice, you'll know it's ready."

She closed the oven door and brushed her hands on the dish towel. "I guess it's a good thing you're married to the rodeo," she finally said. "I think it would be really hard on someone who loved you to watch that."

At least she hadn't told him he shouldn't do it. "Some of the guys are married. I just find it easier not to have to worry about worrying someone."

"So, you recognize how frightening it is to someone else?"

"Definitely." The fear in his mother's eyes was something he'd never forget. Even just talking about it with her broke his heart. He'd had plenty of good women give him ultimatums over the years, and the rodeo always won. "But this is who I am. It's what I love."

"Well, I can respect that. At least you aren't subjecting anyone else to it." Her voice softened. "That would be really unfair to ask someone to watch you face death. It's crazy, but I'm not here to judge you."

"Thank you." A serious moment hung there between them. She must've felt it, too, because she took a step back, then lifted her arms out to the side in a dramatic shrug.

"I just hope our pies turn out a little better than *you* did that last go-round," she teased.

"Funny." He lifted a hefty fingersful of flour and flipped it in her direction.

Her mouth dropped wide. "You did not just do that." She sputtered flour from her lips and brushed her fingers through her hair, trying to do damage control, but mostly it just spread the white stuff more.

"Any other smart comments to make?" he dared.

She pulled her hands to her hips. "Maybe." She grabbed for a handful of flour, but he juked before she could take aim. He grabbed her and twirled her into him, a dance move he'd done a million times that always made the girls swoon.

She stood there, her lips parted, looking surprised.

He twirled her back out, mostly to keep from kissing her.

She giggled as she caught her footing.

He gave her an intense look, and she just smiled back.

He liked her spirit.

8

Merry Anna liked being around Adam. He was fun, and he hadn't been kidding about knowing his way around the kitchen. Even if he wasn't the cup-of-sugar kind of neighbor, she was glad to have him as hers.

"I set the timer," he said. "Let's go outside until the pie is ready."

"Sure." She followed along. The day had grown warmer, but the sky was Tar Heel blue. She'd never really been on a ranch, or horse farm, or whatever exactly this place would be considered. She was captivated by the way the animals moved through the fields. She'd admired them from the bunkhouse, but here, up close, it was different. "It must be a lot of work to take care of this place and all these animals."

"It is, but when it's what you love, it's not so much like work."

He led her down to a long bench with wagon wheels on each side. It looked like something out of the Wild West. They both sat down, and she did so gingerly, careful not to get a splinter in her legs or pull the fabric of her sundress.

"Are all these horses yours?"

"Yep."

"Wow. Are they rodeo horses?"

"You mean like bucking horses? No." He shook his head. "Most are just good old quarter horses that needed a place to live out their days. People bought them to use for roping or for something that didn't quite work out, and I took them off their hands. I have a few really nice horses up on the other side. Nice bloodlines, but nothing I've raised here has been good enough to be a bronco."

"But you've tried?"

"Yeah, but now I'm working on partnering with a livestock contractor who already has a foothold in the business. You think being a pro rodeo cowboy is hard? It's probably even harder to get a stock contract. Those bulls and horses are athletes too."

"Never really thought about it like that."

"You know, the bull gets half the score when I ride."

"What? That doesn't seem fair."

"We're judged on different things. Bulls get points for aggression and speed. If the bull does a good job, I have to perform better. It takes strength, balance, and control. Style plays a part too. Combined, if we both have a good day, then we'll score high."

"What's a perfect score?" she asked.

"Well, 100 is a perfect ride, but that has only happened once. Currently, the highest score ever achieved in the PBR is 97.75, and that's been achieved just a handful of times."

"I saw it with my own two eyes, but it's still hard to picture that it was you, the guy I just baked pies with, riding on the back of a mean, snorting, snot-slinging bull that outweighs you by a ton."

Adam leaned his forearms onto his knees. "It's a dangerous sport, no doubt about it. I like just riding along peacefully on my horses too, though."

"Do you ride them around here?"

"Yeah, I've got trails all up this mountain." He swept his arm across the field. "We should go sometime."

"No, I'm probably worse at that than baking. I've never even touched a horse."

"Not even at a petting zoo?"

She shook her head.

He leaped to his feet and grabbed her hand. "We're going to fix that."

She dug her heels in, trying to slow him down. "No, I'm fine watching from here."

"Come on. You need to experience this."

He had her there, and it would be saying yes to a new opportunity. *I might have to consider adding some parameters to that mission statement.*

He let out a holler, kind of a "Hee-yah!" and the horses started plodding toward the fence.

Fear tap-danced on her heart as she watched the horses stroll toward them, manes wisping back, muscles gleaming. "They come to you, just like dogs." The thumping in her chest finally slowed.

A big black horse was the first to the fence. He hung his head over and lowered his face against Adam's shoulder. "This is Ace."

"He's so regal looking."

A golden-maned palomino pushed his way through two other horses to get some of the attention. Six were all gathered now, and instinctively she backed away. They were so huge, and the fence didn't look like it would hold the animals in if they decided otherwise.

"It's okay," Adam said. "They are just looking for treats. Let me grab them a couple flakes of hay."

She stood there, too scared to approach them, although she really wanted to. It took only a minute for Adam to come back, and she was happy to know that apparently a flake of hay was a big square pad of it. She'd pictured something small that the giant horses might fight over.

He tossed the hay over the fence, and the horses nickered and jockeyed for the best spot to get their fair share—or more.

Adam reached his hand out to her. "Come here. Let me introduce you to Chips."

She took his hand, and he walked her toward the black-maned buckskin. He lifted her hand and placed it on the side of the large horse.

"He's beautiful."

Adam moved her hand along the horse's thickly muscled neck.

"How did he get his name?"

"He has a long registered name. Great heel horses in his lineage, but I just call him Chips because he's crazy about tortilla chips."

"And you know that how?"

"We used to have this Mexican restaurant in town, and one night I had a bag of leftover tortilla chips that I'd brought home. I'd stopped to check on the horses, and this guy shoved his nose into the bag and started snacking. He loves them. That started a tradition of me bringing all the leftover chips on the table for him. He's been Chips ever since."

"That's funny."

"It was great until the restaurant closed down," he said. "Now that little habit costs me an extra thirty bucks a month in store-bought chips to keep my guy happy, since I buy him the organic ones."

"Even those can't be good for him."

"He's a little spoiled, but I make sure he gets all the right nutrition. This old guy deserves a splurge or two. He's twenty-nine years old. I say if he wants chips, he should have them."

"Twenty-nine? How old do horses get?"

"The average life span is somewhere between twenty-five and thirty-five. I once heard a guy claim his horse was fifty. Don't know if it was true or not, but Grandpa had one that was thirty-seven."

She braved placing her hand on the horse's face. Chips blew soft air, making her laugh.

"He likes you," Adam said.

"I don't want anything this big not to like me." She could feel herself smile.

"Come over here, and I'll show you how to brush him. He loves that."

She walked over, trying to look braver than she felt. She stepped up next to the horse.

Adam grabbed a flat brush from the fence rail. "You have to use some pressure, else you'll just tickle him. Use even pressure. One long sweep and then out and away. That'll loosen dirt and debris."

She took the brush in her hand. "Like this?"

He helped her make the long sweeping motions, his hand on top of hers. "Feel the difference?"

"I do."

"Keep doing that. I'll get us some water."

"You're going to just leave me here?"

"Chips is gentle. You'll be just fine. Don't walk behind him—or any horse, for that matter."

"I'll stay right here." She wasn't about to move until Adam got back. Her heart raced, but she kept brushing Chips, and he did seem to like it. She spoke to the horse. "I'll take you riding after a while if you want."

The horse sputtered, almost scaring her to death, but he dropped his head, and she realized he hadn't meant to frighten her. "Don't push your luck now," Merry Anna bargained with him. "I'm a rookie. Give me a break."

Adam brought back two bottles of water. "You're doing good. Sorry, Chips, the pies are ready. Your quarter just ran out."

"That went by fast." She handed him the brush.

"For some reason, time always flies when you're with the horses." He put all the gear in a bucket, then led the way back to the house.

She followed him inside.

The floral, sugary-sweet smell of the fruit mingled with the buttery scent of the crust in the air. She closed her eyes and inhaled deeply. For a moment, she pictured herself as a cartoon character being lifted from her feet and levitated by the scent to the kitchen. When she opened her eyes, Adam stood there grinning ear to ear. "Good stuff, right?"

"Oh yes. I did that?"

"Yes ma'am."

He opened the oven and looked. "What do you think?"

"It smells so good." She peered inside, blinking against the heat. "The fruit is bubbly, and the lattice is golden brown, just like you said it would be. I think it's done."

"Me too."

She grabbed the pot holders and pulled the pie out of the oven. "It looks perfect!"

He put a trivet in the shape of a horseshoe on the counter. "You can set it here."

She did and then laid the pot holders to the side.

"Now the hardest part of all."

She couldn't imagine what the next step would be. "What?"

"We need to wait for it cool so we can cut it."

She swatted him playfully. "Yes, it'll be hard to wait, but not as hard as making the crust. I think that was the trickiest part."

"I know a way to make it easier, but I'm afraid I'm going to have to rain check you on it until next time. Usually I make homemade ice cream, but I can't stand by and let you do all the cranking. If you come for another visit, we can make ice cream too."

"How can I say no to that?"

"You can't. It wouldn't be fair to your taste buds." Their eyes held. "What's your favorite flavor?"

"Vanilla."

"Humph. Didn't have you pegged for plain-Jane vanilla."

"Well then, fancy me up. What do you suggest?" She fluttered her lashes.

"Strawberry or in-season peach ice cream is always a favorite. Maybe vanilla-peach-caramel?"

"That sounds amazing." *I think* you're *kind of amazing.*

"About ten miles up the highway, there's a small orchard that's on the barn-quilt tour. They have great peaches. Krissy knows all about them. You'll have to ask her to show you where that orchard is."

"I will. Thanks."

"Ready to make the other two, or should we save that for another day?" he asked.

"If you have time, I'm up for trying it while I still remember everything."

"Fine by me." He smiled and shrugged. "I have nowhere I need to be."

For two hours, they made pies and Adam shared stories with her about growing up visiting his grandpa in Antler Creek. All the land on the hill used to belong to his grandparents, along with the feedstore where the two met.

She enjoyed hearing about how he treasured his summers and every school break that he got to spend in Antler Creek, and there was no question in his mind that someday he'd live there.

She envied that he was so sure of things, and although the family rift seemed to be about his major decisions, he seemed not to hold a grudge over it. Quite the contrary, he missed his folks and held on to the special things they'd shared, hoping someday they'd understand the goals he strived for.

She looked out the kitchen window, over at his barn. The big red structure had a loft in the middle, but it looked as though over the years, they'd just kept adding stalls, giving it the look of a giant bird with wings that went on and on. "Why don't you have a barn quilt?"

"I think that's more the kind of thing the woman of the place picks out. I never heard of them growing up, but I see them all the time on the road now."

"I think they're neat. I'm trying to paint one."

"Where are you going to put it? On the bunkhouse?"

"Sure, why not?"

"I don't know. I guess because it seems like something people do for the long term, not at a place they're renting. But it's nice."

"It's just a board screwed to the building. Not too hard to take down."

"True. Let me know how it turns out."

"I might need your help hanging it. You could end up being the first person to see how it turns out. That is, *if* it turns out."

"Have faith in yourself. I have a feeling you can do just about anything you put your mind to."

I used to believe that. "Thank you, Adam. It's been a long time since I did something just for fun."

"You've got to balance the needs and wants in order to be happy."

"For a crazy cowboy, you sure have good advice."

"Well, it might look like I'm just throwing caution to the wind on a wild run, but I can promise you that I've planned this out." He rubbed his scarred hands together. "I know exactly what my goals are and how I will get there."

"Did you always know?"

"I've always loved rodeo, but my priorities have shifted along the way. Especially the last few years," he admitted. "My goals are long-term, but I have to hit every milestone if I'm going to achieve them all in time."

"Sounds like you're racing a ticking clock."

"I am. Sort of. It's critical that I make the finals and do well in them this fall. My whole future rides on that."

She wished her future was that focused. She admired him for that, even if it was crazy for someone to want to tie himself to a bull, even for just eight seconds. Then again, what else could you complete in that short amount of time and call it done?

9

Merry Anna enjoyed watching Adam move about the kitchen. He even cleaned up behind himself, leaving her nothing to do but enjoy the process. His comment earlier rattled through her mind until she just couldn't keep from asking, "Adam, why do you say that everything is riding on the rodeo finals? Because of the big payday?"

"No, that's only part of it. My buy-in with that livestock contractor is banking on my brand bringing something to the deal. If I don't win or do very well, I don't have a brand to bank on."

"That seems like a lot of pressure."

"Or a lot of motivation."

"Perspective." She admired how well-thought-out his plans were in contrast to the recklessness of his life. She was drawn to him, and she wasn't quite sure why. Swirling in her mind was his gentle touch while baking, the rugged cowboy spurring that bull in the arena, and the man whose horses came running to him. She pictured herself with him after a week of him away rodeoing. Him with a bandaged arm, riding his horse one-handed. Her galloping along on that pretty palomino—which would probably never happen, because she just wasn't fearless like that. She lived a safe life.

"You know, Adam, just because you don't worry about the risk when you're rodeoing, it doesn't change how others feel watching it."

"Oh, I know that all too well." He ran his hand through his hair. "My folks barely speak to me anymore because of it. I do understand how they feel, but I wish they could at least try to understand my love for it."

"That has to be hard."

"It is. I tried to do everything the way my family wanted. I started rodeoing in high school. My grandpa was one of the best bull riders around. He was my hero. Still is. He had more buckles than anyone I've ever known. I remember how my grandma had them displayed in the fancy china cabinet. No china, just gold buckles and bronze statues he'd won over the years. I was so in awe of that."

She loved how his eyes danced when he talked about it. "I can imagine."

"I was a high school rodeo champ, and I was ready to walk in his footsteps, but my father wanted me to go to medical school."

"So you were a good *student* too."

"Oh yeah. Always honor roll. I rodeoed my way through college. It's who I am. My father begged me to get that degree, so I did. I didn't want to let him down. But I couldn't live that life."

"So that's why you have a medical degree and don't practice? It was their dream, not yours?"

"Yes ma'am. Got my degree in sports medicine. Texas A&M."

"It's hard when your family has those kinds of expectations." She knew how that was, only she'd never even considered pushing back. At least not until recently. Her career in the family business was never posed as a choice. "Hard to waste all that education, though."

"Well, I use it all the time on myself and my buddies. I'm very well aware of the dangers of my sport. I have a great relationship with the doctors that work the rodeo too."

"That took one heck of a commitment to finish medical school. You are a complex man, Adam Locklear."

"I don't know about that. It's hard to disappoint your folks. Dad's a doctor, and Mom was a nurse practitioner until she finally took an early retirement. Dad's still practicing. They just always thought I'd go to college and join Dad in his practice."

"I know how family businesses can be." She hadn't meant to say that and hoped he'd let it go. "Expectations and all. I'm sure it was very difficult for you."

"More difficult for them, I guess."

She respected him for knowing what he wanted to do. She'd just moved blindly toward what her family had expected from her. It was a good career, but if she'd taken time before going to work in the family business, would she have done something different? Would she and Kevin have ever married? If she hadn't had such a well-paying job, maybe he would have stepped up and found one of his own instead of lazing and living off her income.

"You followed your dream. That's really admirable," she said.

His face flushed. "What was your dream when you were a little girl?"

"I don't know." She really didn't. Her family was always focused on the business. There was no room or encouragement for any other thought.

"You had to have wanted to be something. A teacher or maybe a ballerina?"

"No, my parents were very realistic. Very purposeful, and intentional about everything. We even had our family vacations planned four years out."

"That doesn't sound like very much fun." Adam shook his head. "Well, actually that might've been nice. We never took family vacations. I always spent my summers here with my grandfather. We were really close."

"I didn't know any different. It was just the way it was. When I wasn't at school, I was helping with the family business, even if that meant just straightening shelves."

"You're never too old to dream. You can make up for it now."

Why hadn't she ever thought of that? She'd just done as expected, and with Kevin too. She'd let everyone else have a say in her life except for herself. At least she'd been bold enough to stop here in Antler Creek. That was a tremendous first step, and she was making new friends too. Yes, things were definitely beginning to look up.

The kitchen timer buzzed. "Our pie should be ready to eat now," he said. "Are you hungry?"

"I've been trying to make it to the buzzer." She knew it was a lame attempt at a rodeo joke. "I've been salivating since it was baking."

He took a pie server from the top drawer and sliced the pie, then scooped out the piece onto a small dessert plate that had western cattle brands on it. He handed it to her, then served a piece to himself.

She stood there holding the plate, almost afraid to taste it. "It looks perfect. I hate to ruin the illusion if it's not good."

"I'll try it first." He stuck a big forkful into his mouth and immediately started nodding. "Perfect. Go for it."

She raised her fork and took a bite, savoring that first taste. "Wow." Her mouth still full, she gave him a thumbs-up.

"You did good," he said.

"A-mazing! You're an excellent teacher." She took a second, larger bite. "I'm so ready to make this again, with you just there as encouragement. Please let me know when you have time to do it again. Oh gosh, I can't believe I made this!"

"Believe it."

"This is the best birthday treat I've ever had."

"It's your birthday?"

"Technically not until tomorrow, but still. This is so good. I'm glad I let you talk me into this."

"You're welcome." He put a piece of foil over the pie pan.

"This pie looks perfect," Adam said. "I think it's cool enough now to carry. I'll help you take them home."

He set the pies on a cookie sheet, with enough foil over the top that they weren't about to wiggle. He heaved it up on his shoulder like a sack of feed, and they walked back over to the bunkhouse.

"Thanks for spending the morning with me," he said. "I enjoyed it."

"I did too. It's not what I expected at all." That didn't come out exactly as she'd meant it.

"Is that good?"

"Yes. I enjoyed it very much. I just didn't know what to expect, and I never thought I'd not only bake a good pie but also enjoy it." She got ready to walk up the porch steps, when she stopped and turned. "Were those rodeo tags on the wall and the chaps all yours?"

"Yeah, I doubt Krissy had time to clean out anything before you happened along."

"Why wouldn't you save all of it?"

"I've got so much of that stuff now. You can't save it all. Most of that is from my high school days. Some of the chaps belonged to some friends. They're broken or got left behind. We used to crash in that place all the time."

"I bet that was rowdy. It was quite a ruckus down there the other night when all those pickup trucks came rolling in so late."

"Sorry about that. Doesn't happen as often as it used to, but every once in a while you have to blow off some steam. I'm sorry we kept you up."

"Now that I've gotten to know you, I respect that decor more. There's a lot of sweat and passion behind all those paper numbers stapled to the walls."

"You got that right." He handed the tray of pies over to her, and she walked up to the front door.

"Thanks again. I really did enjoy getting to know you." She balanced the tray in her hands. "Have a good rest of the day."

"We'll do it again. Soon."

I hope so.

Adam stopped and turned back to her. "How about you be ready at eight thirty tomorrow morning? I'm going to take you horseback riding."

That was presumptuous. But the idea excited her, and spending more time with him after today would be fun. That little voice in the back of her mind nudged her. *Something new. Got to go for it.* And then Adam saying it was never too late to dream. She swallowed back the fear and let the words tumble out. "Yes. I'll be ready."

"Jeans and a T-shirt. There are wild blackberries along the trail. They're tasty, but those stickers will scratch you up. See you in the morning."

She waved and watched him walk back down toward his house.

I'm going horseback riding? With a handsome, honest-to-goodness cowboy? She held in the squeal, because one thing she'd learned about these wide-open mountain spaces was that sound traveled.

After letting the screen door close behind her, she set the pies on the counter. Her little kitchenette was more than enough for her, but after spending the day in a real kitchen with Adam, it seemed so inadequate.

Later that evening, with hair still damp from the shower, she sat on the porch swing out front. From there, she could see lights on at Adam's house through the trees. Maybe he was fixing dinner.

It had been a really interesting day. He was so easy to talk to. She'd kept her divorce and her leave of absence a secret when she hit town. It just seemed easier, since she wouldn't be here that long, but she'd been tempted to tell Adam about her situation. He'd be the one person who might understand.

She picked up her phone and typed his name in the search bar, and a whole page of links popped up. He had made quite a name for himself in high school rodeo around here. There was even a scholarship named after him and several articles written about him when he was in college in Texas.

On the Professional Bull Rider website, she saw his statistics for the past few years, and he hadn't been exaggerating when he'd said he was a contender this year. Right now he was leading the board. His dreams were certainly within reach.

The goals were lofty, but they looked attainable if he could stay healthy and focused.

His determination was inspiring. She pulled her bare feet up into the seat and hugged her knees.

What is it that I want out of my life?

10

Merry Anna's alarm sounded at seven. It wasn't like her to sleep until it went off, and suddenly she found herself panicked at the thought of getting up and ready on time for this horseback ride she was supposed to go on. *What was I thinking to say yes to that?* A trickle of anxiety stole her breath. *Because I'm trying new things, that's why.*

"Here's to new things." She got out of bed and pulled her hair into a braid.

She was brushing her teeth when her phone rang. A picture of Mom and Dad smiled back at her from her phone. She pressed the speaker button. "Hello."

"Happy birthday to you, happy birthday to you, happy birthday dear Merry Anna—best daughter in the world—happy birthday to you." They held that last out-of-tune note long enough for her to almost beg for mercy.

It was an annual thing: the torturous duet from her parents, followed by the—

"Thirty-three years ago today," Mom started without a hitch, "I was—"

There it was. "Yeah, yeah, I know, Mom. Good morning."

"You always say the same thing," Dad grumbled. "Give the

girl a break. She doesn't care what you were doing the day she was born."

Mom mumbled something in the background.

"When are you coming back home and to work?" Dad always did cut to the chase. "This has gone on too long."

"I don't know, Dad."

"Happy birthday, honey," Mom sang out. "Do you have big plans?"

She didn't really know how to answer that. "I'm celebrating with the girl I work for. I'm really looking forward to it." *Why am I lying to her? I am divorced. I'm a grown woman, and I can do whatever I want to do. Then again, Mom never baked a pie. She probably wouldn't even be impressed.*

"That sounds lovely, dear."

"Why are you still working in that gift shop?" Dad sounded annoyed. She wished she'd never told them about taking the job there. "That bet with Kevin is ridiculous. Living on next to nothing? What does that prove? How long are you going to let this go on? You could own a chain of little gift shops if that's what you want. It's about time you come back and do your real job."

"It's my birthday. How about I spend it the way I like just this once?" She'd never really spoken so strongly to her father before, but this was worth fighting for.

"Leave her alone," her mom chimed in. "This is not the time for you to tell her what to do."

At least Mom was kind of on her side today, although Merry Anna knew full well that her mom was also on Kevin's side. If her mom had her way, Merry Anna would not only come back to work but also go back to Kevin. *That'll never happen.*

Merry Anna glanced over at the clock. "Thank you for calling this morning. I'm meeting someone for coffee, so I'm going to need to run." *Two lies in one conversation? This is not good.*

"You have a great day," her mom said.

"Call us and let's talk about you coming back before people think they don't need you around," Dad added.

"Thank you." She hung up quickly before they could squeeze in any other orders.

Exhausting. Every time she talked to them, it was like that.

She walked back into the bathroom and put some sunscreen on, then got dressed. She still had a few minutes before she needed to leave, so she walked out on the back porch and watered her plants. They were growing so well. She felt good about that.

She actually felt good about a lot of things lately.

She locked the back door and then went out the front. Just as she stepped outside, she saw Adam standing at the bottom of the steps. His smile was easy. He lifted his chin, his eyes squinting in the sun. "Good morning."

"How long have you been there?"

"I'm an early bird." He had both horses tied up out front.

Adam's skin was as tan as the hide of the horse he was standing next to.

"Chips was anxious to wish you a happy birthday," he said.

"Isn't *he* sweet?" She walked down the steps, clomping in the boots that were about a half size too big but doable. She walked straight over to Chips and gave his nose a rub, hoping Adam was wishing he'd admitted to being the one who wanted to come over.

"I don't have any tortilla chips in my house," Merry Anna said sweetly to the horse, "else I'd give you the whole bag."

"No worries. I packed some in the saddlebag so you could treat him to some later."

"Thank you. Am I riding Chips?"

"You sure are."

"You and me, buddy," she said.

"Come over on the stoop. I've got some spurs for you."

"Spurs? I'm not going to need those. I'd never spur Chips." She pressed her hand against the horse's neck. "That would be mean."

"You won't hurt him, but you do need the spurs just to keep him going. Sometimes he has a mind of his own and wants to meander or take a shortcut."

"I don't like the sound of this."

"It'll be fine." Adam sat down on the step. "Prop your foot up here."

She put her right foot up on his knee, and he put the spur on her boot and buckled the leather strap.

"Other foot, please."

She switched feet, and he made short work of getting that one in place. "You're all set. I'll help you up on him."

She took a deep breath. Her stomach swirled, and her mouth had gone dry. *Is this a good idea? What if I fall? Spending the day in the emergency room would not be a good birthday at all.*

"You okay? You look kind of nervous."

"I am."

"No need to be. You will be perfectly safe. I promise. I'm an expert, and Chips knows his way better than any of us. Take a deep breath."

She exaggeratedly sucked in air.

"Good. Now let it out."

He took her hand and led her to the left side of Chips. "He's tied to the hitching post here, so he's not going anywhere until you're ready, and then I'll untie him, okay?"

"Okay."

"Put your left foot up in the stirrup."

She lifted her foot, and it was a stretch to get her leg up that high. "He's a lot taller than I'd realized."

"He thinks you're shorter than he remembered."

"Funny." She finally got her toe up in the stirrup.

"Now grab the saddle horn, and then you're going to push yourself up and throw that leg right over him." She struggled a little, so he gave her a little boost on the seat of her pants, and she sat right in the saddle.

"Wow. This is really high."

"Just relax and get your bearings." He helped her get both feet in the stirrups and checked them, adjusting both sides to the right length, then made sure she was seated comfortably in the saddle. "How's that?"

"That's better." She lifted the reins. "What do I do with these?"

He gave her a quick lesson in neck reining. "Here's the thing. Chips knows what he's doing. Like any good old trail horse, he'll take care of you."

"I don't want to go fast. I feel like I'm going to fall off."

"We'll take it nice and easy. We're in no hurry. We're going to stay right here on the property. I know every twist and turn." He walked his horse, Ricochet, slowly in a circle, giving her time to settle in the saddle. "Are you ready to go?"

"I'm not sure. I mean, yes, let's do this."

He led Chips away from the hitching post. Then he walked over and got on Ricochet and gave him a little kick. Ricochet moved next to Chips. Adam reached over and touched Merry Anna's arm. "Relax. We're going to just walk side by side for a bit. Here we go."

And they did. In unison like two horses on a carousel, they walked around the bunkhouse, then down the hill past Tara's house, through the red pole gate, and back onto Adam's land.

"How're you doing?"

"Okay. I think I've missed everything so far except the back of my horse's head. I've just been looking at these reins and praying I don't slip off."

His laugh made her relax. "Well, that's no fun. Look up. Look around. Wave at me."

She gave him a wave and then rolled her eyes. "It's not as bad as I thought."

He dropped his reins and raised both his arms above his head. "Look, those reins are not going to hold you on the saddle. They're just for steering."

She reached for the saddle horn.

"Lay your reins across the horn and lift your arms in the air."

Chips continued to lumber forward. Merry Anna took Adam's advice and hoped for the best. With her hands in the air, she did feel just as steady in the saddle as with her hands damply clutched to those reins.

"See?"

"Yes." Her shoulders relaxed a bit, and her heart slowed to the point that at least it wasn't deafening her any longer. She blew out a breath. "Okay, this is much better. I'm new at this, so you're going to have to be patient with me."

"You're doing great."

They rode quietly for about ten minutes, staying close to what was familiar to her, thank goodness. She could see the bunkhouse from here. Right now, if the horse went completely nutso, she could jump off and run back home. She wasn't quite sure why that was comforting, but it was.

"Ready to go up the trail?"

"I think so." Both nervous and excited, she copied Adam's actions, lifting her legs and giving the horse a little kick, and darn if it didn't work. Chips picked up the pace, his strength beneath her undeniable and his breaths loud as he hoofed it up the path.

Every once in a while, her horse would do something that sounded like a combination of a snort and a sneeze, and it startled her every time, rocking her back in the saddle.

"He's okay, right?" she asked, laughing.

Adam twisted in his saddle to face her, placing one hand on the top of Ricochet's rump for balance. "Oh yeah. That's just what they do."

"Turn around!" she cried. "You're going to walk right into something."

"One thing you need to know about horses is they don't want to walk into anything or off anything. So, yeah, you have to be careful of low-hanging branches, but other than that, your horse is looking out for himself as much as he is you."

"That is a good point." She'd never really thought of it that way. Now that they were walking up a narrower path, it was nice to know that the horse was probably less worried about the weight of her on his back than about concentrating on being sure-footed so as not to slip down the side himself.

She took her eyes off the path and tried to take joy in the beauty around her.

Cicadas made an electric vibe that seemed to push the birds from one limb to another. Nearby, a squirrel scampered off into the brush, flipping his tail like he was giving her what for, and that tickled her.

They rode to the comfortable melody of the twigs and brush beneath the horses' feet.

Becoming more confident in the saddle, she bravely reached to touch a huge white magnolia flower. Her fingers just grazed its soft petals as Chips walked by, but the sweet fragrance hung in the air around her. So many textures and smells gave her a fresh sense of renewal.

A bright-red bird flew in front of Adam. "Did you see that?" she called out. "That was the reddest bird I've ever seen. Redder than a cardinal."

He slowed, letting her horse catch up to him there where the path was wide. "That was a scarlet tanager, one of the most beautiful songbirds in our woods. My grandma used to say if you saw one that it meant joy and peace would follow as long as you followed your right path." He scratched his head. "Don't know if it's really true or she was trying to trick me out of getting into trouble, but it's a nice thought. Always makes me feel good when I see them."

"Made my day."

"You're doing good," he commented. "You're a natural."

"I can't believe I've been missing out on this my whole life. It's so freeing out here."

"Yeah, I haven't been getting as much riding in for pleasure. All my horses need to be ridden. Most of the time, I'm playing catch-up, so I just ride them in the ring or right around there in the barn to get it done quickly so they all get a chance. The 4-H kids come out and practice tacking them up and riding in the ring too. That helps."

"You can probably twist my arm into this again."

"You like it! That's great!" His head bobbed, making her like him even more since he was so happy just to share something he loved. "I hoped you would."

"I do." She wasn't sure if it was the company or the horseback riding, but it was a day she wouldn't soon forget. "Thank you. I'm so glad you offered to take me."

"Sounds like you're kind of done for the day. I guess it was a long ride for your first time on a horse. I hoped you might want to stick around and let me fix you a real cowboy meal. I have all my cast-iron stuff set up at camp, where I park my horse trailer. It's not much farther."

"Where they put the cast iron down on the coals and then coals on top of it?"

"Yes. Exactly."

"I've always wondered how that was done. Does it really taste different?"

"You can be the judge of that. Up to you. We can either turn back or go on down to camp. I could make us an early dinner. Riding always makes me hungry. What do you think?"

Trying new things was a little nerve-racking, but so far everything she'd tried had turned out well. "Don't know how much help I'll be."

"That's the best part. The dinner practically cooks itself. You pretty much just have to sit back and relax."

"I believe I'm qualified for that. Let's do it."

He spun Ricochet around in a tight circle three times.

"Are you doing that on purpose?" She wasn't sure if his horse had been bitten by something or what, but then she noticed Adam's smile. "What are you doing?"

"Celebrating," he said. "Come on. Follow me."

11

Adam hadn't been sure that Merry Anna would go for the whole-day ride and the dutch-oven dinner he'd planned. If she hadn't, he'd have had a whopping lot of food down there at the horse trailer to cook up and eat by himself. He'd taken the day off from the feedstore, leaving Jim to take care of things. One of these days, he should probably let Jim buy him out completely, but it was his one tie back to Grandpa, and he just couldn't let go of it, even if it was mostly breakeven the past couple of years.

It had been a long while since he'd taken time to just have fun. No ranch responsibilities. No rodeo to travel to. And best of all, with Merry Anna, there were no games and no expectations, so they could actually just relax and have fun. Just friends.

He and Merry Anna rode the trail. The horses did most of the work, and she looked as though she'd been riding for years, sitting relaxed in the saddle, her feet just kind of bumping along in the stirrups. She hadn't complained about a thing.

"Do you know what that sweet smell is?" she asked.

He took a whiff. "Oh yeah, that's honeysuckle." It delighted him how she was taking notice of things.

"I really like it."

He steered his horse over to the right and pointed it out. "See? There's tons of it."

"I smell it. Oh gosh. I don't think I've ever smelled something so sweet."

"I think that's one of those smells those aromatherapy people have missed out on."

"We never slept with the windows open where I used to live. I really love it."

"Where did you used to live?"

Her lips parted, and then she said, "Up near DC."

She seemed to watch for his reaction, which was hard to hold back. "DC? You don't seem like a city girl."

"And what does *that* mean?"

"I don't know. You seem nice and not all frantic."

"I'll take that as a compliment."

"It is one. What made you come to Antler Creek?"

She wiped her hand on her pant leg and regripped the reins. "That's kind of a long story."

She didn't elaborate, and he didn't press. He found that people would tell their stories when they were ready. Pressing never did serve a purpose, and it wasn't all that important anyway.

He took her up his favorite trail, stopping at the top to let her look down across the town.

"It's so beautiful. Peaceful," she remarked. Then she sat quietly.

There was something special about watching someone find a moment of peace. This place had that effect on folks. He let her take all the time she needed. This was his favorite place in the world.

A couple of silent moments passed. He reached into his

saddlebag and took out two bottles of water. After opening one, he handed it to her.

"Thank you."

He sipped from the other, then tucked the bottle back in the bag.

She looked over and then did the same thing.

"Ready to head down to the creek?" Adam asked. "These guys are probably thirsty too."

"Sure."

He gave his horse a kick and turned to head down the path on the other side. "You good?"

"I think so."

He looked over his shoulder to check on her. Chips was already making the turn to catch up.

They rode leisurely down the winding path. Adam slowed to a stop and pointed out a deer to the far right.

Merry Anna's mouth dropped open, and her hands clenched. "Breathtaking," she whispered.

They stood still long enough that finally the buck turned and ran, disappearing into the woods.

She gave Chips a little kick and he stepped up next to Ricochet. "That was so amazing."

"Never know what you're going to see out here." He moved his horse forward. "It's just a little farther to the creek." They rounded the next corner, and both horses walked straight down into the rocky creek bed and began slurping water.

When the horses finally quit drinking, Adam led the way through the creek bed to the other side, right in front of his horse trailer.

He got down from his saddle and threw his reins over Ricochet's neck, then helped Merry Anna down from Chips.

"Your horse isn't tied," she said.

"As long as he has those reins over his neck, he'll behave."

"You better tie mine up. I don't think I could chase him down right now." She leaned side to side, stretching her legs. "That's a workout. I haven't used some of those muscles in a very long time. Maybe never."

He walked both horses over to the trailer, untacked them, and then tied them out on the picket line.

"I'm going to feed these guys some hay. There's a bathroom inside. Make yourself at home. I'll be up in a few."

"Thanks. I'll be fine."

From the hay shelter, he watched her walk inside. By the time he got back over to the trailer, she'd returned and settled into one of the chairs.

She was relaxing with her eyes closed when he walked up. He grabbed a couple of ice-cold waters and snuck up behind her. He couldn't resist pressing one of the bottles against her neck.

She shrieked and jumped up. "You!" She stabbed a finger in the air.

"Oops. Here. It's cold." He handed her the bottle.

"I'm well aware of how cold it is." She took the bottle and twisted it open. "You cannot be trusted."

"Oh, come on. It was all in good fun." He tried to make an innocent face. "Do you forgive me?"

"I don't know." She took a big sip of water. "Maybe, but only because it felt pretty good. You almost got a punch in the gut. You better not do that again. You're still on the mend, and I know your weak spot."

"*I'll* decide what I can and can't do. I have to be back in the arena a week from Friday, so I'd better be in good enough shape to ride a trail horse and take a wild punch from a girl."

"You're going to be on a bull again so soon? Those stitches aren't going to be healed over in a week."

"We'll wrap it real good. That's the way rodeo works. My sponsors count on me to represent them at these rides. If I don't ride, I don't get paid."

"You can't miss even one?"

"Every ride is a chance to win, and each win counts if I'm going to have a shot at the finals. I can't risk giving the other guys an opening to pull ahead. If I get so hurt that I can't ride, that's a different story, but this injury isn't enough to keep me out."

"I'm not going to say anything else about it. It's your choice." She held her hand up and shook her head.

"Come with me next weekend. It's not too far. Cool little town called Boot Creek. Let me teach you about the sport. I think you'll understand it more if you join me."

"Fine. I should. You're right. I'm making assumptions," she reasoned. "I reserve the right to not like it, though I'll give it a fair chance."

He couldn't hold back the grin. "Good. Thank you for that."

"No problem. I know we're neighbors and I probably should've realized this, but I didn't know there was so much land over here beyond the tree line."

"My grandparents owned all this and more. I used to love getting lost out here as a kid."

"It had to be so freeing to be surrounded by this kind of beauty." She took a sip of water. "I didn't have anything like this in my life when I was growing up. That horse trailer is as big as my first apartment."

He laughed. "Yeah, a splurge. I can carry four horses, and the living quarters are so convenient. To be honest, though,

I'm a bull rider. I don't need a horse for my event, and I never have time to go horseback riding on a vacation with friends, so it was overkill. I bought it with some of the money my grandpa left me. He and I used to talk about taking our horses and riding trails across the country. It never happened."

"Sorry about that."

"We're not promised tomorrow." He shrugged. "Grandpa always said that. I just never thought he'd go so soon. No warning. No time to do those things we'd planned."

"I'm sorry."

All of a sudden, heavy raindrops fell, plopping against the awning.

"I didn't see that coming," she said.

"Me neither, and I'm usually pretty good about that kind of stuff."

The rain stopped as quickly as it started, a typical Antler Creek storm.

"Look!" Adam pointed across the pasture. A perfect rainbow stretched over the whole landscape.

"It's beautiful!" They stood side by side, looking at nature's colorful splendor in silence.

"I never get tired of this," he said.

"I can see why." She sat in the chair under the awning. "This whole town is amazing. I feel so different here."

He sat down next to her. "Good people. Great scenery."

"Fascinating friends."

He pointed to himself. "Me?"

She cocked her head. "Yes, you. You're a mishmash of all different things. Fearless when you rodeo. Patient when teaching me to ride. Kitchen savvy. Business owner. I can only wonder what you'll surprise me with next."

"Just wait until I do some real cowboy cooking for you to-night. Cast iron on the firepit."

"See?" Her lips pressed together. "One continuous sur-prise."

"That sounds like a challenge."

She laughed, but he didn't. Instead he reached for her hand. "You can help me gather all the ingredients for our meal. I think you're going to enjoy this surprise."

Adam started the fire, and then together they spent the next hour chopping and dicing and getting things ready. There was an easy vibe between them that didn't require fill-ing the quiet space with idle conversation.

He layered dinner in the cast-iron pots, then insisted she not watch as he put together the last dutch oven.

Merry Anna walked over to the horses and checked their water while he continued working on the surprise dish.

She must've seen him put the last pot on the fire, because she walked back over.

He went inside and turned the radio to a country-music station through the outside speakers.

The coals glowed vibrant orange. "It smells so good," she said as they relaxed by the fire.

"Yeah. Makes my mouth water." He got up and stoked the fire. "Wait until we eat. There's nothing like good dutch-oven cooking, and I'm not just saying that because I'm the one doing the cooking."

"How much longer?" she asked. "The aroma is making me hungry."

"Good. Should be about ready now." He grabbed two plates and heaped a little of everything on each one, hoping she wasn't one of those women who ate like a bird in front of a guy. He turned and placed one of the plates in front of her.

"Wow." Her eyes widened. "That is a lot of food, but I can't wait to try it."

He sat down with his plate. "Pork shoulder, my special cabbage recipe, and potatoes with onion and bacon."

"Sounds like comfort food." She lifted her fork and took a generous bite. She took in a breath as she chewed. "Adam, this is amazing."

"Wait until we get to dessert." He gave her a wink and took a big bite of the potatoes.

It was a long, leisurely evening. They talked after dinner until they lost track of time. Finally, he served dessert—a dutch-oven apple pie.

Merry Anna set down her napkin. "Adam, that was delicious. This has been the best birthday."

"Thanks for letting me be a part of it." He leaned in, wanting to kiss her.

She moved back, putting some space between them. "It's so nice to have good friends to enjoy things with. No pressure and all that."

The move surprised him, but he tried to recover quickly. "Yeah, right," he said nonchalantly. "People always want to make things so complicated."

"They don't have to be, do they?"

He shook his head. "No, they don't." They'd talked so easily all night, but now a silence fell over them. Interestingly enough, complicated was exactly how things seemed right now. Just a little kiss was all that was on his mind, but he didn't want to rush things. "Are you ready to ride back?"

"I have to get on that horse again?" She looked deflated. "I'm so sore."

"We can walk if you want. Actually, it's a really short walk if we go through the field rather than take the horse trail."

"Could we? I'd be forever grateful."

It had been a pretty long ride for a beginner. "Hey, it's your birthday. Anything for the birthday girl." He stood and held out his hand.

She took it and stood, and they headed back to the bunk-house. The evening was cool, and the dew on the ground was so heavy that their pant legs were wet. About halfway there, he took off his jacket and laid it across her shoulders. "Here. It gets chilly in the mountains at night."

He wasn't chilled at all, though.

When they reached her porch steps, she turned to him. "Good night," she said. "This was a great birthday."

"I'm glad you enjoyed it." He leaned in for a kiss. This time she didn't stop him. Her lips were soft and warm. Her eye-lashes tickled his cheek, and he wanted to pull her closer, but . . . she pressed her hands to his chest.

She looked away, letting out an audible breath, then looked back at him again. "My life is really complicated."

"Seriously?" He tapped his chest. "What's complicated about a little birthday kiss?"

"No. I liked it. I—"

"Nothing more than that. Just two people doing some stuff, just because. But that's okay. I'm sorry. Didn't mean to make you uncomfortable."

"I wasn't exactly uncomfortable. I . . . ."

"It's okay." He couldn't take his eyes off her. She wasn't like any woman he'd ever met. This not-dating was beginning to feel a lot like dating, and he didn't mind one bit.

I enjoy spending time with her.

A little voice inside reminded him, *Don't take your eye off the prize, Cowboy. This is your year.*

"Thank you." She placed her hand on his forearm. "This has been a birthday I'll never forget."

She closed the door behind her, and he cursed himself for not having had something perfect to respond with.

He went back down to the trailer, put out the campfire, and cleaned up. Sitting under the stars against an inky-black sky, he was too comfortable to go back to the house. He'd pony the horses back to the barn in the morning. He kicked off his boots. Right then, all he wanted to do was sit there and think about his new neighbor.

12

A week and a half later, Merry Anna got ready for church, then went out and sat on the stoop. She wasn't used to letting other people pick her up, and waiting made her antsy. Finally, she walked down to Tara's.

Tara was already outside, about to get in her car.

"Thanks for offering to drive to church this morning." Merry Anna lifted the handle and slid into the passenger seat.

"I'd have picked you up."

"I know, but I figured since I was ready, I'd meet you."

"Dear, I know you usually walk, but it's so hot this weekend. I just couldn't stand the thought of you sweating out there." Tara glanced over at her. "Okay, really I just thought it would be nice to have the company."

Merry Anna pulled two small fans from her purse. "Just in case they haven't gotten the sanctuary air-conditioning working any better this week, I picked us up a couple of little fans while I was shopping." Merry Anna flipped open a blue one and fluttered her lashes as she fanned herself dramatically.

Tara laughed. "You do look like quite the Southern gal."

"Why, thank you so very much," she said in an overly

breathy Southern accent. She turned and fanned Tara. "Seriously, they work really well."

"Oh, they do." Tara lifted her chin, enjoying the cool breeze. She motored down Main Street so slow that Merry Anna was pretty sure that if she'd left at the same time on foot, she may have beat Tara to church.

Tara put on her turn signal a block from the turn. The incessant clicking accentuated the snail's pace at which they were moving, and it took everything Merry Anna had not to say something.

Finally, Tara swung wide, almost into the other lane, and turned into the church parking lot.

Merry Anna clung to the door, silently vowing never to ride with Tara again after today.

They got out of the car, and the two of them started toward the door. Tara stopped and greeted just about everyone along the way. Like a pair of bumblebees pollenating a field full of flowers, they zigged and zagged their way inside.

The church was pretty packed, so they took a seat near the back. Merry Anna pulled out the hymnal and started tagging the songs listed in the bulletin. She handed the hymnal to Tara. "I marked them for you," she whispered.

"You are so sweet. Thank you." She clutched the book in her lap.

Merry Anna put placemarks in her own hymnal. The pipe organ bellowed in a rich tone that made Merry Anna hitch a breath.

It was right about then that something on the other side of the sanctuary caught her eye.

Adam walked in with his cowboy hat in his hand and took a seat at the end of a pew near the front.

Her stomach swirled. His dark hair curled just above his collar. It had been over a week since the horseback ride, and she found herself smiling. She hadn't expected he'd be back in town in time for church after riding this weekend.

Tara elbowed her and gave her a knowing smile.

It's not like that. But she didn't say it out loud, because, well, it didn't seem a hundred percent honest, if the way her insides were jiggling around was any indicator.

Merry Anna did her best to keep her eyes on the pastor, if for no other reason than to be certain Tara didn't catch her gawking again. That painstakingly long mile-and-a-half ride home would be even more miserable if she had to listen to Tara speculate about her and Adam.

The pastor stepped up to the front and welcomed them, starting the morning with a few announcements: prayers for members sick or in the hospital, a reminder about the adult Bible study every Tuesday night, a mention of the potluck next Sunday after church, and last but not least, a call for help with the teen youth group gathering that night.

Adam's hand shot into the air.

"Thank you, Adam," the pastor said. "Anyone else?"

Merry Anna had no idea what came over her, but her hand lifted.

"Thank you," came the pastor's reply.

Adam spun around to see who would be helping him, and his face pulled into a wide look of surprise when their eyes met.

She wiggled her fingers in a wave.

What the heck do I know about teenagers and youth group?

She swallowed hard, hoping her face wasn't turning red.

"If you two can meet me out front after the service, I can

give you some instructions. Great. Let's begin our worship this morning with a word of prayer."

All heads bowed.

Lord, help me be of service this evening. I have no idea why I volunteered. I'm not well equipped for this.

Had that been a nudge from God that had urged her hand into the air, or a self-serving move to spend more time with Adam? She wasn't interested in him like that. That couldn't be it. No, this was good for her, and honestly it was a little uncomfortable to be volunteering with Adam. They probably would have so much to keep them busy that they wouldn't even have a minute to talk.

She pushed her thoughts aside and tried to focus on the sermon. The service ran long, and those fans came in handy. Finally, the pastor offered his blessings and guidance, the organist began playing, and everyone rose. Merry Anna and Tara were some of the first to leave since they were seated at the back.

Merry Anna stepped outside and then moved to the edge of the sidewalk.

Tara said, "I know you need to stay and talk to them about the youth group. You just take your time. I'm going to wait in the car."

"I can walk back home, Tara."

"No, I don't mind waiting," Tara insisted.

Then from over Merry Anna's left shoulder, she heard, "I can give her a lift when we're done." It was Adam. "If I'd known I'd be back in time for church today, I could have given you both a ride."

Tara touched his arm. "It's good to see you."

"Yes ma'am." He tipped his hat back just a bit. "How's it going over at the house?"

"Still in the demo and planning stages, but I've started buying some new fixtures that fit the period of the home. Don't you worry. I'll have you over once I make some good progress."

"I'm counting on that."

"Well, I guess I'm not needed. Looks like you'll get home one way or another," Tara said to Merry Anna with a hint of mischief in her eyes.

The pastor stepped next to them. "Thank you both for doing this. It's great to have a couple of the younger adults step up. I think these teens can identify with you. It'll be good for them and you."

"You're welcome," Merry Anna said.

"Absolutely. Happy I'm in town to help out," Adam said.

"You ever done anything like this before, Merry Anna?"

"Never. I'm a quick study, though."

"Well, not much to it, really. The event is going to be held down near the pond. We'll have all the canopy tents set up. We'll fog for mosquitoes about an hour before it starts too. Merry Anna, you're going to want to wear long pants. We have mosquitoes the size of nickels in this town, and for all the spraying in the world, they'll still pester you."

Adam laughed. "You'll feel them land."

"Oh my gosh," she said.

"I'll bring some extra mosquito spray from the house. Least I could do. I'm happy you volunteered." Adam lowered his voice. "Last time it was just me and Mrs. Ragsby, who happens to be about eighty-four years old."

"Hey, ol' Mrs. Ragsby probably has more energy than I do," the pastor said with a laugh. "We've got the men's Bible-study group cooking the burgers and serving the meal starting at six. They'll do the cleanup too. I just need y'all to chaperone, more or less, and manage the campfire and s'mores. Make sure everyone disperses by nine."

"I'm an expert at s'mores," Merry Anna said. "I can pick up all the stuff for those."

"Don't even need you to do that," the pastor assured her. "We've got them all in little individual baggies all ready to go. Just show up, make sure everyone is enjoying themselves and being kind to one another, and have some good fellowship. If you could get there a little before six, that would be perfect."

"I feel like I'm getting off light here," she said.

"That's how I reel you in to be a volunteer again," the pastor teased.

"I think it's working already." She turned to Adam. "I'll just follow your lead."

"Yep. We'll be fine."

"Thank you both so much," the pastor said. "This is a huge help. I think you'll enjoy this group of young adults." He lifted his hand in a wave. "Thanks again."

Merry Anna waved, then turned to Adam. "Well, that seems easy enough."

"I've done a ton of these. I *was* one of the boys that would wander off and stir up trouble, so I'm one step ahead of these rookies." He smirked. "Figure it's my duty to make up for my past."

"I can't imagine that your past was all that bad."

He nodded toward his truck, and she walked with him. "It wasn't, really, but a lot of that had to do with the chaperones. So I'm just paying it forward."

She got in his truck for the short ride home. She hopped out as soon as he stopped the truck. "Thanks for the ride," she said. "I'll see you there tonight."

"We may as well ride together," he said. "I'll zip by and get you on my way out."

"Okay, and don't forget the bug spray."

He dropped down the glove box. "I never leave home without it. This stuff is as necessary as toothpaste around here."

"I'm still learning."

Dust kicked up from his tires as he backed down her driveway to go home. She was glad he'd be back to pick her up in just a little while.

That evening, while helping the youth group, she realized there was yet another side to Adam. He was patient and playful, but the teens respected him. It was interesting to see, but more than that, it surprised her how much she enjoyed just a few hours of passing out s'mores around a campfire.

She was grateful she'd raised her hand to volunteer, even if it may have initially been motivated by the chance to be around Adam. There'd been one girl who had been hanging back from the group. In a short conversation with her, Merry Anna learned that she was in town for the summer to help her mom with her sick aunt. Merry Anna knew that uncomfortable look. When she was that age, she'd been so awkward in social situations. It did her heart good to motivate the teen to join in the volleyball game, and by the end of the night, she was laughing and palling around with the locals like one of them.

Merry Anna came home feeling as though the couple of hours she'd shared at that youth-group gathering meant something. She got more out of it than the kids did. *Now that my life is simpler, I'm going to do that more.*

The weather was so nice that she opened all the windows.

The lights shone from the back of Tara's house. The shrill whirl of a drill sang into the air. That woman kept some strange hours.

A loud slam startled her. She pictured Tara under a ladder or, worse, having fallen through rotted boards, her legs dangling through the first-floor ceiling. Merry Anna ran out the door and down the hill.

She yelled for Tara as she got close to the porch. She ran up the front steps and pounded on the door. "Tara?" She twisted the doorknob and stepped inside. "Tara? Where are you? Are you okay?"

Tara walked into the front room, a thick leather tool belt hanging from her hips. She had a hammer in one hand. "Hey there."

"Oh my gosh. I heard a loud bang from my place. I was afraid you were hurt and trying to signal for help."

"Don't be silly. If I get hurt, I'll call the police or the fire department. I wouldn't sit here banging in hopes someone might get nosy."

Is she calling me nosy? "Well, thank goodness you're okay."

"How was your little s'mores party?" Tara asked.

"It was fine." Look who was being nosy now. "What do you know about it?"

"Nothing. That's why I asked. I saw the way Adam looked at you after church."

"We volunteered to help with teen night. It was not a date. Believe me, those kids kept us on our toes."

"Mm-hmm. Nothing sweet went on around s'mores time?"

Could that woman read minds, or had someone from the

church been gossiping already about the fact that Adam had swept a melted marshmallow from the side of her mouth? *His fingers were as light as a feather against my cheek* . . . No. Tara was just digging for information and wishing for something that was not going to happen.

"Nothing to speak of," Merry Anna said as casually as she could manage with the memory of his touch hanging in the forefront of her mind. "We went through a lot of marshmallows, and the kids had a great time."

"Well, that's good," Tara said, looking a bit disappointed. "Doing your part for the community and all."

"Right." Community was the last thing on her mind when her hand had shot up in church to volunteer. She knew darn well that if Adam hadn't been the first to volunteer, she wouldn't have offered.

"You're not going to tell me about you two going to the rodeo together next Friday?"

Merry Anna hadn't told a soul. "How do you know about that?"

She shrugged. "People in a small town talk."

"Tara, you are newer around here than I am."

"Yes, but I made friends with the men, and they are way bigger gossips than women. They cannot keep a secret." She pinched Merry Anna on the cheek. "It's okay. He's very cute. I'm not your mama. I'm not judging you. If you hang out with that handsome cowboy for a while, maybe it'll loosen you up a little." She swatted Merry Anna on her rear as she turned and walked back into the kitchen.

"I don't need loosening up." Merry Anna followed her.

"Sure you do. What are you going to wear?"

"To the rodeo? Jeans, I guess."

"Merry Anna, you need to drive down to the western-wear

store on the other side of the mountain and get you a bright-red pair of boots and great-fitting jeans. What's that song? 'Blue jeans and pearls are my kind of girl' or something like that. You'll figure it out."

"That'll seem like I'm trying too hard."

"No, it'll just show that you want to look your best. And who knows when you'll meet your next true love? Maybe this bull rider isn't it, but who's to say Mr. Perfect won't be there selling T-shirts or photographing the event for some fancy magazine? Got to always be ready."

Somehow the thought of her next true love selling T-shirts was a bit disappointing. "I'm not looking for love. I'm just going to support my friend and understand the sport a little better."

"What's there to understand? Guys tie themselves to a mad bull and then try not to get thrown to the ground and gored in eight seconds flat."

"There's more to it than that."

"And more to life than being alone. Which is why I made friends with those breakfast-club guys." She shook her finger in Merry Anna's face. "You need someone."

"I really don't. Even when I was married, I was the one who took care of us financially. My ex did nothing. I don't need anyone."

"Just because you had one loser doesn't mean you're a loser magnet."

That stung.

"God Himself said we weren't meant to be alone. Quit all your resisting and let life happen. He's got it all planned out, you know." Tara turned toward her kitchen project. "I've got to finish this up so I can call it a night."

"What is it you're doing?"

"Putting up those lights we picked out for the kitchen. Come look. They are perfect."

"They are." Merry Anna didn't tell Tara that when she'd said she was going to put sconces in the kitchen, it had seemed like an old-lady look. She was glad now that she hadn't mentioned it, as the carriage house–style lights were stunning against the brick. "It's beautiful."

"Sometimes it just takes the right accessories to bring something back to life."

"Are you referring to this house or me?"

"Take it how you see fit."

Really? She was a spitfire, but it probably wasn't bad advice. "You know, my ex-husband was like an entitled teenager. We were teenagers when we got married, so I guess I just never realized that he didn't grow up. I made so many excuses for him over the years that my parents, to this day, have no idea that I was the only one paying for things." *That sounds pitiful. How embarrassing.* She wasn't sure that she'd ever admitted that to anyone else. "He'd take a job for a while and then quit, always on to the next thing. Part of why I'm here is to figure myself out. I made some horrible decisions, and my priorities were crooked. I didn't even know it until I took myself out of the situation. Being here has been a real eye-opener."

Tara took off her tool belt and sat on a stool. "Thank you for confiding in me. I'm sure you haven't shared that with many others."

"No one."

"It'll eat you up if you keep it inside like that."

"My parents think I've been totally unreasonable with Kevin. He cheated on me. He never contributed to our marriage anyway, so I don't know why it surprised me. All I ever asked was for him to honor the vows we'd made. Why is that so hard for some people? How do you forgive that?"

"Only you can be the one to judge that, and it's no one else's business but yours. Not even your parents'." She picked up her hammer. "Come here."

Merry Anna walked over to her.

"You are going to love demolition. Tell you what. You take this hammer in your hand like this and swing for all you're worth right there on that big *X* I have on the wall. You give that past a heaping hard hammer hit goodbye, and don't ever think about it again."

Merry Anna laughed.

"I'm not kidding." She held out the hammer, shaking it toward her. "Take it."

"Really?"

"Yes."

When Merry Anna hesitated, Tara turned, pulled the safety goggles from her head over her eyes, and wielded her hammer like it was nothing. Plaster, dust, and pieces of wood flew into the room. She looked like a giant bug with her safety glasses on.

Merry Anna stood there in shock.

"Your turn."

After putting on Tara's safety glasses, Merry Anna grabbed the hammer and hit the wall.

"That's all you've got? That guy cheated on you."

She reared back and really slammed it this time. A big chunk of plaster dropped to the floor with a thud. "That felt really good."

"I knew it would." Tara patted her on the shoulder. "I'm not saying you and Adam are a thing, but promise me you'll relax and just listen to your heart. You might be delighted by where it leads you. A man that is worthy of you will make you feel like a treasure. You do not want to miss out on that."

"I can't even imagine."

"You deserve it, Merry Anna, and a healthy relationship is equal. I'm not saying it has to be fifty-fifty financially, but you'll find your balance. One of you will excel where the other falters, and together you will add up to be more. I had that. I'm telling you that you want it."

"It sounds like a fairy tale."

"Well, I'm not saying Adam is the guy, but he does ride a big white stallion. I've seen him." Tara winked at her. "You can write your own fairy tale."

"Thank you, Tara."

"Now finish knocking out that wall. I've got work to do there."

Merry Anna didn't hesitate. She swung that hammer until she thought she might cry, but the relief of each powerful landing was like snipping the ties to Kevin, her past, and everyone's opinion about it.

If I ever do have another relationship, it'll be someone worthy of writing home about.

13

On Monday morning, Merry Anna put on slacks so she could ride to work on the bike Krissy had loaned her. Retro green and cream with a cute stained-wicker basket on the front, the old Schwinn was probably worth a fortune. She coasted down her driveway and then pedaled up the street. Was it her imagination or were the birds singing extra loud today?

She pedaled on past the colorful metal rooster statue in front of Memory Lane Antique and Crafts. If she had time after work, she'd stop in and see if she could find a new project for the bunkhouse or maybe even a little housewarming gift for Tara.

Slowing in front of Hardy House, she felt a sense of pride for her tiny part in this little store that she'd never felt as COO of the Supply Cabinet. *Why is that? I don't even have an investment in this place.*

Maybe that was the problem. She had a major investment in the Supply Cabinet, but it was never *her* financial investment. Her uncle had been the one to put the sweat equity into that business. She'd been expected to carry it on, an unspoken promise of sorts between her mom and dad and her mom's brother. There'd never been a time when Merry Anna had been allowed to entertain doing anything else for a living.

Was that because working for her family's business was her duty? She'd thought she was happy, but then, she'd thought her marriage was okay, too, and that had been a hot mess.

The sad part was that now that she realized how joyful she felt doing these other things, how was she supposed to go back to her old routine of ten-hour days? Gosh, the more she tried to figure out who she was and what she should be doing, the more confusing it became.

She went inside, grateful for her life today and trying so hard not to get hung up on why.

"Good morning, Merry Anna." Krissy was dressed in a summery yellow sundress and sandals with daisies on them. "How was your weekend?"

"So good." She brushed her fingers across the stack of new pillowcases. "These just came in?"

"Yes! Aren't they fabulous?"

"I don't think I've ever felt anything softer." Each case had tiny flowers embroidered at the edge. It was such a simple and delicate design that it made them feel even more precious. "I'm definitely going to need a set of these."

"I already put aside the ones with the tiny bluebells on them for me. I just got off the phone with Liz. I know she's going to want them for Angels Rest too."

"This is the only bad thing about working for this place. I could spend my whole check in here."

"I have the same problem," Krissy said. "But isn't that a great problem to have?" Her laughter was light. "I love Hardy House."

"Me too. You don't know how much meeting you and staying here in Antler Creek has meant to me."

"I never wanted to pry, but I knew you needed something." She pressed her hand against her heart. "I'm not asking for details. But I do want you to know that you have been such a treasure to me. Which brings me to something very important that I need to talk to you about."

Dread tensed Merry Anna's muscles. "Is everything okay?" Was she going to lose this wonderful little job? Was this the sign that she was supposed to go back to work like Mom kept saying? Deflated, she tried to hide her concern. "What can I do?"

"Everything is perfect. More than perfect. I don't even want to think you might leave me someday. I heard through the grapevine that you've made some new friends—wait, more specifically, a very handsome, fearless friend."

Adam. She started laughing.

"I know it's none of my business, but if you were to meet someone here in Antler Creek and that meant you'd be around forever, well then, wouldn't things be great?"

"Yes. Yes, they would." She exhaled a sigh of relief. "Oh, Krissy. I was just outside this morning, looking at this store and wondering how I ever thought I was living before I came to Antler Creek."

Krissy walked over and hugged her. "I feel like we've been friends forever."

"I was so broken when I got here." Merry Anna couldn't fight the memories flooding back, as fresh as if she were standing there watching Kevin lean into that woman's car and kiss her. Not just a peck either. He'd lingered long enough that she realized she was standing in the middle of the parking garage in plain sight. She'd hopped behind a pillar, but she couldn't make herself look away. It was clear that it was something that had been going on for a long while. She'd felt so tiny and insignificant.

That evening, she confronted Kevin with the information, and they'd fought all night long. He lied to her face, accusing her of not trusting him. He'd been the one to break the trust, and had she not seen it with her own two eyes, he'd have convinced her that it wasn't true. How could she not have known? She questioned everything now.

"You know, it's a long story," Merry Anna said, "but I was searching for something when I got here. I didn't know what. Still don't, really, but I do feel different. Happier."

"And Adam?"

She grinned. "Adam. That's a sticky situation." His thumb on her cheek against that sticky marshmallow had made her insides swirl. That kiss on her birthday—it was so nice even though she'd cut it short. She didn't know how to let go and allow it to happen. She'd been married her whole adult life. Not being married wasn't easy.

"How so?"

"He's fun to be with, but he said he's got room for one commitment and that's rodeo. I'm not sure getting tangled up with him is smart. Friends is all it can be. I'm fine with that."

"He's very handsome." Krissy raised her brow. "So?"

"So, he's a good neighbor."

"I heard you two baked pies together."

Small-town gossip. It was no joke. "We did. Strawberry pies, and they were delicious." She turned away from Krissy's hopeful stare. "And we may have spent a day riding horses . . . on my birthday."

"Your birthday? It was your birthday and you didn't even tell me?"

"It was no big deal. I wasn't even going to celebrate it, but then Adam started talking about horseback riding and I'd never been, and, well, one thing led to another."

Krissy plopped down in the white Queen Anne chair sitting next to the front counter. "All this was going on? You sure have some explaining to do. Tell me everything."

Merry Anna felt the heat rise to her cheeks. "It's nothing."

"If it was nothing, you wouldn't be blushing right now."

She dropped her head back, then closed her eyes. "I don't know what it is. It's nice." She crossed her arms, not even wanting to say it out loud.

"It's nice. Oh my gosh. You do realize that Adam Locklear is the most available bachelor in three counties but doesn't date. I mean, yeah, he might have a few girls hanging around once in a while, but never anything serious. And never anyone like you." Krissy covered her mouth. "I can't believe this."

"Stop. No. You're out of control."

"Fine. But you are attracted to him, right?"

"Well, yeah. Who isn't?" She thought of the women lining up around him after the rodeo. He had his pick.

"Exactly my point."

"But I think the reason we've had so much fun is that neither of us is looking for anything. He has some lofty goals for this year. Did you know he has a shot at winning the whole bull-riding final thing this year?"

"I knew he was having a good year, but that's really something."

"And it requires focus. He doesn't have time for anything, and you know what? I am in no position to be dating or starting something. I just got out of a bad relationship, and I—"

"Okay, okay. I get it. But I hope this means you're thinking about sticking around."

"I am very happy here, and as out of character as it might seem for me to live at the bunkhouse, I love that little place."

"How are your plants doing?" Krissy asked.

"Wonderful. I still can't believe they are doing so well. Every one of them is thriving. The little cherry tomatoes are really springing up."

"Like you. You seem like a different person. It's like you can do anything. I'm sure the people you worked for before are missing you like crazy."

If you only knew. "They've mentioned they'd like me to come back, but I'm not so sure I want to." She looked right into Krissy's eyes. "When I left, it was supposed to be temporary. They wouldn't accept my resignation."

"Well, they can't make you go back. It's your choice."

"Yes, but sometimes it's complicated."

"Why do you think things are so different here?"

"I don't know. It's a slower pace. It seems more real. You're great, and this store is amazing. I love all the feminine stuff. It's all just so pretty. It's nice. This town is small, and I guess with it being small, I notice and enjoy more things. Does that make sense?"

"I know. When I was in Hilton Head, things were so busy that I didn't even have time to enjoy myself."

"Right. Like walking to work, or today I rode the bike. That's so nice. And church. I don't even remember when the last time was that I'd gone to church before I moved here. I love it. I feel so grounded, and I'm doing things I normally wouldn't do."

"I saw you volunteer to help with teen night."

"And I had a blast. I think I may have even helped someone. That was so gratifying."

"You fit in so well here. Whatever it is you think you want to do or be or try, you can do it here in Antler Creek."

"Would you mind if I committed to sticking around and renting your bunkhouse through the summer? By then I'll be prepared to sign a lease or find another place to live if you're ready to flip it. Is that fair?"

"Totally, and I'm not pushing you for a decision, but I'm so thankful you're going to stay a while longer." Krissy bounced with delight. "I have a feeling Adam is influencing this decision, whether you admit it or not."

"If I stay, it won't be because of Adam. It will be because it's right for me."

Krissy flung her hands in the air. "Good. You're right. That's how it should be. We have to take care of ourselves before we can consider including anyone else in the equation. That's how it was for me and Grady too. It wasn't until I got back here and opened the store and kind of got my feet under me that I could take my hands off the brakes and start coasting into that possibility."

"You two are so perfect together."

"It's funny how things work out when you least expect it. I'd all but given up on having someone like him in my life, and then there he was." She reached over and patted Merry Anna's hand. "I won't push, but just don't turn your back on the possibility. I never knew life could be this good with the right partner. I want that for you too."

"Thank you." The chimes on the door jingled. "We have a customer. I better get back to work, or my boss might fire me." Merry Anna walked over to greet the customer, excited to spread a little Antler Creek hospitality. "Looking for anything special today?"

"I'm not sure what I'm looking for. My mother-in-law's birthday is next week, and my husband always dumps that on me. Like, how am I supposed to know what to get her?" The woman spun around, too harried to even really see anything.

"Oh my goodness. I'm sure that makes you crazy, but you've come to the right place. I just know we'll be able to pull together something she'll love or, even better, can't complain about."

"Do you know my mother-in-law?" The lady let down her guard. "Thank you. I appreciate the help."

"I'm Merry Anna, and it's my pleasure."

"You can call me Jessica."

"Well, Jessica, let's start over here." An hour later, not only did Jessica have the perfect gift for her mother-in-law, but she'd also treated herself to some very nice things.

Merry Anna wrapped the present for Jessica's mother-in-law, then carefully folded the other things in beautiful tissue paper. Jessica was sure to feel special when she rediscovered all her goodies later at home. Merry Anna walked the woman all the way out to her car, then came back in to a very happy Krissy.

"And this is the selfish reason I want you to work here. My sales have never been this good."

"That's only because it's still a new business. You are doing everything right."

"Well, it's more fun with you here. I'm going to head upstairs to the studio and work on that barn quilt for the Ogburns."

"Sure. I've got this."

Merry Anna's phone rang, startling her since it so rarely

did these days. It was her mother, and since she wasn't up for a discussion with her, she let it go to voice mail.

At the end of the day, Merry Anna got on the Schwinn to go home. The neon sign at the antique store beckoned her.

It wasn't as though she had anything better to do. With her plants on the back patio, she could even take care of them late at night under the porch light. She swerved the bike into the lot and pulled it up onto the sidewalk next to the front door. She put down the kickstand and went inside.

A booth of cinnamon brooms was right across from the register. Not exactly a smell she usually associated with summer.

"Hello." Flossie raised her bony arm in the air. "Merry Anna! Good to see you. Let me know if you have any questions."

"Yes ma'am. I will." The front half of the store was mostly twelve-by-twelve-foot craft booths on consignment. The back half was where the real money was made. Flossie had dealt in antiques in this region for most of her years. Everyone in town said this was the place to find the good stuff. Rumor had it she cherry-picked most of the estate sales before they even went public.

Merry Anna had no idea what she was looking for, but she wanted to make that bunkhouse feel more like her own, even if it was just temporary. Maybe she'd find a nice piece of furniture. There was a beautiful sideboard, with all original hardware and hardly any wear. She pulled the drawers out and inspected the piece. It was a little pricey, but once this wager with Kevin was over, she could spend whatever she liked. This would definitely be on her list.

Merry Anna turned to go chat with Flossie about the sideboard, when something else caught her eye: the most beautiful, elegant bed she'd ever seen. She stood there picturing it with fine linens and a billowy, crisp-white comforter.

Flossie's instincts must've been ringing up dollar signs in her mind, because right about that moment, she poked her head around that old sideboard. "Find something you like?"

"I did, but then I turned and saw this bed."

"Oh yes. It's one of my very favorite pieces." Flossie walked over, twisting the diamond on the dainty golden chain around her neck. "An estate piece. Rumors were flying that Liz Taylor had slept in it. No idea if that was true or not, but it made for an interesting day of speculation. Drove the price up, too, I'm afraid."

"I love how simply elegant it is. I don't think I've ever seen a wooden bed that looked so feminine but not ornately so. Does that make sense?"

"That's what initially drew me to it too. It's the burled walnut that gives it the unique look. Very rich looking, but with simple lines. Truly exquisite. This is an 1880s Victorian Eastlake."

Merry Anna ran her fingers across the wood. "I didn't see a price on it. Don't tell me it's not for sale."

"It's for sale." Flossie hooked a finger, and Merry Anna followed her to the headboard. She slipped her hand behind the wood and pulled up a hangtag on a string. "I might even be able to do you a little better on this piece, with you working down at Hardy House and all."

"Really?" She stepped over and read the price tag. "What can you do?"

"Ten percent off?"

"It's out of my budget for this month." *Stupid bet with Kevin.* She had half a mind to cheat and sneak it, but then she'd never be able to lie to him. "Could I put some money down to have it held for me? I could do three payments."

"Three equal payments? One now and one each of the next two months?"

"Yes. I'm sorry to ask you to do that."

"Don't be. I'd love for you to have this bed." Flossie leaned in and nudged her with an elbow. "I like you. I can do that for you."

She hated that this stupid bet with Kevin was making her buy time, but she couldn't risk her amazing find slipping away. "I can't believe this will be mine. I hope the time flies."

"You don't have to wait," Flossie said. "Pay me that third, and I'll schedule delivery and setup immediately."

"Really?"

"Yes. That bed deserves to be somewhere besides this store. I think it's a perfect fit." Flossie smirked. "Don't really think you're much of a flight risk anyway."

"I promise I'm not. Thank you so much, Flossie."

Merry Anna wrote Flossie a check, then walked out of that store with a spring in her step.

In a couple of days, she'd have her new bed. On her way out of the store, she spotted a stained glass panel. "Flossie, can you deliver this with my bed? I can pay you today for it."

"Sure can. Salvaged that from an old church. The white paint has charm, with the multiple layers and slight curling at the edges, but aren't the colors vivid?"

"They are. When the sun comes up in the morning, it shines through my bedroom window. I'm going to hang this from a wire in front of the window. I bet it will cast those colors across the whole room and my new bed."

"Now, that's the way to greet a new day," Flossie said.

14

Merry Anna spent the better part of the week working on updates to the bunkhouse. Krissy volunteered Grady to go pick up the old bed and a couple of other things that Merry Anna wasn't using and store them upstairs at Hardy House. In the meantime, Merry Anna and Krissy went to work picking out new bedding and a rug for the room.

That evening, her new bed was delivered, and Tara came over to help Merry Anna and Krissy get everything set up.

"I'd almost forgotten about this stained glass panel," Merry Anna said. "I saw it as I was leaving the store. Isn't it beautiful?"

"It is," Tara said. "Where are you going to put it?"

"I thought it would look so pretty hanging right in the center of the window here on the inside, so the colors would stream through in the morning."

Tara walked over and examined it, lifting it and looking at how it was made. "It's heavy, but I think I can do something for you." She really did know as much as any handyman. She cut and shaped wooden pegs with hooks that allowed them to clip the heavy frame in front of the window a few inches, allowing her just enough room to open the window if needed or remove it to clean the glass.

It took Tara less than an hour to have the stained glass panel in place, and during that time, Merry Anna and Krissy had made the bed and hung a couple of pictures.

"It doesn't even look like the same room," Krissy remarked.

"It's gorgeous. Just like I wanted it to look." Merry Anna plopped onto the bed.

Tara and Krissy joined her, and they all sat on the bed and marveled over the way the light came through the stained glass—and it was almost dusk. The morning was sure to be even more glorious.

"It's perfect."

"Heavenly," said Tara. "I think you're going to feel so at peace in here."

"It would have to be better than what it was," Krissy said. "I feel bad for not thinking to at least glam up the sheets and stuff for you before you moved in."

"Don't be silly. I was thankful for the place to stay, and I love this place. I'm not gonna lie. I'm going to really love sleeping in this room now and reading. I think I might order a couple new novels."

"You need a nice comfy chair. It would fit perfectly right over there," Krissy said.

"That would be good. I'll have to go back down and see what else Flossie has. That place is filled with wonderful stuff."

"That funky rooster out front of her antique shop is misleading," Tara said.

"Yes, it is a little crazy looking, but the quality of the furniture is amazing. You'll be able to outfit your whole house."

Tara looked intrigued. "Let me know when you go back down. I'd love to tag along."

"I will," Merry Anna said.

"This room is pretty enough to entertain in, if you know what I mean." Tara raised her brows, nodding at the two women.

"She talks like this all the time," Merry Anna said to Krissy.

"Well, she's not wrong. It will be lovely and very romantic." Krissy shrugged.

Tara nodded, then interjected, "Speaking of romantic, did you ever get an outfit for the rodeo?"

"I'm just going to wear a pair of jeans and a T-shirt."

"Aren't you going with Adam?" Krissy asked.

"Yeah, but just as friends."

"Right, but he's kind of a celebrity around the rodeo." Krissy's eyes became slits. "Women in three counties have been trying to get his attention. If you show up with him, you need to at least look the part."

"What part?"

"Interested, maybe?" Krissy said.

"We're just neighbors," Merry Anna reminded her.

"It couldn't hurt to bling up your look a little," said Tara.

"If you don't want to buy something new, come over to my house," Krissy said. "I've got tons of that stuff. Blouses, hats, jewelry. Lots of turquoise. How about tomorrow night? We'll have a girls' night. You too, Tara."

Merry Anna did not want to make a big deal out of this. "Y'all are killing me."

"I'm in," said Tara. "I could use a night off from swinging a hammer. I'm sore." She rubbed her shoulder. "I'm not as young as I once was."

"See. It's the neighborly thing to do. We need to make Tara take a break." Krissy smiled. "You're outnumbered."

It did sound fun to have a girls' night. She didn't like being outvoted, but this time, what could it hurt? "Next time, we need more voters, but count me in."

Friday rolled around, and the outfit Krissy and Tara had voted as "Most Likely To" was lying on top of the white comforter of her new bed.

Merry Anna lifted the blouse. It was pretty, but there was a lot going on with it. *What exactly are you 'most likely to' do?* The shirt had attitude. It was way louder than she'd ever been.

"Okay, here we go." She'd seen Adam drive down the lane a little earlier. She wondered if his friends were pushing him to wear a special shirt tonight.

She washed off her daytime makeup and then got in the shower. As she let the water run over her, she thought of Adam. The bruises and scars on his body. A man with no fear. She lifted the scented soap to her nose. It smelled of flowers, fruits, and herbs. She swept the bubbles, as smooth as lotion on her skin, across her body. These little niceties were about the only thing she missed from her old life.

She let the water run until it ran cool. She stepped out and wrapped her hair in a towel, then put her bathrobe on. In her bedroom, she blew her hair dry, letting the waves curl the way they liked. She wasn't sure if she could pull off the cowboy hat that Krissy had lent her, but Krissy had taught her how to sweep her bangs back before she put it on so her hair would still fall nice when she took it off.

Her heart pounded, sending her nerves into so much of a tizzy about this "not a date" that she was sweating. She turned on the little USB fan that sat on her desk, but it wasn't very helpful. She went back into the bathroom and turned on her blow-dryer, pressing the little blue button to cool the air. She aimed at the dampness at her hairline, being careful to just blow underneath her hair so it didn't get too big and puffy.

The alarm on her phone went off. *It's go time.* She needed to finish getting ready.

She put on her makeup first, then got dressed, stepping into the boots last. The Dan Post Bluebird boots were well broken in. Krissy said they were her favorites, and Merry Anna could see why. The leather was so soft that it was like butter from years of wear.

Tiptoeing in front of the bathroom mirror, she checked herself, then clasped the necklace around her neck and slipped the two bracelets Krissy had picked out over her wrist.

Her phone dinged.

She picked it up and laughed when she read Krissy's text. It simply read,

Wear the hat! Embrace the rodeo!

Merry Anna picked up the cowboy hat from the bed and twirled it between her fingers. It was pretty, but she'd never been the type to really call attention to herself. *Quit being safe.* She walked back into the bathroom to put it on just the way Krissy had showed her. Talking to herself in the mirror, she said, "Adam, I hope you don't think I'm crazy."

She heard his diesel truck rumble up the drive.

Her hands tingled. *Breathe!* She walked out the front door and down the steps to meet him in the driveway.

He pulled to a stop right next to her.

Feeling like the only one in costume at a formal party, she

began second-guessing the advice Tara and Krissy had given her.

The door on the Ford truck swung open, and Adam hopped out, his eyes wide and his mouth quirked to one side. At first she thought he was laughing at her.

"You look amazing!" His smile widened. "I mean, you always look beautiful—ya know, good—but wow!"

It took a second for his words to sink in. "Are you making fun of me?"

"No." He tugged the cowboy hat from his head. "Absolutely not. You always look very nice, in the dresses and conservative stuff, but this is an unexpected surprise. The bright colors make your eyes sparkle." He kicked his foot forward awkwardly. "That sounded better in my head."

And she thought she was the one making a fool of herself. "I'm glad you like it. It's kind of a new look for me."

"It's appealing." He walked around to the passenger side and opened the door for her. "Let's go."

She jumped into the truck and sat, crossing her legs. The snip toe of the sanded leather with the turquoise inlay stitched on the boot made the tip look like a little fox face. She did love these boots.

When Adam slid behind the wheel, he gave her an approving nod.

She sat back, rather enjoying the attention.

There weren't very many people there when they arrived at the stadium. Adam walked her through the back, showing her how the livestock was handled and explaining how the handlers would move the animals from place to place for the event. A maze of chutes and gates remained empty at the time, and it was a little hard to imagine how it all worked.

Adam led Merry Anna inside one of the chutes, and one of the other guys pulled it open to give her an idea of what it was like when a cowboy was riding.

"Adam, there is so much more to all this than I'd imagined."

Next, Adam introduced her to the announcer, a man with a quick smile and a voice to die for. "She can sit up in the box with us," the man said.

Adam looked to her for an answer.

The announcer said, "We do have the best view in the place. I mean, if you don't mind not being in the crowd."

"Thank you. That would be great."

"Good. Just come on up when you're ready. We'll have a chair for you." He tipped his hat before he walked off.

"That was nice." She smiled at Adam.

He nodded. "Good people. All of them."

"I'll be fine here. I know you need to get ready."

"I have to check in and attend the riders meeting." He handed her a twenty-dollar bill. "Get yourself a snack and a drink."

"I'm not taking your money. I can pay for my own drink."

"It'd make me feel better if you let me."

She let out a breath. "Fine." She wasn't used to anyone else picking up the tab, but if she wasn't going to repeat her past mistakes, this was a pretty good first step. "What am I supposed to say? I'm not thinking 'Break a leg' works in this situation, although, honestly, I've never really understood it for actors either."

"How about you just pray for a safe ride? That's what I do."

Pray. With a nervous tickle in her gut, she watched him walk away. *Please let him have a safe ride.*

By the time she walked around and bought a T-shirt and a bottle of water, there was still about thirty minutes before the event would start. She stood off to the side of the bleachers, people-watching. She recognized a couple of folks from Antler Creek, and a couple of the riders looked familiar from last time.

A young boy, probably ten or eleven years old, walked by, wearing shiny blue-fringed chaps and pulling a red wagon full of cattle-dog puppies.

"How old are they?" she asked.

"Ten weeks. They're for sale." He stood there, one hip jutted out, looking like a regular cowboy.

"Can I hold one?"

"Depends. Have to warn you, most of the girls who hold one end up buying one." He shrugged.

"I'll take my chances." She picked up a blue-spotted one. "Oh gosh. They are sweet." It didn't take but a minute for the wagon to be circled by cowgirls. Merry Anna handed the pup off to another girl and slipped away.

She heard the announcer welcome the crowd, which was beginning to pour in pretty steadily now. She went over to the booth and climbed up the stairs, knocking as she entered. "Still have room for me?"

"Sure thing. Come on in, Merry Anna."

"Thank you." She took a seat at the end of the long table. "If there's anything I can help with, feel free to put me to work."

"No need. I've got a couple helpers coming. You just enjoy the show."

Excitement rose in the arena as the noise from the increasing crowd grew. The bleachers were full. A bright array of western wear and cowboy hats dotted the stands. She noticed the schedule posted on the glass partition. Adam was riding seventh.

That's lucky, right?

He'd drawn a bull named No-Frills Freak, who weighed in at 1,994 pounds.

Although some sporting events had put a big pause on the national anthem and color guard, there was no such behavior in Archdale, North Carolina, that night. The national anthem was sung by a young lady while another girl dressed in red, white, and blue carried the American flag as she rode a white horse through the arena under a spotlight.

". . . and the home of the brave."

The crowd screamed and applauded.

The announcer welcomed everyone again and said the Cowboy's Prayer. Who knew there was even such a thing? She'd never heard of that. Curious, she listened intently. The announcer's deep voice and Southern twang came over the speaker loud and clear. "Our heavenly Father, we pause at this time, mindful of the many blessings You have bestowed upon us. We ask, Lord, that You will be with us in the arena of life."

The truth and sincerity in those words sent a chill through her. It might be a crazy sport, but being around these people—there was something more like family than she'd ever felt before.

"Amen."

An amen rose from the stands.

Not even thirty seconds after that, the first chute gate swung open for a twenty-three-year-old from Advance, North

Carolina. Unfortunately, he wouldn't be advancing tonight, because by the time the clock got to 4.1, that guy was on his hind parts in the dirt.

"No score," the announcer said over the speakers. "Everyone, give this cowboy a big round of applause, because that's all he's going home with tonight."

The cowboy picked up his rope and slinked out the gate.

The next rider didn't even make it past the chute before he self-ejected from his bull, and the third one didn't do much better.

Finally, the fourth rider, wearing a vest with sponsor patches and flashy chaps, dropped down on a big black-and-white bull in the last chute on the far side of the arena. The bull jumped, clanging the gates so loudly that Merry Anna wondered if he might break free. Thoughts of a bull running through the stands worried her. There were so many people that it would be hard to escape.

But nothing like that happened. The bull finally seemed to settle down. It was then that she noticed Adam at the top of the chute helping the rider get set, pulling the rope and nodding. The rider put his hand in the air and gave a nod. The gate flew open, and loud rock-and-roll music pumped through the arena.

There wasn't anything settled or calm about the animal that catapulted out of that gate. He vaulted straight up into the air, all four of his legs at least three feet off the ground, his body twisting, coming down so hard that the man tied to his waist flung like a rag doll.

The power forced a sound from Merry Anna. She covered her mouth and nose with her hands. The bullfighters were already closing in, making sure the rider wasn't in trouble. The bull gave one big buck, then sort of moved in one direction, hopping and stopping. Somehow that guy stayed on the whole eight seconds, but it wasn't pretty.

When it was Adam's turn to ride, the announcer made a big deal of it, mentioning all his buckles and previous wins and his golden path to the PBR this year.

Merry Anna held her breath. *Please keep him safe through this ride.*

The *Rocky* theme song played as Adam got down on the bull, and the guys pulled his rope tight.

Merry Anna took a slug of her water, trying to swallow.

She glanced up, and the chute slammed open. The song switched, which only seemed to amp up the crowd and that bull. As if in slow motion, she watched every twitch, hop, buck, and spin, in awe of the strength of the snarling, drooling animal. Adam had his chin tucked, arm up in the air, and legs spurring as the bull spun in circles as if they were in some twisted ballet. Each time Adam's spur connected with No-Frills Freak, Merry Anna sucked in another breath.

The buzzer sounded, but for a moment, Adam remained in place, his hand still there on the back of the bull. She heard one of the bullfighters yell the words *hung up.*

The other bullfighter raced in front of the bull, waving his arms, as another cowboy ran in to assist Adam. It seemed as if it took only one tug before Adam leaped from the back of the bull, sticking the landing in a squatted position. At least he landed on his feet.

Everyone in the whole place stood and cheered wildly.

She jumped up, clapping.

"Adam Locklear scores a 91!"

The crowd got even louder. It was the highest score so far, and as each rider took his turn the rest of the night, no one could beat it.

Afterward, Merry Anna hung out in the box. Just like before, a group of girls flocked to the area where the cowboys came out. She was prepared for it this time.

Adam separated himself from the herd, raised a hand in her direction, and waved her over.

She met him halfway. "You were amazing. I about had a heart attack."

"Well, don't do that. We need the EMTs ready out here in the arena in case someone gets hurt." He bumped her shoulder to shoulder. "Your prayers must've worked. No one got hurt. Thanks for those."

"You bet." It seemed she had a lot more to pray about since she'd arrived in Antler Creek.

On the walk back to his truck, she observed the other people leaving. There was a general atmosphere of fun in the air, but Adam seemed contemplative, probably coming down from the exhilaration of it all. They got into the truck and rode home, the radio taking the place of any conversation between them. When he pulled up in front of her house, he turned down the radio. "Glad you went?"

"I am."

"I'm glad you did too. We'll do it again sometime if you like." He reached for her hat and gave it a slight tug down over her eyes. "You looked real pretty tonight. I meant it when I told you earlier."

She lifted her face, hoping the hat might camouflage the blush that was certain to show she'd never been good with compliments. "I hope we will. I know you have a lot on your plate this year, and you need to stay focused on those goals."

"Man, you are special. I'm riding nearby again next week. Maybe you can come with me then."

"That would be nice." She scooted out of the truck. "Congratulations on your win tonight." She sensed him watching her. Spinning around to see, she took a couple of steps backward and waved to him.

Adam waited to leave until Merry Anna got inside. She turned on the porch light and waved again.

She watched as he rode off into the dark, but instead of being on a white horse, he was in a big Ford pickup truck. It was almost like a romance novel, the way it left her a little breathless.

15

Adam was in his workout room doing sit-ups, when it sounded like there was a knock at the front door. He hesitated, then dismissed it. He wasn't expecting anyone.

He grunted out four more reps. Another knock, and this time there was no mistaking the sound.

"Hold your horses," he mumbled. He'd gotten so he didn't take kindly to people just dropping in unannounced, especially during his workouts. Normally, he'd ignore the interruption.

He finished the last two of his set, then laid the twenty-pound plate next to the workout bench and jumped to his feet. *What if it's Merry Anna?* He mopped his brow with a towel and slung it back over his shoulder to the bench.

"Just a minute. I'm coming!" he yelled.

He opened the door, and a woman wearing a straw Charlie 1 Horse hat with a soft-pink band stood there looking down at the little girl clinging to her right hand.

He'd hoped it had been Merry Anna, because really no one came to the front door, but this was most certainly not her. "Hello?"

"Hi." She lifted her face, the hat shadowing it still slightly, but the smile, those eyes—they were familiar. "Did I wake you?"

"No. I was up. Working out," he said, suddenly aware of his sweat-drenched shirt. She just stood there, as if waiting for him to say something else.

She leaned away, her smile pulled into a tight line. "It's me, Adam. Carly."

Carly? Barrel racer from South Carolina. A wilder female version of himself. "Carly?" He ran a hand through his hair. "Wow. What's it been? Years?"

"A long time."

"How've you been?"

"A lot has happened. Some good. Some not so good."

"Oh yeah, well, life's like that. Had my share of ups and downs too. What are you doing here?" He didn't remember her ever having been to the farm before, but here she was. Her eyes didn't dance like they used to, but other than that, she looked the same. Memories of how her thick braid hung from beneath her hat as she raced through those barrels galloped through his mind. Her body would hug the horse, like an extension of it, the barrels and her legs flailing as they raced for the finish. No one could beat her, and then she just kind of disappeared from the circuit.

"Can we come in?"

"Uh, yeah." He'd been distracted by the memory. Why had she just up and left? "Sure. Come on in."

She stepped inside, and the little girl—wearing blue jeans, a ruffly pink T-shirt, and matching cowgirl boots—hung close at her hip. Those tiny boots clomped against the oak flooring.

"I hope we didn't interrupt you," Carly said. "I'd have

called, but I didn't have your number. Somewhere along the way, I guess I lost it."

He dug his wallet from his back pocket and handed her a business card. "Here's my number. Yeah, it's been a while." He wondered if he still had her number in his phone.

"You're having a good year."

Pride pulled at him. So, she'd been keeping up with him? "I am. Thanks." Silence hung awkwardly between them. *Why didn't I just step out onto the porch and talk to her? It's a pretty day. I'm out of practice.* He led them into the living room.

"You riding tonight?" she asked.

"No, I won the round last night. I don't ride again until tomorrow night."

"That's great," she said. "You look good. Always did." Her eyes traced his chin.

He scoffed. *You're just digging for a compliment.* He'd throw her that. "You look good too, Carly."

They sat on the couch, the little girl hanging so close that you couldn't fit a carrot between them. He took the seat across from them.

She pulled her shoulder up, lowering her lashes. He remembered that look.

The little girl stared at the longhorn bull head mounted over the fireplace.

"Why are you here, Carly? I heard you gave up barrel racing."

"I did. I've been doing some training." She shook her head. "That's a lie. I don't know why I said that. I haven't ridden in a long time."

"So then, you're not here looking to buy a horse. What's up?"

She looked down at her fingernails, which were the color of the turquoise beads around her neck. "I had this all thought out—ya know, rehearsed in my head."

"All what?"

Her hands shook. Her eyes were glossy, with the threat of tears.

Please don't cry.

Carly pulled the little girl to her in a hug. "This is Zan. Isn't she beautiful?" She swept a graceful hand across the little girl's cheek, brushing back a curling lock of nearly white hair.

"She is." He leaned forward. "Hi, Zan. I'm Adam."

"You're a cowboy." The word had come out more like *kah-boy*, the emphasis on *boy*.

He grinned. "Yes ma'am, I am. How old are you?"

She spread all the fingers on her right hand wide.

"Use your words," Carly said.

The little girl whispered, "Five," and then hid her face in her mother's body before she turned to face Adam again.

"You look just like your mommy."

Zan giggled, already an ace at flirtation, just like her mother.

"She's my whole life," Carly said.

"I can see why." He still didn't know what any of this had to do with him. "Last I heard, you were living in Tennessee."

"I did for a while. I'm not really living anywhere right now." Her words caught. "Adam, I hate to ask, and I know this is unexpected, but I need your help."

"What?"

"I need a place to stay, a—"

"I just sold the bunkhouse."

"No, you don't understand. I need a place that's safe and clean for Zan." Her eyes held his. "For our little girl."

Our? Carly's words repeated in his mind. "Our?"

"Please don't hate me. Mom threatened to tell you at least a hundred times, but I thought I could do it alone. I've done nothing but make a mess of it. I can barely make it through each day. I should've told you about her before. At least before now. I'm so sorry."

"She can't be mine." He looked at the little girl sitting there completely unaware of the game being played. Not a game he took kindly to either.

"She is, Adam."

If there was one thing he'd never been wild and free about, it was that kind of thing. He knew guys who had been less than prepared or not careful over the years. That wasn't his way. "No, I've always been careful. Why would you say she's mine? If you need money, I can—"

"Because I know she is yours. I've always known."

He hung his head. *What is happening?*

"Adam, we can do a paternity test if you want. I know this is unexpected, but if you look at her, there's no mistaking that dimple in her left cheek and the shape of her lips."

"I'm going to need some time for this to sink in." *Like until after I get to the finals.* "You need some money for a place to stay?"

"Adam, I can't do this anymore. I just can't. I need a break. Or something. Can we stay here? Just until I can breathe again?"

"Carly, I don't—"

"Please, I'm really at the end here. I can promise you I wouldn't have shown up otherwise." When she swallowed, she looked as though she might choke. "Just even one night. Something."

As much as he wanted to believe that this child wasn't his

own, an unexpected fury began bubbling in his gut. *Five years? How could she have kept that from me? Maybe I'm not the father type, but wasn't that my choice, not hers to make for me?* Part of him wrestled with the idea that it might somehow be true. Carly said he was her last option?

"Carly, how many other places have you shown up unannounced like this?" He looked into her eyes, and for the life of him, he couldn't read them.

"None."

"Why now? She's five, for cryin' out loud." He flung his hand wide.

"I'm desperate now." Tears streamed down her face.

"Mommy, don't be sad," Zan whispered, patting her tiny hand on her mother's leg.

"Why not while you were pregnant and making life-altering decisions?"

"You were chasing titles and buckles and riding bulls. What kind of father would you have been?"

"I guess we'll never know, will we? You took that choice away from me." His voice tightened, and so did his throat, with emotions from deep inside. "And I still am riding, so there's that."

Zan buried her face in Carly's lap.

"I'm sorry." He leveled his tone, pausing to catch a breath. "We shouldn't be having this discussion in front of her." He stood and walked around the room while Carly sat with her head down, softly stroking the little girl's back but not saying a word.

He stopped and looked to the ceiling, praying for some kind of guidance. He'd always been so careful. This couldn't be happening—and not now. He had a plan for his life. He was on track for everything he'd worked so hard for.

She's desperate. No sense jumping to conclusions. I can help her out, and a paternity test will sort out the rest. It won't kill me to extend a helping hand. Lord knows I've had my share of blessings.

He spun on his heel, walked to the front door, and gave out a whistle. A moment later, his little dog came running to the door. "Come on, Shorty."

The canine raced through the door, his hind end skidding past his front, when he spotted the strangers in the living room. He slid to a complete stop, then let out a woof that lifted him right off his front feet.

"Puppy?" Zan pushed away from Carly.

Adam walked over and squatted next to Shorty. "Do you like dogs, Zan?"

She nodded shyly.

"Want to come say hi to Shorty?"

Zan looked up at Carly, who suddenly looked fragile.

"It's okay, baby." Carly nudged her toward the dog. "Go on."

Zan walked over and mimicked Adam's squat, although she was so tiny that it wasn't really necessary. She reached over and put her hand on Shorty's head. "I love puppies."

"Shorty is an old man," he said.

That made Zan giggle.

He stood and slapped his hand on his hip. Shorty jumped to his feet and followed him. "Why don't you two come sit on the couch and visit?" He grabbed the remote and turned on the television. "I'm sure there's a kids' station somewhere on this thing." He clicked until something suitable came on. "Your mom and I are going to be in the kitchen. Okay?"

"Yes sir." Zan had her arms wrapped around Shorty's thick neck. The dog lifted his head sideways and licked her face.

"Come here, Carly. Let's talk this out."

She rose to her feet and walked into the kitchen, her boots clicking off each step.

In the kitchen, he lowered his voice. "Look, I didn't mean to yell in front of your kid. My dad was a yeller. I hated it. I'm sorry. You took me by surprise."

"She's not just my kid." She lifted her chin. "She's your daughter."

"Carly, I'm not running from responsibility here, but it's a little hard to swallow that news nearly six years after the fact. I'll take the paternity test. Not a problem. But I'm feeling quite certain she's not mine."

"I wouldn't lie about it, Adam. You know me better than that. I—"

He held his hand up. "We're not going to argue or be mad. If it comes back that I'm that little girl's father, we'll deal with it. Right now you said you're desperate. That you need help. I'll help you. I *am* that kind of guy. We were friends."

She stood there but didn't say anything.

"Do you need some money?"

"I need you to step up. I can't do this anymore. I simply can't." She closed her eyes and dropped her head back. "We've been sleeping in my car for two weeks." She dropped the purse from her shoulder to the kitchen table. "Look. I've got money. I'm feeding her. I'm doing my best, but I don't know what to do anymore." She clung to a handful of dollar bills, shaking them, then stuffing them back in her hand. "I'm a Happy Meal away from just . . ." She broke down in tears.

He looked away. If there was one thing he couldn't handle, it was a lady crying. He heaved in a breath, wishing she'd stop and hoping that little girl in the other room couldn't hear her.

"Carly, settle down." He reached out to comfort her, but she swung her arm up and away.

Through gritted teeth, she said sternly, "Don't tell me to settle down. I'm not overreacting. You don't know what I'm feeling. I need your help, not your money."

He held his hands out. "Okay, I'm hearing you. Quiet. It's not going to help, you getting all worked up like this."

She shook her hand down to her side. "I'm sorry. I know I should've told you. At the time, I thought I was doing the right thing. It's more than I can handle. I don't have anything anymore. No life. No friends. I sold my horses."

"That's where all the money came from?"

She nodded. "You have to do *your* part. *You* have to take care of her too."

"I don't know a thing about raising kids. Yours, mine, or the neighbors'." He laughed, trying to lighten the moment. He felt bad for her, as she was clearly feeling overwhelmed, but he wasn't good at these kinds of situations.

"It's not funny."

"I'm not making light of it. Look, let's slow down. I'm sure we can figure it all out."

She snatched her purse up, hugging it to her chest like a child. "Don't patronize me. Just do what a man is supposed to do. Take care of your family. Why is that too much to ask?"

"I . . ." But before he could respond, even really think of what to say in a situation like this, she was out the door. He stood there a moment too long, because by the time he got to the front door, she was in the seat of her pickup and barreling out of his driveway.

"Carly!" He raced onto his porch and down the stairs. "Carly!" There was nothing but dust. "What the heck?"

He turned around and stomped back up. When he stepped inside, Zan stood there staring up at him. "Where'd Mommy go?"

Wouldn't that be nice to know?

"I'm not really sure."

Zan continued staring up at him. She wanted answers. So did he. He hated making empty promises, so what could he say?

He stood in the entry to the living room. "I'm sorry I made her cry."

"She cries a lot." She brushed her hair back from her face.

Does she run away a lot too?

Zan asked, "Can I go on the front porch?"

"Um, yeah. Sure." She was just a little kid. What did he know about taking care of a kid?

"Shorty too?"

"Okay, we'll all go." He let Zan lead the way. She was a confident little thing. He'd expected her to be frightened with the way her mother had just up and run off.

She opened the door and hopped over the threshold as if it were some sort of superstition, landing on two feet with all the heft of something twice her size.

Adam let Shorty out behind her and walked over to the railing. Where the heck was Carly?

Zan raced off to the left side of the front door. She plopped down on the deck and began rummaging through a pink Roper bag.

Oh no. Why did Carly bring that bag up to the house? And when?

Zan lifted a small stuffed horse from the bag and bounced it in her lap. Shorty walked over and rested his chin on her knee. "Is Mommy coming back?"

"Of course she is." The words had tumbled out without a

thought, but then the idea of the child asking made him wonder. *Why wouldn't she? That was silly. A mother doesn't just leave her child behind.* "We'll make the best of it until she does, okay?"

"Okay." Zan bounced the horse in a circle around Shorty, who didn't seem to mind either.

16

Carly never did come back that night, and Adam was thankful that Zan didn't seem bothered by getting tucked in on the couch with Shorty for the night. She was a sweet little girl, so well-behaved that it was difficult to believe parenting was half as hard as people made it sound.

But then it hadn't even been twenty-four hours yet, and so far he'd only had to feed her, which he was pretty good at. She'd slept in one of his T-shirts, which dragged on the ground when she walked, a sight he wouldn't soon forget.

She ate four silver-dollar pancakes for breakfast, and he'd have thought the bacon was candy the way she gobbled it up.

"Do you have a bunch of horses?" Zan asked.

"I do. Have you ridden before?"

"Tons of times with Mommy. I like horses."

"Me too," he said. "I have to go feed all mine. Do you want to come with me?"

"Okay." She slid down from her chair. "I better put my jeans and boots on."

"Do you need help?"

"Nope. I can do it." She walked into his bedroom and shut the door. He sat there waiting for her, wishing Carly would get back soon. She'd made her point.

Zan walked out in the clothes she'd been wearing the day before. "I'm ready." She lifted her hand in the air for his.

He took her hand, and they walked outside. He fed and watered the horses and used the tractor to put some hay out for the cows. It was a little tricky with Zan underfoot, but her infectious giggle made it worth it.

"All our chores are done," he said.

"We did good." Zan looked happy with the accomplishments. "I'm hungry."

"Already? Where do you put that food? You ate more breakfast than I did."

"In my mouth." Her head cocked. "It must get used up in my boots, because the more I do, the hungrier I get."

"Is that right?"

"I think so." She propped her hands on her tiny hips in a way that made her look even more like Carly.

Adam took Zan back up to the house. As luck would have it, he still enjoyed several kid-friendly foods, so he had some options. "How about we make sandwiches? I've got turkey, or I can make peanut butter and jelly."

"PB&J!"

"You're my kind of girl. Crust or no crust?"

"I don't know what that means."

"That must mean crust. We'll know in a minute." He made the sandwiches, cut them both in fourths, and served them up on paper towels. He lifted Zan to sit at the bar-height table in the kitchen.

"Wheeee." Her feet swung, and her eyes danced with excitement at the sandwich.

He poured two glasses of milk and sat down with her.

"Can we say the blessing before we eat?" he asked.

"I can do it."

That warmed his heart. "By all means, please do."

She sang, "Thank You, Jesus. We love You. Many, many blessings. We thank You. Amen."

"That was beautiful."

Zan lifted her sandwich and chomped the corner of it, crust and all.

He hadn't taken two bites of his sandwich when his phone rang. *Has to be Carly. Thank goodness.* "You wait right here, okay? Finish your lunch. I'll be back."

Adam grabbed his phone and walked into the other room, ready to give Carly a quiet piece of his mind and tell her exactly what he thought about her little disappearing act.

"Adam Locklear? I'm a nurse at Southeastern Regional Medical. I've got a patient here who's asked me to contact you. Carly Fowler."

"What's going on?"

"Do you know Carly Fowler?"

"Yes. She was here at my house yesterday afternoon. I expected her to come right back, but she never showed up."

"She was in an accident. Her car went off the road."

"Is she okay?"

The nurse quickly responded, "Yes. I'm sorry. I should have started with that. She's banged up and upset. She asked me to call you and let you know."

He pressed his hand to his chest. "How long will she be there? Her daughter is here."

"Zan. Yes, she said you're taking care of her. We're not sure how long she'll be here. They may be transferring her to another facility."

"She's your daughter."

"I know she is yours. I've always known."

"Mom threatened to tell you at least a hundred times."

"I'm desperate."

"I need your help."

"Did you call her parents?"

"Yes, they've been informed. Maybe she'll feel up to calling you later. Until then, she wanted to be sure you knew what happened and that she'd need you to take care of your daughter for the time being."

My daughter? That remains to be seen. He ran a hand through his hair.

"Thank you for letting me know. Please ask her to call me as soon as she can."

"Yes sir." The nurse gave him the phone number and hospital information. "She can't have visitors right now, so call before you make the drive to be sure you're on the list."

That seemed so odd, but right now his main concern was how he was going to care for a little girl.

"Thank you." He turned around to go into the kitchen, and Zan stood in the doorway, looking at him.

Adam swept Zan into his arms. "Hey, little one. Did you already finish your sandwich?"

"I'm full."

"Good deal. Don't want you hungry. Your mom was in a little car accident. She's okay, but she's going to be away for a little while to get well. Are you going to be okay here with me?"

What am I supposed to do with a little girl?

Tears welled in her eyes. "Did Mommy say it's okay?"

"She did. Are *you* okay with it?" *Please don't cry.* But her lower lip was starting to protrude, and one tear slid down her cheek.

"Yes sir." She brushed it away, then placed her hand on his cheek with a smile.

His heart ached for her. This had to be so confusing. He put Zan down, then walked over to the window as he tried to figure out how he could handle this and not miss the rodeo in Dare County tonight. That just wasn't an option. But he couldn't leave this little girl behind either. Even if she turned out not to be his, he couldn't do that.

He pulled his phone out and tapped a number. "Hey, Squatch. Your family coming to the ride tonight?"

Adam fist-pumped when Squatch answered with a groaning yes.

"I need a huge favor. It's a long story, but can you ask your wife if she can keep an eye on a five-year-old girl while I ride tonight?"

"Better to just spring it on her. She won't say no to you. She'll come unglued if I ask her."

"You sure?"

"Yeah. She'll be there. What's one more?"

"I owe you, man. Big-time." He ended the call and let out a breath. "Okay, I've got this." Zan had spread out on the floor next to Shorty, explaining each page of a magazine to the dog, who looked bored. Adam watched as Zan made up stories for each picture. She had a good imagination.

"Let's see what kind of pretty shirts you have in your pink cowgirl bag, because guess what we're going to do tonight?"

"See Mommy?"

That pierced his heart. "No, she can't have visitors yet. But as soon as she can, we will go see her. We're gonna go to the rodeo."

"The real rodeo?"

"Yes!"

Her lips bunched. "I don't have my hat. It's in the car."

"How about I get you a new one. They sell them right there. They might even have a pink one for little girls."

"Really?"

"Really. Let's get you dressed, and then I'll get all my stuff together. I have to work."

"You work at the rodeo?"

"Mm-hmm."

She didn't ask any other questions about it. The tiny clothes in the duffel bag looked as if they were made for a doll, but they fit Zan fine. Dressed in a ruffly white shirt with pink snaps, jeans, and her pink boots, she was ready.

Zan stretched her hand out, a brush clenched in her tiny fist. "Can you make my hair pretty? I love braids."

"I'm afraid that's above my pay grade."

"What's pay grade?"

"It means I'm a boy and my mom never taught me how to do braids. Come here. Let me see what I can do." He brushed the tangles from her hair and pulled it back over her shoulders. "It will look perfect like this when we get you that hat."

"Okay."

Thank goodness for hats. When they got to the arena, he was relieved to see the vendor already opening shop, and there was a whole stack of pink felt cowboy hats right on the counter. "I'm going to need one of those for the little lady."

"Hey, Adam. Isn't she a pretty thing?" the vendor said, smiling.

"Thank you," Zan said. Then she touched her finger to the glass case. "Is that you?" She looked up at him wide-eyed.

Sure enough, there was a line of stickers with his face on them. "Pro Bull Rider" arched around his mug. It was still weird to think kids wanted to walk around with his image on their binders and book bags.

The vendor pulled a sticker out of the case. "Sure is him. Here, I'll stick this on your hat."

She clapped her hands and jumped with excitement.

"Thanks, man." Adam took the hat and pushed it down on Zan's head.

She tipped her chin up, white-blond curls framing her face. "Am I pretty?"

"The prettiest cowgirl in the whole state." He laid a gentle hand on her shoulder. "Come on, I've got to get signed in. How about we get you a corn dog for dinner? Do you like corn dogs?"

"I like corn."

"You've never had a corn dog?"

She shrugged.

"You're in for a treat." He bought two corn dogs at the concession stand and got a cup of ketchup for dipping. They sat on the bleachers and ate their corn dogs. He kept dabbing his napkin on her face. If he'd realized how messy this would be, he'd have skipped the ketchup altogether, but Zan seemed delighted with being able to eat a hot dog on a stick, and she was so cute that he hardly cared if she wore it all.

Zan held the half-eaten hot dog out toward him. "I'm full."

"I can take care of that." He took a giant bite that made her laugh. This wasn't how he usually spent his time prepping for a ride, but she sure was an easy handler. *I probably shouldn't be comparing this kid to a horse.*

"You wore a lot of that ketchup." He wiped the last of it from her cheek and forehead.

"Like lipstick."

"More like blush. Come here." He tipped a bottle of water over on a napkin and used it to clean up the sticky mess. "That's better."

She giggled, and his heart bubbled unexpectedly. "You are a good little girl."

Squatch texted him. They were over at check-in.

"We're going to go meet up with some friends." He took Zan by the hand and wove through the bleachers. Fans were already starting to come in to get good seats for the night's event.

"Squatch!" Adam waved.

"Hey, man. Good to see you." He turned to his wife. "Honey, look who's here."

"Adam? Who do you have there with you?"

"This is Zan. She's the daughter of a friend of mine. I'm watching her tonight." *It better just be for tonight. She's a cute kid, but if I don't get my head in the game, it's not going to be good.*

He watched Zan stiffen.

"Hello, Zan. You can call me Miss Darla."

"Hi, Miss Darla." She shrank back behind Adam's leg.

"Oh my gosh. All these boys. I'd die to have a sweet little girl like her. Zan, do you want to sit with us while Adam and my husband ride bulls tonight? We can cheer, and we usually build a little tent fort at the corner of the bleachers. I think you'd have fun."

Adam was so glad he didn't have to ask. This was going better than planned.

Zan looked up at him and hooked her finger. He stooped down. "What is it?"

"Can I sit with them?" she asked.

"You sure can. You're going to cheer me on, though, right?"

"Yes!"

Adam walked off, but he couldn't help but keep looking across the arena to where Darla and the kids were making their own little party. He helped Squatch get set, and Adam was pretty sure it took longer to get Squatch on the bull than the amount of time he actually stayed on. No score for him. The next three guys didn't cover their rides either. Sometimes it seemed it wasn't the cowboys' night. Adam needed that mojo to change, as his turn was coming up.

He walked behind the chutes and took a moment. His mind wasn't clear right now. Thoughts of Zan. Merry Anna. Carly. Every cowboy that hit the dirt tonight.

Things are changing. I need focus.

He got up and tossed his rope over one of the panels in the alley and began heating it up. Racing his glove up and down the length, the rosin softened, getting stickier against his glove.

His thoughts zoned in on the end goal: finals.

He heard the buzzer sound for the last rider and the consolatory applause for another loser. He didn't even have to look to know. There was a resounding difference between the cheer for a cowboy who covered the ride and one when the bull was victorious.

He stood up, took the hat off his head, and twirled it around, then set it hard down on his head. A silly little something he did before every ride. His signature. His rope and glove were so sticky that he didn't even need to close his hand around the hat to keep it from falling.

He climbed the pole gates and went over to the platform. His buddies clapped him on the shoulders as he stepped one leg over the gate. He was one dusty boot away from his ride.

Earlier, he'd got the best draw of them all: Tail Biter. This bull had more twists than a mountain road. He'd jump high and swivel around close enough to bite his own tail.

Adam knew that if he allowed himself to predict Tail Biter's moves, he'd be bucked off in a quick hurry. He needed to stay in control and maintain balance no matter where that old bull went, and if that meant swinging left and then right, he needed to wave like a flag.

He let out three quick breaths, ignoring the talking around him. Tuning out the noise and the music, he dropped into the box until his rear end hit the bull's back. He felt the power beneath him. After heating up his rope again, he pulled it tight. One more extra turn around the thumb for good measure. He pounded his fist into the rigging. The bull rocked and snorted.

Adam huffed back, clamping his legs to the sides of the beast.

He lifted his free hand up near his ear and tucked his chin so low that he couldn't see anything but the brim of his own hat and the shiny black shoulders of Tail Biter.

He gave the nod.

The click of the chute releasing and the slam from the gate flinging open sent Tail Biter catapulting out.

Adam had laser-like focus on the bull's shoulders, willing his body to move as one with it. Red dirt from the arena flew through the air as the formidable animal dug his feet into the ground to hurl himself back in the air again. The bull let out a long, deep groan.

This time Tail Biter twisted to the left, his body like a U in that telltale move he was known for. Adam stared that bull right in his left eye, the white wide and the pupils huge and filled with anger. Adam didn't blink. He didn't breathe. He let that animal groan a howl as he flung his heavily muscled neck in the other direction.

Adam's body whipped around, his own knee bouncing to his shoulder on the recoil. He stretched out his leg and spurred that bull. The animal flung him with fury. Adrenaline masked the pain of his recent injuries.

When the buzzer sounded, Adam pulled the rope of his rigging and let go, flying a good ways in the air before landing in the dirt against the fence. He stood, brushing the dirt from the seat of his pants, caught his breath, and scrambled to safety, then looked back to check on his opponent.

The bull pawed the ground. Dirt rose beneath its heavy hooves, and its eyes were lasered in on Adam. The bull huffed.

Adam jumped for the gate, reaching the top just as Tail Biter hit it.

The pickup guys raced their horses up the arena to assist. The bullfighters distracted Tail Biter, allowing the cowboys to funnel the bull out of the ring.

Adam's heart pounded. He could see the crowd cheering, but he heard nothing. He took the hat from his head and tossed it into the air.

All the spectators in the stands were on their feet.

He pumped his fist in the air.

Thank You for giving me a safe ride.

That ride felt like the ride of a champion—the champion he wanted so badly to be.

He grabbed his rope and bell from the ground and headed to the back, stopping to wave one more time at all the fans, who were still standing.

The announcer drawled out his score. "Adam Locklear is

owning this night. Tonight he has done it again. A whopping 94.5!"

The other cowboys slapped him on the back as he walked to the locker room. Doc was there too. He'd seen Adam through some of his best and worst rides.

"Wow, you did it! I think that may be the highest score ever ridden in this arena."

Adam shook his hand. "Got my head right. Don't know how I did it. I was so distracted. I had to muster everything I had."

"Well, distraction worked for you tonight."

"I guess."

"You okay?" Doc already had his penlight, checking for issues.

"Not a scratch from tonight. Still have the stitches in my gut, but they're fine." He nodded toward his rigging shoulder. "It's out again."

"Good. You can't take many more hits to your head. You know that." Doc worked his magic, guiding Adam's shoulder back into the socket.

Adam gritted his teeth, snorting relief when it fell into place. "I know. Still not wearing a helmet. I'll get more hurt with it on. It throws off my balance."

"I'm not going to preach at you, son. You know the risks. What's got you so distracted anyway? New woman?"

He looked over his shoulder. Everyone else was packing up. "An old one, actually. Remember the barrel racer from six or seven years ago?"

"Pretty blonde. Crazy-eyed?"

"Yep, that one. Carly. She showed up with a five-year-old kid. Swears she's mine."

Doc shifted his weight. "Simple paternity test will answer that."

"I know. It's my next move. But if I do that in town, everyone will know." He lowered his head. "Problem is, we had an argument at my place. She stormed out and left the little girl with me."

"She coming back?"

"She better. She was in an accident. They called from the hospital. I'm taking care of her daughter until she does."

Doc looked speechless. "I can't believe you're even here. Where's the kid?"

"Squatch's wife is looking after her. I don't know what I'm going to do. I swear if I can just make it to the finals, I'm done with riding. I'm going to pay into that partnership with the livestock contractor."

"Adam, that's a risky investment."

"I've got to do something. I love this sport, and running the feedstore isn't going to make me happy. I can't sit around in one place all week long. You know that."

"You can use that medical degree and years of experience in this sport," he said. "I'd hire you tomorrow, man. You have options. It'd take some time to get you certified, but you'd be on the payroll. And your experience and passion makes you the right guy to help these boys make good decisions when their health and dreams don't align."

"I've got a mess on my hands."

"I'll arrange the paternity test for you. No one else needs to know."

"Thank you."

Squatch ran through the door, carrying a red-faced Zan with huge tears in her eyes. Her little pink-and-white outfit was covered in dirt.

"What happened?" Adam leaped to his feet and took her from Squatch.

"Sorry, man. Darla said she looked away for a split second and she was gone. In all the ruckus after your ride, she went missing. Next thing I know, someone said she almost got trampled in the back here. I guess she was looking for you."

He hitched her up on his hip. "Zan, you okay? Come on, girl. Where's my cowgirl smile?"

She patted her mass of tangled curls. "My hat's gone!"

Doc bent down on one knee. "Hey there, little one." He pushed her hair from her face and put a cool compress on her forehead. "It's okay. You're okay." He checked her arms and legs. "I don't see any blood or anything, Adam. I think she's just scared."

"Are you scared?" Adam felt his own eyes moisten. "I'm right here."

She touched his face with her hand, then gobbled back tears before pushing her face into his shoulder.

"I think she had a big day," Doc said. He placed a comforting hand on Adam's shoulder. "I have no idea how you rode tonight. You do have a lot on your plate. Let me know if I can help."

"I will. I'm gonna get her home."

Squatch ran ahead and grabbed Adam's bag. "Here's your stuff. Sorry. Darla feels horrible."

"No, tell her not to. I shouldn't have put this on her anyway. Tell her thank you."

Adam hooked his bag over his other shoulder and strolled out to his truck. A minute later, Squatch ran up behind him. "Found her hat." He was swatting dirt off it, but the sticker with Adam's face on it was still clinging to the side.

Zan grabbed it, a little smile coming through.

"Thank you," Adam said.

"Thank you," Zan whispered.

Adam put her in the truck.

"You don't have a car seat for her?" Squatch looked appalled. "Dude, you can't do that. Wait a minute." He ran off and came back with one. "Take this. We've had so many kids that we have them in every car."

"Thank you. I'm in uncharted territory here."

"Oh, I know what you mean. I couldn't figure any of it out without Darla. She's the one that keeps us all going." He held up a finger. "Let me strap it in. These are tricky." Squatch strapped the seat tight, and then Adam put Zan in it.

Zan pulled the strap up and buckled it.

"Looks like she knows more than you, man," Squatch said.

"I'm beginning to think I know less than I ever did."

On the ride home, Zan fell asleep, clutching her pink cowgirl hat.

Adam carried her inside and laid her on the couch. Shorty made himself at home, curled up at her feet.

Adam pulled his phone from his pocket and turned the sound back on. He scrolled through the missed text messages and emails, then noticed the missed call from Carly's folks.

"Adam, the doctor told us Carly had a nurse call and give you an update. Honey, I'm sorry I let her keep me from calling you and that she didn't tell you about Zan. She's a sweet little girl. She's yours. Carly knew it from the moment she was pregnant. In her own way, she thought she was doing you a favor." Mrs. Fowler sighed. "I've got Zan's birth certificate here. Might make you feel a little better to know that even though your name isn't on it, her legal name is Zan Locklear

Fowler. Carly had been on the road for the past few weeks. I wondered if she might be heading your way. She's in a mess of a mental state right now. Physically, she's just banged up, and she sprained her wrist. They've moved her to the psych ward, though. I don't know how long they'll keep her there, but I think it's the best place for her right now. I'm so thankful that Zan is there with you. Call me when you get a chance."

He sat down in the kitchen chair and cried. Tears for Carly. Her family. That baby girl in the other room. The longer he was with Zan, the more he began to see that reflection of his own image in her face. He felt a connection stronger than he could have imagined when he thought she'd been hurt. He'd believed it impossible that she was his, but not anymore.

The paternity test will only make it official.

He stood and walked to the doorway. Standing there, he watched her sleep, wondering what she dreamed of, as his own dreams slipped ever so slightly out of reach.

17

It was late June, but it was so hot and muggy that Merry Anna hadn't even made it to the mailbox and her thin cotton blouse was already sticking to her. She had to drive to work, breaking her streak of walking or riding her bike each time. She could only imagine how oppressive the heat was up in DC today. At least here they had the trees and the mountain air to keep things somewhat bearable.

Not today, though.

She drove down to Main Street and found a parking space in the alley behind Hardy House, leaving the prime spots for customers.

Krissy had said this week, the week between the first and second summer sessions at App State, usually brought her big-spending customers in. Merry Anna wondered how many would venture out with the intense heat wave going on. She walked inside to find Krissy setting up an extra fan near the front window to keep the air moving.

"Who stole our weather?" Krissy asked.

"I know. I drove today. That's how hot it is." Even just the few minutes from the car to the shop had left her glistening. "We might want to set up one of those big jugs of ice water for customers."

"That's a wonderful idea. Would you mind running down to the hardware store to see if George has one in stock? If not, maybe even the Feed & Seed. They've got all kinds of random stuff in there."

"Not at all. I'll pick up some cups and a bag of ice while I'm out," Merry Anna offered.

"That would be great."

She went to the hardware store first, but George was sold out of dispensers, so she went to the feedstore. She hoped she might run into Adam. She hadn't spoken to him since he dropped her off Friday night, and she couldn't wait to hear how his rides went the rest of the weekend.

Her silenced phone buzzed in her pocket. Thinking it might be Krissy adding to the list, she picked it up without looking. "Hello?"

"Merry Anna. How've you been?"

His voice caught her by surprise, but she knew exactly who it was. "Kevin? Why are you calling?"

"I can't call to say hello?"

Why would you do that? "I think that usually subsides following a divorce."

"Well, we've known each other our whole lives. Surely, that counts for something."

She wasn't buying the cordial act. She'd already agreed to extending the alimony wager, but that wasn't over until September. So why would he be calling? "What's up?"

"Your parents' wedding anniversary is coming up. I was thinking maybe we could do something together for them."

He couldn't remember our *anniversary. Why would he remember my parents'?* "No, that makes no sense at all."

"It's just that when I was over there this weekend, they

were talking about when we all went to that inn on the Eastern Shore. Remember that?"

"I do. You bellyached the whole time."

"I wasn't that bad."

"You were."

"Well, they remembered it quite fondly, and I was thinking, *Hey, why not?* We could all do it again. Get the same neighboring cottages. I checked and it's available."

"Kevin, we're not doing that."

"Why not? They'd love it."

"*I* wouldn't."

"Come on. Not everything in our marriage was bad. It'll be my treat."

That would be a first. "Kevin, we aren't married anymore. We're not buying gifts together, and we're definitely not going on trips together. And why exactly were you at my parents' house this weekend?"

"They invited me for dinner."

"Why did you go?"

"Because they are family."

"Not yours."

"A divorce doesn't erase all that history, Merry Anna. Your mom said you haven't been keeping in touch with them."

"Kevin, I'm sure you have something better to do than hang out with my parents. You certainly had no problem staying busy when we were married."

"Things change."

"How so?"

"I think you'll be happy to hear that I've been working."

That's it. He's probably running some kind of get-rich-quick scam and wanting to get me to invest. "Really, and where are you working?"

"I'm working for the Supply Cabinet. They hired me to oversee all location updates to the new brand."

"What? You don't have a lick of experience managing projects." She felt the heat rise inside her. She'd never have let that happen.

"It's not that hard. There's a plan and a timeline, and I make sure people do what they are supposed to do on time and not spend too much money."

Neither of which he handled in his own life. "Who is going to make sure you are doing what *you* are supposed to be doing?"

"It'll be fine. Come on. Your mom helped me get the job. You should have done this for me years ago."

Her head pounded. This would be a disaster. One more mess he'd make that she'd have to clean up. "I've got to go. You are on the clock. You should get back to work."

"Speaking like the COO of the company again. Does that mean you're going to come back and make sure I do my job?"

"Goodbye, Kevin." She hung up the phone and dialed her mother.

"Hello, Merry Anna." It was as if she knew she'd be calling. Was it possible Kevin may have called from her parents' house?

"What have you done? Kevin just told me you put him in the project management position over the store remodels. He can't do that job."

"Why not?"

"Because he's lazy, Mom. Why do you think I never let him work for our company all those years?"

"You're exaggerating. He had that job over at Chart Brothers. I remember him telling us about all the big projects he worked on there."

She couldn't and wouldn't go into the details of her ex-husband's lack of motivation but expertise in embellishment and pretending to work.

"Look, you're on leave," her mother said. "Decisions have to be made. We're making them the best we can."

"Mother, is this your way to get me back home?"

"Well, if you were here, you could certainly make sure things went the way you'd like them to, couldn't you? And Kevin told me he was going to talk to you about going to the Eastern Shore to celebrate our anniversary. I'm so excited!"

"Mom, Kevin and I are divorced. We won't be doing things together."

"Doesn't mean you can't still be friends."

"Yeah, it kind of does. If you want to go with Kevin to the Eastern Shore, enjoy yourself."

"Oh, Merry Anna. It's time you came back. He's gotten rid of that woman. You know she was trying to manipulate him and come between you. It was really her conniving that started that whole wedge between the two of you. I think with just a little work, you could get back what you had."

"I don't want what I had. Not Kevin, and you know what? Not being the COO of the family business either."

"Don't say that."

"Well, don't go teaming up with my ex-husband to sway me. I've found a real peace here in this small town. I'm happy. I don't think I knew what real happiness was before."

"Relationships take work."

"Yes ma'am. They do. I can't argue with you there, and both parties in that relationship have to work equally hard."

"Seems to me that Kevin is the only one working on it."

"Mom, if he wanted to fix our marriage, he had plenty of

time to do that before we were divorced. That ship has sailed and is at the bottom of the sea. Shipwrecked."

"Please come home for a little visit."

She didn't want to, partly because now she didn't trust that her mom wouldn't have Kevin hanging around, and partly because she knew Adam would be in town this week and she hated to miss a chance to see him again. "I can't. I've made other commitments."

"I don't want you to take this the wrong way, Merry Anna, but I would think your commitment to the Supply Cabinet would come first. Kevin has really been a dear the past couple of weeks, spending time with your father and helping him. He even took him to the doctor last week."

"I thought he was working."

"Well, yes, but he's made time for us too."

Her jaw pulsed. Kevin was just going to sponge off them. That was his new job. She wanted to scream. "You're breaking up. Mom? Hello?"

"Can you hear me?"

"Hello? I can't hear you. Oh gosh. This connection out here is so undependable. Think . . . you . . . conn . . ." She grimaced at the little white lie about the connectivity, but she couldn't take a moment more of the Kevin parade.

After those two phone calls, she was so flustered that she could barely speak. She'd leave, except that Adam's truck was parked at the far end and he'd wonder what was up if she left now.

I'll just go in and look for the beverage dispenser, and if I run into him, then I'll politely wave and promise to catch up later in the week. Easy.

She pushed her car door open, then lunged to catch it before it bumped into the car next to her. Thankfully, no damage was done. The owner of a green pickup walked by her to get into his truck. By the stink eye she got from him, he must've seen the almost incident. She smiled and then ran into the store.

Remembering from her visit before that there were picnic and cookout supplies to the right, she headed in that direction. Luckily, there were two beverage dispensers on the shelf. She took the larger of the two and carried it to the counter.

She'd just walked out the front door when Adam came jogging up the loading dock toward her.

"Merry Anna! Hi. How are you?"

Just seeing him made her smile. His shoulders looked broad in his work shirt. "Good. How about you?"

"I don't know," Adam said. "It's been a really bizarre weekend. I feel like I've been in the twilight zone since Friday night."

"Is that the song they played when you came out of the chute Friday?"

"I don't know. I tend to blank that out, but I may have to request they never do that again. I was going to call you today. I . . . wait, let me carry that to your car for you." He took the large glass drink dispenser from her and walked down to her car. He set it in the passenger seat and belted it in. "Shouldn't go anywhere."

"Thank you." She watched him come back around to the front of the car. He seemed harried. Frazzled. Not like Adam at all.

"Saturday morning I had a surprise visitor. Actually, I thought it might have been you. I wish it had been, but it wasn't. This barrel racer that used to hang around at all the bull-riding events, Carly, showed up. I haven't seen her in five or six years."

Was he getting back with an old girlfriend? Her heart dropped to her gut. She tried to manage the tremble in her lip.

"Out of the blue, she showed up at my place," he repeated. "I don't even know how she knew what town I live in. I say 'Winston-Salem' on the forms because some of those fans are a little crazy."

"I wondered why they announced you were from Winston instead of Antler Creek." She tried to concentrate on that part rather than on Carly. She even had a fun name. Not like Merry Anna. She'd always hated her goody-two-shoes name.

"Yeah, and no one knows where any of the small towns the riders really live in are, anyway."

"Well, it must have been nice to see your old friend after all that time." Pressing back her disappointment, she tried not to overdo her enthusiasm. So, she'd slipped and fallen for a cowboy. Age-old problem. She should've known better.

"I don't even know where to begin." He sat on the edge of the two-rail decorative fence next to the parking area. "We never had anything going on. Nothing serious."

She wasn't sure she wanted to hear all the sordid details.

"I mean, we hung out a lot. I really liked her family too. But then she just kind of disappeared from the scene. Someone had said she ended up in Tennessee. There were rumors she got married, but no one talked about her."

"And then she shows up at your house?"

"With a little girl, who she proceeds to inform me is mine."

Merry Anna put her hand out on the rail and leaned against it. "Wow."

"Yeah, exactly! I've had my share of women—not bragging,

just being honest—but I've always done the right thing. I don't play wild and risky with that. It would be one of those .09 percent situations if that child was mine."

"It does happen."

"Well, I'm not the kind to run from responsibility. Man, this is such a convoluted story. Let me back up." And he did, taking Merry Anna through all that had transpired, with the hospital calling about the accident and the voice mail from Carly's mother. "I've been a wreck."

"I bet. Adam, I'm so sorry."

Her irritation with Kevin and her mother seemed negligible in comparison. *There's always someone who's going through something worse.*

"You'll have a paternity test?" she asked.

"Yeah, and I spoke to Carly's folks a little while ago. Her dad had a stroke last year, and her mom hasn't been in good health for as long as I knew about them. Carly had been staying there with them and helping out. Her mom said Carly had been dealing with depression and just sort of snapped and took off with Zan."

"And now you have her?"

"Yes. My friend Ginger is watching her today. Zan's a good little girl, but I don't know what the heck I'm doing." He twisted his hands together. "Even if she isn't mine, I want to help."

"Of course."

"I'm going to take care of her until I get the paternity test results back, and then I'll go from there."

"That's a lot to take in." Her head was swimming, her emotions swirling. She could only imagine how he felt. She had feelings for this man, and this was one messy situation, but it made her feel closer to him that he told her and trusted her with the information. Small-town folks were funny about stuff like that. They liked to keep things close to themselves, although it seemed as though everyone always knew everyone else's business. "I admire the way you're handling this."

"Well, don't be too impressed. I'm just taking one step at a time, and some of those steps have felt like greased logs."

"Good thing you're known for your excellent balance."

"Put me on a bull any day of the week. Cakewalk compared to this."

"You know," she said, softly because she knew it was going to be a touchy point to make, "you can't spend your time risking your life on bulls if you're a father."

"There are plenty of bull riders with families, Merry Anna."

"That would be a really unfair thing to do to a little girl who just met her dad."

He shook his head. "Well, that's true. I hope Carly won't be gone too long. Zan's a little confused about her mom being in the hospital, but then, so am I."

"Kids are smart. They take in way more than you think."

"Merry Anna, I know we haven't known each other long, but I need and want your help through this, if you can find it in your heart to give it."

That was asking a lot. "I don't know a thing about kids."

"Me neither. Also don't know a thing about relationships. I've pretty much succeeded in not relationshipping."

"I don't think they give badges or belt buckles for that."

"No."

"When's the paternity test?"

"I'm going this afternoon. Because of the situation, they are going to expedite it. Doc said we might know as early as Wednesday, but probably not until Friday."

"Are you going to take some time off until you get this figured out?"

"I feel like I can't take my hands off the wheel. I'm so close to winning. There are big changes coming in my life no matter what the test says. I don't want to take my eye off any single part of all this."

She admired his tenacity, but realistically there was too much for any one person to handle. "What can I do to help?"

"Really?"

"Yes, really. I can't guarantee I'll pick up on things as quickly as I did baking strawberry pies, but I would be happy to help you, under one condition."

"Anything."

"Adam, you have to promise me that if she is your daughter, you will come up with a backup plan."

He held his hand out to her. "I'm really glad you rented my old bunkhouse and became my neighbor."

"Me too."

"How about you come over for dinner tonight? You can meet Zan. I'll cook."

"I can do that. What time?"

"How about six? I know that's early, but I read that children her age should be in bed by around seven thirty, and I don't want her to go to bed on a full stomach. Well, couch. She's sleeping on the couch."

"You know more about this stuff than you think." Suddenly he was the sexiest father she'd ever seen, and she couldn't wait to meet Zan. "Does anyone else know about this?"

"Adam, we need you in here!" one of the sales guys hollered from the loading dock.

"A few people. I'm keeping it kind of quiet until I know the results. Sorry, I gotta run."

He hooked his pinkie to hers, then dropped an unexpected kiss on her cheek as he got up and ran inside.

She got in her car and touched her cheek where he'd pressed his lips for that second. That kiss had made her almost out of breath. *A real one might have given me a heart attack.*

18

Merry Anna brought the beverage dispenser back to the shop. "Here we go. I got the big one."

"I like the spigot on it," Krissy said. "That's cute."

"It is. I'll be right back. I've got the ice and stuff in my car." She ran out back and collected the bags and carried them inside. Merry Anna started setting up the beverage station on the small table in the middle of the store. The farther she could lure the customer inside, the more likely the person was to buy something. Some retail knowledge expanded across all types of business.

There had been a steady stream of customers all day, despite the heat. As they were closing shop, Krissy asked, "Want to come over and have dinner?" She put the unused cups back into the plastic sleeve. "Matt is doing a big cookout at Angels Rest tonight. He's got ribs smoking, and he'll be barbecuing chicken. And I hear they've got a huge pot of fresh green beans and shoepeg corn. Matt is the best cook."

"What is it about these guys in Antler Creek? Do they all cook?"

"Just about all of them, and you'll never hear us girls complain about it either."

"Oh, I'm not complaining. I'd love to come, but I already made plans. Adam is cooking for me tonight."

Krissy twisted in delight. "Oh! I love how y'all are getting along. You may just be the woman to tame that cowboy."

She'd never met anyone like him before. "He definitely has my attention."

"Well, you go have your romantic dinner, and I'll sneak ribs off the grill for us for lunch tomorrow. You've got to try them."

"Sounds great." The one thing she knew for sure was that, under the circumstances, there'd be no romance this evening, but that gentle kiss on her cheek this afternoon had made her swoon in a way that she'd be feeding off of for a while.

"I'll finish closing up. Why don't you head on out?" Krissy suggested. "Go on."

Merry Anna grabbed her purse from under the counter. "I'll see you in the morning." She went out back and got into her car. Since she wasn't walking, she had a little extra time, so she drove to the other end of town to the department store.

She loaded a handbasket with crayons and a coloring book, a princess tiara, and some alphabet flash cards. At the last minute, she grabbed a fluffy plush goat from an endcap. This little splurge wouldn't crunch her budget for the month too bad. That stupid bet with Kevin was becoming inconvenient. She swerved over to the linen aisle on the other side of the store and found the perfect set of frilly little-girl sheets, a small white blanket with a pink pony on it, and a small pillow, and she still came in under budget. That little girl might be sleeping on Adam's couch, but they could make it seem like her special little princess place.

"Need any of this wrapped?" the salesclerk asked as she scanned the tickets.

"That would be so fun. Not the sheets and stuff. They can go in a bag. But the toys—yes, that would be great."

"A little girl?"

"Five years old."

"Oh gosh. I remember when mine was just five." For a minute, Merry Anna thought the lady was going to drag out her phone and show her pictures. "Five is such a sweet age. They still love being read to and snuggling in your lap. I'm going to warn you, that whole mama crying when the baby goes to school is not a myth. I cried like a baby."

Merry Anna didn't bother to tell the woman that the little girl wasn't hers.

With a bag of wrapped packages and the other with the linens, Merry Anna had run out of time to go home and change, so she went straight over to Adam's house.

"Yoo-hoo." Merry Anna knocked on the front door and pushed it open. "It's me. Merry Anna."

"Come on in." Adam popped his head out of the kitchen. "We have some gourmet stuff going down in here."

"Well, don't let me interrupt." She followed Adam into the kitchen, and what she saw caught her by the heartstrings. She knew immediately that the paternity test would come back positive, and it wasn't just because they were in matching aprons. There was a remarkable likeness, especially the set of their mouths and the chin. "Hey there. I'm Merry Anna."

"I'm Zan. We've been making dinner for you." She lifted a dramatic hand to her head to sweep the bangs from her face.

"Oh, you have! Well, aren't you awfully young to be such a fine chef?"

"Yes, but I have a good teacher." Her lips pursed as she

sprinkled grated cheese over a long french loaf. "It's been kind of like school."

"Do you go to school?"

"No ma'am, but next year I can."

"How exciting." Merry Anna took one of the stools. "You are very pretty."

"Thank you. I love your dress." She reached for the fabric, touching it tentatively. "You look like a fairy princess."

Merry Anna looked down at the simple A-line sundress. Compared to how most people dressed these days, she probably did look a tad overdressed. But rather than make an excuse, she owned it, making a curtsy. "Why, thank you."

Zan lifted her hand to her mouth and whispered to Adam, "I think she *is* a fairy princess. Did you see her curtsy?"

"I hope fairy princesses eat spaghetti!" Adam called out.

"I heard that," Merry Anna said. "And I adore spaghetti."

Zan gave Adam a relieved look. "We have salad and bread too. I'm not having salad. I'm just having cucumbers."

"I think that's fine. Is there anything I can do? Set the table, maybe?"

Adam piped in, "We already set the table in the dining room."

"We're eating like grown-ups." Zan's lips made a tight bow.

"Wonderful," Merry Anna said.

They ate dinner, and it was hard to believe that Adam and Zan had met only a few days ago. Zan was quick to explain that her mother had left Saturday and didn't say when she'd be back. That broke Merry Anna's heart. She wondered what kind of life this little girl had been living.

They ate dinner, which was delicious. By the time they cleared dishes, Zan was yawning.

"It's getting close to somebody's bedtime," Adam said.

"I brought a few presents for Zan."

"For me?" She stood on tiptoe, her eyes as wide as quarters. "Why?"

"Because I wanted to welcome you to Antler Creek," said Merry Anna.

"I love them." The words exploded from Zan's mouth before Merry Anna could hand her the gifts.

Adam laughed. "She hasn't even given them to you yet."

Zan spun toward Adam, lifting her hands to her hips. "But she's going to."

"Yes, I'm going to." Merry Anna took the bag with the sheets and blanket in it over to the couch. "First of all, I heard you were sleeping in here, so I got some girlie things for you. We love pretty stuff, right?"

Zan dropped her arms to her side and grinned. "Yes. Totally."

Merry Anna started taking things out of the bag.

Zan went straight to the ruffles on the edge of the pink-pony blanket. "It's the most beautiful blanket in the whole world." She threw her arms around Merry Anna's neck and then ran to Adam and hugged him too.

Merry Anna stretched the bottom sheet over the cushions and then pulled up the flat sheet and put the ruffly pillowcase on the pillow.

"I have a feeling you're going to have beautiful cowgirl dreams tonight, Zan." Adam lifted her in the air. "It looks pretty, doesn't it?"

"Like a dream cloud." Her lashes flashed as she looked at everything.

"After you get your sleep shirt on, you can open the other stuff." He set her on the ground, and she ran into the bathroom.

It took Zan only a minute to come back wearing a Cheyenne Rodeo T-shirt.

Merry Anna had laid the packages on top of the new blanket. Each white-wrapped box was tied with a pretty pink bow.

Zan climbed up on the couch, her little bare feet wiggling to get underneath the covers. "I'm ready! This is like Christmas, only pink."

Adam and Merry Anna shared a glance. He mouthed, "Thank you."

Merry Anna gave Zan a nod. "Go ahead. Open them."

She ripped into the paper, squealing in delight and disbursing hugs after opening each gift. "I'm so excited I might not be able to sleep."

Adam took everything and set it on the coffee table. "You have to go to sleep. Little girls need lots of dreams."

She kicked her feet under the blankets. "I'll try."

"Prayers?" Adam reminded her.

"Yes sir." She shut her eyes and folded her hands.

Merry Anna's heart squeezed at the precious sight of Zan's sweet hands folded in prayer, tucked under her chin with her eyes closed.

". . . and thank You for good people like Adam and Merry Anna, and take care of my mom and help her get well and come home soon. I love You, Jesus. Amen." She rolled over, hugging the plush goat.

"Is she asleep already?" Merry Anna leaned in to see. Zan's eyes were still squeezed tight.

Adam shrugged, then nodded toward the kitchen. "Thanks for coming tonight."

She followed him, clearing the wrapping paper on the way. "That was a great dinner. You two are a good team."

"It was fun." He pressed his hands on the island. "That was really nice of you to get all that for her."

"It has to be confusing for her. I thought the crayons and stuff might make her days a little more fun. I don't know. I just wanted to do something to help."

"You are amazing. I did also pick up a little something for *you* today."

"You did?"

He went to the refrigerator and took out a bouquet of bright-colored flowers.

"They're beautiful," she said.

"So are you."

"That was smooth."

His eyebrows wiggled with each word. "And this." He scooted a new five-pound bag of sugar toward her. "Since I said I might not be the kind of neighbor you could borrow sugar from, I wanted to make up for it in advance with a starter kit. I want you to borrow anything you like from me. Anytime."

Her breath stopped mid-intake. "Well, thank you." She took the sack of sugar into her arms, cradling it. She heard Zan turn over in the other room, taking Merry Anna's attention off the romantic gesture. "I probably ought to go so she can get some sleep."

He reached for her as she stood. "There's one other thing I wanted to ask you."

"Sure, what's that?"

"I need to ride this Friday night. It's a one-night event. Would you watch Zan?"

Was this why he was being so flattering and sweet? Or was she just jaded from her own baggage? *He's not Kevin. Maybe he should be trusted. Give him a chance.*

"Well, I promised myself I'd say yes to new opportunities, and watching kids is definitely new for me. You sure you want to leave her with me?"

"Positive. You're very capable. But, honestly, I don't have many options."

She hesitated, but only for a moment. "Yes, I'll watch her. How about I come over here? That way she'll already be tucked in and asleep when you get home." She picked up her purse and keys. Was she setting herself up for a big disappointment?

"Thank you so much." He walked her to the door, and she left a little uncertain of how she felt about everything and not sure why.

Merry Anna didn't hear from Adam all week, and that gnawed at her. Had she read more into his signals than was ever there?

By Friday, she was almost perturbed with him. Wouldn't it have been the polite thing to do for him to have stayed in touch and then confirm that she'd be coming tonight to take care of Zan? Or maybe she was just bent out of shape because she'd hoped to hear from him.

She tortured herself with the internal dialogue until she saw Adam walk through the front door of Hardy House full of apologies and carrying a bucket of strawberries.

"I'm sorry I haven't been in touch this week. It's been really hectic." He glanced around, looking tired. "I brought you some strawberries. Forgive me?"

She couldn't stay mad at him when he looked so beat up. "Hard not to. Maybe I'll make you a pie. I have a great recipe."

A smile played on his lips. "Yeah?"

"Mm-hmm. Talked a good-looking country boy into giving up the family recipe. So, what time should I come over tonight?"

"I need to leave here by four. Do you think you could get away that early?"

"Yeah, Krissy won't mind."

"I made dinner. It's in the refrigerator. All you have to do is heat it up."

"I should be able to manage that."

Work dragged by for Merry Anna. She wasn't sure if it was because she was looking forward to taking care of Zan for Adam or because she was anxious to see him. At three o'clock, she couldn't take it another minute. "I know I told you I didn't need to leave until three thirty, but would you mind if I left now?"

"To go see Adam? Not at all," Krissy said with that hopeful smile.

"Quit matchmaking. It's not like that."

"Yeah, right. You and all your 'just'-this-and-that excuses." Krissy tossed her head. "Believe what you want."

Merry Anna made the walk home to the bunkhouse in record time. A quick change and she was out the door, taking the shortcut to Adam's.

When she arrived, he was already putting his things in the truck.

"Thanks for doing this," he said with a lift of his chin.

"Just remember you need a backup plan. It's part of the deal."

"I haven't forgotten."

Zan came running out of the house carrying a piece of paper. "Miss Merry Anna! I made you a picture."

Merry Anna crouched down to see it. "That is very pretty."

"I colored the dress just like the one you were wearing the other day. When I grow up, I want to wear dresses like that."

"Then you shall." Merry Anna took her by the hand. "Are you okay with a girls' night with me while Adam goes to work tonight?"

"Yes. I like you."

"I like spending time with you too. Should we color first?"

"Yes!"

They went inside as Adam drove off. Zan colored and then insisted Merry Anna color a picture for Adam. By dinnertime, they had a table full of drawings.

Adam had made hamburgers and had cut cucumber strips for Zan and made a salad for Merry Anna.

They ate in front of the television, watching a movie, and then it was already bedtime.

Merry Anna mimicked the routine from the other night and let Zan say her prayers. "Sweet dreams, little one. I'm going to be right there in that chair watching television until Adam comes home, okay?"

"Yes ma'am. Sweet dreams to you too."

Merry Anna flipped through the hundreds of channels Adam had. At the bunkhouse, she only had antenna TV. Not that she minded. The break from television had been one of the first things she realized she didn't miss. Not watching had quieted her mind. She felt like she was more creative and actually had time to think.

She turned on a movie and pulled her feet up in the chair. As the movie credits ran, she noticed it was after eleven. She'd really expected Adam home by now, and her mood swayed from worried to miffed. By midnight, she knew if something had happened, she'd have heard from the hospital. As annoyed as she was, she resisted the urge to call him.

Finally, headlights swept past the front windows. The unmistakable sound of the diesel engine got closer and then shut off.

A few minutes later, Adam came through the front door. He almost looked surprised to see her. "Hi," he whispered.

"How'd you do?" she asked. She hadn't meant for the words to come out so clipped, and by the look on his face, he must've picked up on it. She softened. "Are you okay?"

"I made the buzzer." He didn't offer anything else.

"You're so late. The rodeo ended hours ago. I was worried that something had gone wrong."

"Some of the guys got together after." He paused, but he must've realized how mad she was, because he quickly added, "Squatch, the guy who helped with Zan last week, wanted me to stay."

"And you thought that was the right decision to make? When you had a child here waiting on you?"

"You were here."

"As a favor." She crossed her arms, pressing them tight against her chest. "And you let me worry."

"I'm sorry. I figured you were already here." He tossed his hands in the air. "What's the big deal?"

"The big deal is I was doing you a favor and you took advantage of my good nature."

"Well, I didn't have a great night either. I didn't even score in the high eighties. Not good enough to win. I was distracted."

"I bet you were. Were all your little girlfriends hanging around afterward with the guys too?" *Why did I throw that in his face? I have no right.* She hated jealousy. No one wore that well.

"No, not like that. My mind was here."

"Then maybe you should've been here."

"I don't know what to do about this. Look, you might not know this about me yet, but I'm a responsible guy."

"So it would seem." The words pressed her lips.

"This is not my fault. I never knew she was pregnant." He let out a huff and dropped his hands to his side. "I'm just trying to do the right thing here."

"But you didn't. You talked *me* into doing the right thing for you. You need to be the one making this work." She got up and snatched her purse from the table.

For all the cowboy reputations and warnings about how unattainable the most eligible guy in this town was, she had to go and fall for him. Maybe this was just a rebound thing and she'd get over it as quickly as she fell into it.

19

If the amount of anger welled up in Merry Anna's gut was any indicator of how deeply she'd fallen for Adam, she was in trouble.

Thank goodness it was Saturday and she had the weekend off. She stayed huddled down in her sheets, unwilling to face the day or her decisions.

Disappointed in herself for falling for the charms of a cowboy, she'd embarrassed herself by admitting as much to Krissy even after she'd said Adam couldn't be settled down.

Who do I think I am?

She thought about how she'd dressed up for the rodeo that night. That wasn't her style—at least not who she used to be. And although she'd come here hoping to discover who she really was or wanted to be, maybe she was trying too hard.

For a moment last Monday, it had been like playing house—the homemade dinner, tucking Zan into bed, and the flirtation in between the serious-life-decision talk.

All likely just his way to get her to be a free babysitter. He probably only asked her because she didn't know everyone in town, so the scandal might stay dormant a little longer, until he ran out of favors and had to start hitting up other people for help.

I'm an idiot.

She didn't care one way or the other if that little girl was his. It wasn't her business anyway. For all she cared, he could just hit the road with Zan in his duffel bag.

Only that wasn't true. She wished she could take the negative thought back.

That was a horrible thing to think.

She went back to sleep, not even bothering to get up and have something to eat.

The sun had set when she awoke with her phone ringing. She grabbed it from the nightstand and looked at the display. Adam.

"Hello."

"Hey, Merry Anna. I wanted to apologize about last night. You're right. It was unfair to leave you hanging like that. I'm really sorry."

Her throat tightened. "Thank you."

"Look, I'm just a cowboy doing what he loves. I don't have the best track record with women, and I can be a selfish somebody, so I've been told on more than one occasion. I'm probably going to make some mistakes, and with everything that's going on, I'm not even sure which way to lean."

"There is a lot going on."

"But I mean well, and I will always be honest with you. I usually keep everyone at arm's length. Ask anyone. But I feel different when I'm around you. You've been completely open with me about things, and I respect that."

Most things. Her guilt for being less than open with him about her divorce had her second-guessing Adam's intentions. Or was she giving herself a reason to push away? Now that Adam's situation was rapidly changing, it wasn't necessarily going to be at an arm's distance. Before, when he was completely focused on his rodeo goal, it was safe to say that he was unattainable until the end of the year. That had bought her time to avoid considering the situation.

"I want you to know I really appreciate your help with Zan, but more than that, I like you for who you are. I just wanted to apologize. I hope you'll forgive me."

"I don't appreciate being used. I did worry, but—"

"It's fine. I was in the wrong. I know that. Look, I don't know if Zan is going to be around here long or not, but until I do know, I want her to be safe and happy, and I don't want her to be afraid about anything. I expect you and I will be friends for a long time no matter how everything else shakes out. I want to be a good friend to you."

Friends? If that's all this will ever be, that's fair.

"I'm frustrated," he admitted. "I didn't get the test results on Friday. I guess I should've known it might take longer even if they tried to expedite things."

"I'd be going crazy," she admitted. "I know this is a lot to have on your mind."

"I can't promise I won't make other stupid mistakes, but I hope you'll stick it out with me. I decided that the right thing to do is to take Zan to church tomorrow. I mean, if the test comes back positive, then why would I wait? Carly clearly had her in church. She knows to pray, and I think she needs that continuity. If she's not my child, at least I tried to do the right things for her while she was in my care."

"Yes, and really, isn't that all that matters?" Merry Anna said. "Just be honest about what's going on. It's better than the alternative of people assuming."

"I agree. Well, I'll see you there tomorrow. I know Zan will be excited to have you there."

"I'm looking forward to it also."

On Sunday morning, Merry Anna picked up Tara for church. The older woman came out carrying a large wicker purse that looked more like a lunch basket than a pocketbook. Merry Anna loved how Tara had the confidence to pull that kind of thing off. With a pretty scarf wrapped around her head, Tara ducked to try to outrun the raindrops on her way to the car.

"Whew, this weather is crazy!" Tara hollered as she jumped into the car and ripped the scarf from her head. "Hot and muggy, and now rain. I'm glad I got those windows replaced last week."

"It's supposed to be a whole week of rain." Merry Anna had just heard that on the news. "I guess we shouldn't complain, though. Folks around here have been talking about the drought they've had the past two years. I think it's probably a good thing we're getting some rain."

"Yeah. I guess you need to have the whole picture to keep it in perspective," Tara said, slapping her hand against her knee. "But I don't have to like it much."

"No, you don't."

Merry Anna and Tara sat in the back pew of the church. It had kind of become their unspoken spot. Usually, Adam sat up toward the front on the right, coming in just as the service started. Merry Anna kept one eye on that part of the church, hoping he would show up as he'd planned. It was a selfless act to bring Zan here, where there would surely be tongues wagging with speculation.

She felt a hand on her shoulder. She turned to look behind her. Adam stood with Zan, who was dressed in a pretty floral sundress. "Think we could sit at the end of this row with y'all?"

"Absolutely." She tapped Tara on the leg. "Scoot down a little."

Tara looked confused, then scooched. Her eyes bugged out when she realized Adam wasn't alone but had a little girl with him.

Merry Anna leaned forward and gave Zan a little finger wave. The girl waved back, then placed her folded hands in her lap.

The sermon seemed to speak directly to Merry Anna. It was about love.

The pastor leaned forward as he spoke. "In life, to be loved is one of the most desired human needs. Love can cause us to climb mountains, cross seas, and do the unthinkable."

She resisted the urge to glance over at Adam and Zan.

Her mind wandered.

She'd struggled with her shifting feelings about Adam—analyzing them, judging them, and even fighting them. Before the divorce, she'd identified herself as COO of the family business. She was proud to have such an important role within the corporation her family built, which included hundreds of stores across the nation. *That's what I did, not who I am.*

Being here in church was a good step. It was something she and Kevin had stopped doing years ago, maybe the first year they'd been married. She couldn't even remember why they'd stopped going. Maybe it was Kevin's passion for Sunday football games and getting the gang together for them. Or maybe they'd just gotten busy.

Who am I? Am I living a meaningful life?

"Relationships take work," the pastor said. "I'm not just talking about your relationship with your husband or wife here either. Just like you have to work at your marriage, you have to put the effort into your relationship with God. Think about that. Are you really putting in the effort?"

It was true. She had let most everything, other than work, run on autopilot. She blamed Kevin for their divorce, but had she ever really put in the effort? The final blow that took their marriage to its knees could have just been a symptom of years of neglect. That realization weighted her chest.

After the service, the four of them walked out of the church, and Tara had barely made the last step before swarming in to get the scoop. "Who do we have here, Adam?"

"I'm Zan."

"Nice to meet you, Zan. I'm Tara. I live in the big house next to Adam."

Zan nodded, but Tara wanted the details. "Adam, is this your niece?"

"No, just an extraspecial little cowgirl who is staying with me for a while. Right, Zan?"

Zan dipped her head in a giant nod. "Right. And with Shorty."

Tara laughed. "The dog. I wondered why he hadn't been to visit me this weekend."

"He's my best friend."

"You're a very lucky little girl."

Adam took the moment to exit. "We've gotta run. We have big plans this afternoon. Good seeing y'all." He and Zan took off for his truck, leaving Merry Anna there with Tara.

"Humph." Tara didn't say another word.

"Ready to go?" Merry Anna hoped she was in the clear.

"Yes." They got into her car, and Merry Anna hadn't even put it in gear before Tara started in with questions.

"So, what is *that* all about? Zan is absolutely the most adorable little girl, but how does a cowboy end up with a five-year-old and no one in town know anything about it? That's odd, if you ask me."

"Guess your morning group of gossiping men at the church hasn't been talking about it?"

Tara blushed. "Maybe. Can't believe you didn't tell me about it."

"Wasn't my place to tell, which is why I'm not in the morning church group. I don't gossip much."

"Touché." Tara fidgeted. "I know you know the story. Are you going to tell me?"

"All I can say is that she's the daughter of an old friend of his who's in the hospital, and he's caring for the little girl until his friend can get on her feet."

"There's more to it."

Merry Anna pulled in front of Tara's house. "I'm sure more details will become clear soon. Stay tuned."

"You're a party pooper."

"You won't say that when I'm keeping a secret for you one day."

Tara scowled. Apparently, she got the hint, because she shifted the topic to her renovation. "Well, I was hoping you could help me hang curtains. It's a bear to do by yourself."

"I'd be happy to." She got out of the car and followed Tara inside.

"When are those tomatoes going to be ready?" Tara asked. "I've been dying for a good BLT on toast. Doesn't that sound good?"

"It does. We're getting close," Merry Anna said. She'd been checking them twice a day. "I think I should have my first ripe tomato in the next day or so if the birds don't mess with it."

"That's wonderful. So the boat planter is working out for you?"

"It is. I put a little plastic bag on a stick next to the plant to keep the birds away. You were so right about the raised bed. It wouldn't be nearly as pleasant if I was all bent over on my knees on the hard ground. I find it really relaxing standing out on the back patio, tending to the plants in the SS *Fresh Veggies*."

"You named the boat? That's great." Tara walked over and grabbed a ladder. "The curtains I want to put up are in here. You haven't seen the progress I've made. A home just doesn't feel like a home until the kitchen is complete."

Merry Anna followed along. The original cabinet boxes had been painted a navy blue, and new fronts in a beautiful wooden tone looked striking against that dark backdrop. All the light fixtures had been updated, as had the cabinet hardware.

"It looks like something out of a decorating magazine."

"It came together so nicely. No one would ever believe the rest of the house is in such a mess, would they?" Tara looked pleased.

"No, they wouldn't. *I* can hardly believe it."

"This is exactly why I like to start with the kitchen to set the tone." Tara opened a box and pulled out curtains in a lovely toile. "These are going to really bring things together."

Merry Anna got on the four-foot stepladder by the window, and Tara climbed up on the other one and began pulling the curtain onto the heavy wooden rods. The tab-top panels hung splendidly, and it didn't take long to get them all on.

"Thank you so much for the help," Tara said. "It's always much easier with a friend."

"You're welcome."

"So, are you worried?"

"About what?"

"Zan?"

Merry Anna sighed. It was hard to keep anything from Tara. She had the interrogation skills of a lawyer. "Look, he doesn't even really know what the whole story is yet. An old girlfriend showed up saying Zan was his daughter. He took a paternity test. He hoped he'd get the results back Friday, but they haven't come yet."

"Does that worry you?"

"I don't know. Maybe a little. I guess it's just such un-charted territory for me. I don't know anything about kids."

"He probably doesn't either. New parents don't. Everyone starts at ground zero."

"I guess that's true. She's such a sweet little girl, but I don't want to get attached."

"Well, don't hold back. Even if this is short-term, some-times we're tapped to be an angel for a season to someone. You're needed. You can make a difference, Merry Anna." Her eyes seemed to twinkle. "It's an opportunity you don't want to miss out on."

Merry Anna imagined Tara as sort of an angel to her who was speaking from experience. It didn't make the compli-cated situation any easier, though. "I don't want to be taken advantage of either."

Tara leaned back. "That's your ex-husband baggage talking right there. Adam is not Kevin. You do what's right in your heart for the right reason, and no one can ever take advantage of you. You trust that."

Merry Anna nodded. It was hard to trust that about her-self, but she was trying. "What if we got serious? Being a step-mother is harder than being a mom. You're raising a child under someone else's rules. That can be tough."

"Or it can be a blessing." Tara reached over and held Merry

Anna's hands. "I can see the worry. Don't be afraid, Merry Anna. You are falling in love. Put your arms out, close your eyes, and just glide."

"That sounds so beautiful." Merry Anna laughed. "And scary. Did I mention I have a fear of heights?"

Tara shook her head. "Soar over the water, then, if that'll make you feel better."

"And water," Merry Anna admitted. "I'm scared to death of water. I don't even know how to swim."

Tara blinked slowly. Then, with a cluck of her tongue, she added, "Have I told you that you can be a real downer sometimes?"

"Maybe just a little while ago. Party pooper is the same thing, right?"

"Yeah. We'll work on that." Tara let out a sigh. "Thanks for helping me hang the curtains. Why don't you get on home and tend to our tomatoes?"

"I was going to say that." Merry Anna walked over and gave Tara a hug. "I'm so glad we're friends. Thank you for everything."

"It's my pleasure. I like having you around."

Merry Anna went home and changed out of her church clothes into shorts and a T-shirt. She went outside to tend to her plants, checking them and pinching off dead leaves. She was delighted to see more tomatoes beginning to ripen on the vines. She wondered how long it would be before she could pick a few. With the morning rain, she was careful not to overwater them. She found the mindless work to be relaxing.

She thought about today's sermon, and it made her reflect on the anger she'd felt when Adam came home so late Friday night. Her heart was getting in the way of her good judgment.

She'd been worried—a little—but more so, she'd taken it personally. She wished she'd gotten her point across without losing her temper. *I'll try harder next time something happens like that.*

She woke up on Monday morning to the sun shining through that wonderful stained glass window. A bird chirped outside her window with such exuberance that she got up to see what all the fuss was about. She spotted him right away, sitting on the fence line. His head bobbed, his neck stretched, and with each of his movements, the sounds from the songbird dipped and rose.

She stood there, smiling and watching, until the bird finally lifted his wings and flew across the way. Maybe Tara was his next stop.

She stepped outside. Thankfully, the weather finally broke and it was almost bearable. She got dressed and headed out a little early to give herself enough time to walk down to the coffee shop and enjoy a cup while sitting outside, overlooking the river, rather than guzzling the brew inside the store between tasks.

There were two people working the counter, and the line was moving fast. She ordered a cup of coffee and a slice of breakfast bread, which looked a lot like carrot cake without the yummy cream cheese frosting. She carried her purchase outside and took a seat near the railing. It wasn't easy to sit still and just listen to what was going on, but she did it, and she felt good about that.

She opened up the store and went through the orders that had come through the online site over the weekend. Those orders kept her busy until Krissy came in at lunchtime.

"How's the morning been?" Krissy asked.

"No customers, but we had a ton of orders over the weekend. I've got almost all of them packed up and ready for the post office." She pointed to the stack against the back wall.

"How'd you get all that done so fast?"

"No interruptions, I guess. It was so quiet that I actually went to the front and double-checked that I'd turned the sign to Open on the front door."

"Thank goodness for the online store. I'd love to expand that. It's been going so well. I originally created that website to move a bunch of hand-painted scarves that I got an amazing deal on. They were so beautiful that I couldn't pass them up, so I put some in the store and then put the rest out on the internet. It was perfect timing, being close to Mother's Day. I sold out of them in just a few weeks. That online store has proved to be a nice secondary income stream."

"It's certainly a great sales funnel. You might find, too, the broader your online reach becomes, the more customers you may gain by way of people adding this town to their itinerary just because they love the online store."

"When I'm able to get to it." Krissy looked around the store. "It's a tiny shop, but it takes all my time searching for unique products."

"It's a big job being owner, buyer, marketer, tech support, and cashier." Merry Anna had a team of people working on those things in each store back home. "You know, that's something I could do on days like this when we don't have many customers. I wouldn't mind. I like to be busy."

"Really? That would be awesome. I'll make a list of the items and show you where to update the database that feeds the website." Krissy's smile was all Merry Anna needed to move forward on that project.

"Yes! I could also check vendors for sales and things like that in case you want to do something like a special overstock item each quarter, since that worked so well last time." Merry Anna grabbed a pen and made a list with checkboxes next to each one.

"What did you say you used to do back in DC?"

"I don't think I ever said. Mostly a little bit of this and a little bit of that," Merry Anna said.

"Well, you are most certainly a treasure, and I'm so thankful you landed here for a while."

"I am too," Merry Anna said.

At the end of the day, Merry Anna felt as though she had put in a good day's work and balanced it with some quiet time working on ideas for Hardy House.

On her way home, she decided to stop in the feedstore to see if Adam could tell her what kind of birdseed to get for the songbirds.

Adam must have seen her walking up, because he greeted her at the door. "How are you doing?"

"I'm great," she said. "I woke up to the prettiest serenade this morning."

"Oh, sorry. I don't usually sing that loud in the shower," he said, pretending to be embarrassed.

"Ha, no, it was definitely not you, but I was thinking maybe I'd get a bird feeder and some seed for songbirds. Can you help me with that?"

"I can."

She followed him down an aisle to a whole wall of bird feeders and different types of seed. "This is a little overwhelming." She twisted the tag on one of the bird feeders. "My first apartment didn't cost that a month."

"Somehow I doubt that."

She pressed her finger and thumb together, then widened it. "Slight exaggeration."

He showed her his favorite bird feeder. "I can give you a ten percent discount on this one."

"Sold."

Adam lifted a big sack of seed over his shoulder. "It's a better deal in the big bag, and you'll be surprised how much they eat. Did you walk down?"

"I did."

"I should have known. I'll drop this off at your house on my way home."

"That would be great." Humming from the next aisle over caught her attention. "What is that sound?"

"That's Zan. She's being artistic in her Cinderella fort."

"*Cinderella* and *fort* are not two words I'd usually associate with each other." Merry Anna followed the humming around the corner. Sure enough, Zan was sprawled out across the floor on her belly, coloring on a large piece of paper. Her tongue was working as hard as the crayons, and one foot was in the air bouncing and flexing. Now that Merry Anna was closer, she could make out the song. *"Old MacDonald."*

Merry Anna realized that the fort was actually a tarp over a fence-style dog kennel. "Adam! You can't put her in a dog kennel!"

"She's fine. And it's six feet wide. Hardly a crate. She's having a ball, and it's not like she can't get out. Watch this." He made a little whistling noise, then said, "Zan, do you want a snack?"

"Yes!" She jumped up, abandoning her art in less than a heartbeat to run for the door. She lifted the latch, stepped over the gate, and ran over to him.

He picked her up and swung her in the air.

She screamed, in a giggling girlie way. "Do it again!"

"Look at her fly!" He lifted her higher, leaving her up there for a two-count before crashing her downward.

Adam turned to Merry Anna. "See? I'm being responsible. You told me to figure this stuff out, so that's what I'm trying to do. We come to the store, and she works on her coloring while I help customers." He handed Zan a fistful of coins. "And I pay her in snacks."

Zan grabbed the coins and ran toward the vending machine. Her shoes slapped the concrete floor as she ran.

"She looks perfectly happy," Merry Anna said. "So why is it that *you* don't?"

"Part of figuring it all out is considering all the ways this could go." He shook his head. "I wasn't looking for a ready-made family right now, but I don't know. She's a great kid. If I wanted kids—or had a kid—I'd want a little girl just like her. She's special. I am happy, but I'm also a little worried."

"Because of Carly?"

"No. It's about Zan. Her energy and heart. I . . . I just can't imagine if I'm not her father. I feel so close to her. Is that strange?"

"Not at all. I completely understand. Don't get ahead of yourself. Whichever way this goes, it will be as it should be. You've got to trust that."

"That paternity test is a big deal. Lives are going to change."

"That's true, but lives change all the time—an accident, losing a job, a natural disaster, winning the lottery, divorce, falling in love." *Did I say love?*

Their eyes held.

"Unexpected things happen," he said.

Is my imagination going wild, or did he feel that too?

"It's a lot," he said.

"Adam, I think you have less scenarios to worry about than you think. I think she's your daughter. She looks just like you."

"You think so?" He didn't look disappointed.

"I do. I noticed right off when I saw you two in the kitchen together. Sometimes things get shaken up and you just have to trust the journey. It might feel like the worst thing in the world, but it could be a good change, more wonderful than you could have ever imagined." She knew that was easier advice to give than take.

"I think that's something people say to friends when things go wonky in their lives . . . to make them feel better."

"Yeah, probably is, but in this case, it's true." She'd thought going through the divorce with Kevin was the worst-possible thing that could happen to her—selling the house, splitting up belongings, the embarrassment that went along with it all—but now she could see that it was a necessary change in her life. And here on the other side of it, things were bright and promising. If he knew what she'd been through, he'd understand. "I need to tell you something," Merry Anna said.

"What is it?"

"I—" She stopped as he stepped in closer to her. She wanted to tell him everything about her past—the divorce, her job—but she couldn't bring herself to do it. Lies of omission were lies, and she was so far into the mess now. What was he going to think when he found out the truth about her? "I know you'll make the right decision. Quit thinking so much. Pray about it, and trust it's all going to be okay."

"You're the best." He hugged her with one arm. "I almost believe you. And I should, because you are the most honest person I've ever met. How has no one ever snatched you up?"

Wonderful. Everything you love about me is a big fat lie.

20

Adam had missed a call on his cell phone while Merry Anna was in the store. He played the message. The doctor's office said the paternity results were in, and they wanted him to call back.

He lowered himself into the chair, slack-jawed. He'd been waiting for this call for days, but now that it was here, he wasn't sure what he hoped for. Before he returned the call, he walked back out to Zan's Cinderella fort.

"This has been a fun day," Zan said.

"I'm glad. We're going to leave in a little while, so you need to start putting your crayons back in the box and cleaning up, okay?"

"Okay!" She ran over and picked up the empty box of crayons and started sliding one in after the other.

He walked back to the counter. "Hey, Jim, can you just keep an eye on her for a minute? I need to make a call."

"Sure."

Adam went into the office and closed the door. After he punched in each number, his mouth went dry. The phone rang twice before someone answered. "Hi. This is Adam Locklear. I had a message that the doctor called. I have some test results."

He was put on hold. His knee bounced. He leaned back in the chair, then forward. It seemed like he was waiting a long time, when finally the doctor picked up. "Adam, I'm not sure what you were hoping for, but you are indeed that little girl's father. You can pick up the report. I'll leave it in an envelope at the counter for you, but I wanted to let you know as soon as I got the results."

Adam let out a breath. "Okay."

"Are you all right?"

"Yes sir. Thank you. I don't know what exams she's had or anything. I'll see if I can get Zan's records. I guess I'll be bringing her in for a checkup, and wow. Okay."

"Well, I always like to think people with livestock make the best parents. They know how to keep stuff alive because they pay attention to the little things, and that's half the battle. Our office is here to help however we can. At least you're skipping the diaper phase. I never was good at that myself."

"Yeah. That's definitely a plus." He hung up the phone.

I'm a father.

There was no sense wasting time. He called Carly's mother to tell her the news and find out how to get in touch with Carly.

Mrs. Fowler's voice quaked a bit. "Honey, I know this must be such a surprise for you, but it's really not for us. We've always considered you her father. Carly was sure Zan was yours. You'll be a good father."

"I'll have to be. I need to tell Carly. How can I get ahold of her?"

A heavy sigh came over the line. "She's really struggling, Adam. The doctor seems to think this has been getting worse over time. We thought she was just being irresponsible, but that wasn't it. Mentally, she was in way more trouble than any of us realized. I know you were worried about the argument you had before her wreck. Don't be. I really think in her heart she believed that leaving Zan with you was the right thing to do for everyone, and she intended to take the easy way out."

"You think she wrecked her car on purpose?" Adam couldn't imagine someone doing that. Especially someone so full of life, the way he'd known her to be.

"The doctor thinks so. I'll see if she'll put you on the list. You can't even talk to Carly on the phone unless you're on that list. Let me call them now."

A few minutes later, Carly's mom finally called back with the number.

He dialed it and asked for Carly. A moment later, she got on the phone.

"Carly, it's me," he said. "How are you doing?"

"I'm doing better. I'm really sorry about all this. I never meant to create chaos in your life."

"It's okay. I would never run from a responsibility like this. Carly, you had to know that."

"I did," she said. "Look, I've got a long way to go. I was a good mother, as good as I could be, but Zan should be with *you* now. I need time to get well."

"I got the paternity test results back," he said. "I'm Zan's father." The words felt so foreign, but there was a sense of pride and hope in them too.

"I know," she said. "I always knew."

"I don't want to upset you, but I do wonder what it is you expect from me. I mean—"

"I'm not trying to get us together, if that's what you're asking. I thought what I was doing was right, but I realize I was robbing you of your rights as a father. I also realize dropping it on you all at once was not the best way either. What I will promise you is that when I am well, I'll do my part, but I will always make sure *you'll* be in Zan's life too. We'll figure it out."

"That little girl is amazing," he said. "I can't believe how smart she is."

"She is something," Carly said. He could hear the choked sob in her voice. "She's the best thing I ever did in my life."

Mine too, I think. "I don't want you to worry about Zan. She's fine. Do you want to see her? Should I bring her to you?"

"Not yet. I need time." Her voice shook. "Adam, this isn't going to be just a one-week stay. It could be a long time. I'm kind of a mess. They're recommending at least ninety days, maybe longer."

"Okay. Just say when. I told you I'd help you. I meant that whether I was her father or not. I'll do the right things by her."

"I know you will. Thank you, Adam. Mom and Dad can't travel, but if sometime this summer you could get Zan down to see them, that would be great. I feel so bad for taking her from them. She's the best part of their days."

Carly must feel so lonely. How did a girl who seemed so strong on the outside get to a place like that? He couldn't imagine her like this, and he was drawn to help. First Zan, and now this. For the first time, he wasn't the priority. "I'll come up with a way to get her out there for a visit."

"That would mean the world to me and them," she said, sounding as though she were starting to cry. "Our little girl needs you. Promise me you'll be careful. Please don't let anything happen to you."

"Don't cry, and don't worry." He knew she was talking about the rodeo. "I'll be careful." His eyes teared up, and his voice caught as he said goodbye. He sat there in his chair for a good long while. His whole world was spinning out of control. He couldn't promise that nothing would happen. It wasn't a matter of *if* you got hurt in bull riding, just a matter of when and how badly.

A knock at the office door pulled him out of the moment. "Yes?"

Zan's little head poked around the corner of the door. "I cleaned up all my stuff. Do you think we can have a fort tomorrow too?"

He waved her over. "Come here."

She ran over to him, and he lifted her to his lap. "You like coming to work with me?"

"Yes. Everyone is nice."

"How about until summer is over and you get to start school, you come with me to work. Would you like that?"

"Yes! Can we bring lunch?"

That seemed out of left field, but she had him already wrapped around her little finger. "Sure. We can pack lunches."

"That'll be good practice for when I go to school. School kids get lunch boxes."

"They do?"

"Mm-hmm."

"Well, we could probably get you one of those now. You know, for practice."

She nodded.

"So, Zan, I have something important to tell you."

Her big blue eyes looked straight into his brown eyes.

"I didn't know this before, but you're my little girl. That means I'm your father. Your dad."

"Mm-hmm. Mommy told me. I already told Shorty." She placed a finger to her lips. "Does that make him my brother?"

"I guess so." This little girl absolutely stole his heart at every turn.

He had a lump in his throat so big that he couldn't hold back the sorrow he felt. He hugged Zan, hoping he could get himself pulled together enough to keep talking.

"Zan, I'm going to try really hard to be a good daddy. I might need your help. Deal?"

"I'll help you, but you're a very good daddy. I love you already."

He almost choked on those words. "Oh gosh, Zan. I love you too. I promise I'll take very good care of you. You might have to help me. I've never had a little girl before."

"That's okay. I've been one for five years. I know a lot about that."

"Yes, I believe you'll probably teach me things I never even knew I needed to know." He laughed. She made it easy, but this was a serious moment. "I talked to your mom today."

"You did?"

"She's still sick, but she wants you to know that she loves you and we're going to see her when she's better. Okay?"

Zan's eyes welled, her brows pulling together. "I miss her."

"I know you do." He pulled her into his arms. "We need to give her time to get better, though. Can we do that together?"

"Yes." She nodded, sniffling back the tears. "Tell her I know how to talk on the phone," Zan said. "I could tell her to get well."

"Maybe you could draw her a picture and we'll send it to her. Would that work?"

"Yes. I'll draw lots of them for her to decorate her room."

So much kindness in one tiny little girl. Would I have thought that when I was that age? Doubtful. "That's very nice."

Jim knocked on the office door. "We're closed up. You're the last one here."

"Got it. We're leaving too," Adam told him, and then he turned to Zan. "So, should we celebrate being daddy and daughter with a treat?"

"Ice cream cones?"

"I think it's a perfect day for ice cream." He stood up, and she put her hand in his and they walked to the truck. When he opened the door, she climbed right in and buckled herself in the car seat.

"What's your favorite flavor?" she asked.

"Cookies 'n' cream."

"I want the very same thing." She sat there grinning, then looked up at him with a serious expression on her face. "You should have two scoops. You're bigger."

"Anything you say."

"I'm glad you're my daddy."

He nodded, because he couldn't utter a word with all the emotion that was finding its way past his bachelor heart to make room for this little angel.

21

"Hi, Adam." Merry Anna hugged the phone against her chin since she had a paintbrush in one hand, and the other hand wasn't in much better shape.

"You busy?"

"Actually, I'm trying to paint this barn quilt. It's a bigger job than you would think, but so far it's going quite well." The more she worked on it, the more she felt that Antler Creek was a forever place for her.

"Krissy better be careful. You'll take over that place."

"No. Absolutely not. If there's one thing I have figured out about myself, it's that I like keeping things simple. In balance. I am committed to making this barn quilt beautiful, though."

"Admirable goal. Pretty big commitment too."

It was, and she knew there was more than just this quilt beginning to anchor her to Antler Creek. "You sound up today."

"I am."

"Did you—"

"I got the paternity results. Zan is my daughter."

"Adam, I told you! She looks just like you. Even her mannerisms. So funny. I knew it." In the midst of her excitement about being right, she paused. "And you're okay, right?"

"Yeah. I have no idea what I'm doing or how I'm going to make this all work, especially in the short term. Long term, I've got it, but we have a ways to get there. By the time I got the message, the results were in. I was almost afraid to get them in case I wasn't her father."

"I think there's an unspoken bond between family—one so strong that even if you don't know it, you feel it."

"You and your theories."

"I'm full of them. I have no idea where I read it, but that's what a lot of reading gets you."

"I'll leave that to you."

"So, have you told Zan that you're her father?"

Adam gave her the update about talking to Carly and Zan and the details Carly's mom had shared.

"Wow. Well, she might have been going through something psychologically harrowing, but she loved that little girl enough to make sure she had a soft landing. You have to respect her for that."

"She did her best. I believe that. I guess my biggest regret is that I really don't know that much about Carly to tell Zan. We only knew each other at the rodeo. It was casual at best."

"Well, at five, Zan has her own bond with her mom, and I'm sure Carly will get back on her feet soon and play a role in her life again."

"Yeah, I hope so. I'm trying not to overwhelm myself, but, man, there's so much to consider."

"Well, congratulations! You missed Father's Day this year, but just think, next year you'll get a ceramic handprint kitchen trivet or something."

"And I'll love it," he said. "We've got the Fourth of July festival coming up. Do you want to go with Zan and me? It's a whole day of activities, but I'm thinking we'll go late in the afternoon to make it a shorter day and then watch the fireworks."

"That sounds great."

"Thank you for being such a good friend through all this. I met you at just the right time."

It had been a whole lot less complicated when she only had to worry about him falling off a bull. "I think Antler Creek has a rescue mission statement. This place rescued me at the right time too." *How could I ever leave this town? These people? I could buy my own house and put my barn quilt there.* She pictured a quaint Cape Cod up on the mountain, where she'd have a view of the town and the heavens all from the porch. Simple and elegant.

"Could be," he said. "I've always known there's something special about it."

"Is there anything I can do for you? I'm getting pretty good with this paintbrush. I could probably help you transform a room into a glittery girl space for Zan."

"That is definitely on the list, and I will take you up on that. There is one thing you could help me out with tomorrow after work."

"What's that?"

"I've got guys coming over to the practice ring tomorrow. I don't want Zan anywhere around there. Do you think I could send her and Shorty over? They can just play outside in the front yard. I'll send her with some bubbles. She'll chase them until she's too tired to walk."

She had to bite her tongue to keep from telling him she thought he needed to put Zan first and all those cowboys second. It wasn't her place. But she'd be lying if she didn't admit to herself that it disappointed her. She pressed her lips together and pasted on a smile that hopefully translated over the phone. "Sounds easy enough. Can I have some bubbles too?"

"I'll get two of the big bottles."

"You're on."

The next day was rainy, so instead of getting out the bubbles, Merry Anna took Zan shopping to get her a couple of Sunday dresses, or, as Zan liked to call them, "princess dresses." It was like playing house, something Merry Anna had never actually done as a little girl. She played office and inventory, which were not as fun as this.

They had a modeling show of all their purchases when Adam got home.

"You're the prettiest little girl in the world," he said.

"Thank you, Daddy."

That one little word—*Daddy*—made Merry Anna almost cry, and it had the same effect on Adam, from the looks of it. "We should go to the Creekside Café and celebrate," he said.

"Can I have chocolate milk?" Zan asked.

"You can have whatever you want."

"Me too?" Merry Anna wasn't sure if she was invited to this little celebration.

"You can have chocolate milk too," he said.

She laughed as she walked with them out to the truck. The three of them got in, and as they all buckled their seat belts, she said, "People are going to be asking questions, you know."

"Just gonna tell it like it is. Not even going to worry about it."

"All righty, then."

"Gossip tears through this town faster than a wildfire on a windy day, and folks don't mind adding their spin to the story either. I'm sure people are already speculating."

"Oh, they are." She didn't sell out Tara, though their conversation came to mind.

"Which is why we're celebrating at Creekside Café. Gossip central, Antler Creek."

The three of them walked into the restaurant. Adam marched over to the counter and helped Zan onto a stool. Then he turned, catching a lot of lookers, smiled, and said, "I didn't bring cigars, because I don't believe in smoking, but I'd like to introduce you to my baby girl. This is Zan."

There was a sweet mumble, then one congratulation after another.

Zan smiled, and Merry Anna went ahead and ordered the chocolate milks, because from the look of things, it might be a while before Adam got to sit down and have something. An old woman offered advice, young girls offered babysitting duties, and several men clapped him on the shoulder. One even asked if he was getting married.

It's going to be okay.

The Fourth of July rolled around, and even though it had been only six or seven weeks that Merry Anna had known Adam, she felt as if she'd known him forever. She loved his cowboy stories—well, most of them. She could do without the ones where he wrecked on the bull and ended up bloody and broken. And she found his manners and cowboy charm to be delightful. He took his apology seriously and had been on time ever since, and she loved that about him. He was good to his word.

That afternoon, they weren't supposed to get together until three, so she took advantage of the free morning to work on another barn quilt. She'd been thinking about it for a while, and this morning, the shapes and colors finally became crystal clear in her mind.

She created the design on her computer first, trying out different combinations until it was perfect. With a color printout in front of her, she used a ruler to mark the outline with a pencil, then made a list of all the colors and numbered them. She stepped back from the half sheet of plywood. It was a big undertaking, but now it was just a giant paint-by-number.

All she had left to do was order the paints. She was searching online for the best deals, when there was a knock at the door.

"Hey, did I get the time wrong? I thought we said three."

"We're surprising you!" Zan lifted her horse lunch box in the air in front of her. "With lunch!"

Adam lifted a cooler. "Ours is in here."

"What a nice surprise," Merry Anna said. "Come in, or should I come out?"

"Let's eat under the tree. I brought a sheet to sit on."

"Great. I'll be out in a second. Give me a minute to put away what I was working on." She rushed back and propped the board against the wall in her bedroom and tucked everything else back in the craft box.

She ran outside to catch up with Zan and Adam, who were already spreading out the sheet.

Zan opened her lunch box. "This is how big kids take lunch to school."

Of course it is. Merry Anna could still remember her first lunch box. It was pink with little yellow daisies all over it.

"I'm going to make lots of friends in school."

"I bet you will," Merry Anna said, then noticed Adam open a container. "Oh my gosh. You made fried chicken, Adam?"

He grinned. "Fourth of July food. We've got fried chicken, potato salad, watermelon chunks, and cake."

"I helped make the fried chicken. I put the pieces in the milk and flour. It was a mess." Zan spread her fingers wide and made a face.

"It truly was the messiest batch I've ever made." Adam pressed the tip of his finger to Zan's nose. "But we cleaned it up together too."

A yellow butterfly flew across the picnic. Zan seemed mesmerized by it, staring and smiling as it looped up and away.

After the picnic, the three of them rode in Adam's truck and parked near where the fireworks would be later that night. With Zan between them, they walked down Main Street, through all the vendor tents. There were crafters, food tents, and activities.

"Look!" Zan turned to Merry Anna. "They are doing face paint. Can we?" Her eyes were filled with hope.

The next thing Merry Anna knew, she and Zan were both getting butterflies painted on their cheeks.

It was a full day, and by the time they sat down on Mill Hill to watch the fireworks, Zan was losing energy fast. She fell asleep, and even through the explosions and whistles right above them and the oohs and aahs, she never moved. Adam carried her, and Merry Anna toted the blanket and all their purchases back to the truck.

"Thanks for coming," he said. "That was a good day."

"It was a blast. Get it?" she teased. It was a bad joke, but she couldn't resist. She'd found lately that she liked being a little silly.

Adam pulled in front of her house. "I don't remember that light being on when we left."

"I probably left it on. I do that all the time."

"Oh no, you're one of those?" he moaned.

"What? Wait." She pointed her chin toward him. "You're the light-and-thermostat police! My dad was like that growing up. Drove me nuts. So I guess that's that."

"That's what?" he asked.

"We could never be a couple. I am constantly leaving lights on. All the time."

He shrugged. "Oh yeah, that would never work. Total deal breaker."

"Impossible situation." The playful banter between them seemed so natural. She grabbed her things, including an insulated shopping bag with two Moravian chicken pies she'd bought at a vendor earlier, which were just bake-and-eat. Even *she* couldn't mess that up, hopefully.

She put her things away, then pulled back the curtain and watched Adam drive over to his house across the way. His life was going through a metamorphosis more elaborate than that of a butterfly. She watched until he and Zan were in his house, and then she washed the blue butterfly from her cheek and climbed into bed.

I love my life here.

The next evening, Merry Anna harvested the first tomatoes from the SS *Fresh Veggies,* and they were beautiful. She cut one into thin slices, piling them high in a sandwich for Tara. She wrapped it up, then hopped into her car. On her way down, Merry Anna saw Tara racing toward the car.

Merry Anna swung into Tara's driveway and lowered her car window. "Everything okay?"

"Marvelous," Tara said. "The new front doors were delivered today. You've got to come see them."

"You scared me, the way you ran out! I was getting ready to stop by anyway." She pulled her keys from the ignition and got out.

Tara herded her inside. The new doors were propped up against the wall in the living room.

"Wow! Can't miss those doors," Merry Anna said. "They look huge in here." She'd just entered through a standard single door, but this was a set of double doors with seeded glass.

"I decided to splurge," Tara admitted. "It means hiring someone to open up the front and install them, but I think it will really showcase this place."

"You're so right. And the light will change this room too."

"It will."

"I can't wait to see them installed," Merry Anna said.

"I went for those big carriage lights for the front too."

"The high-dollar ones you loved so much?"

Tara gave a sheepish grin. "Yes. I kept going back to them. I really think they'll be the crowning touch."

"Well, if anyone deserves it, Tara, it's you. You're working so hard on this place. You are an amazing woman. I don't know how you do it all."

"I'm an old lady with lots of experience. Hey, I picked up a couple of those Moravian chicken pies today at the farmers market. Never frozen. I got you one."

"You didn't have to do that." She already had two in her

freezer, but it was such a nice gesture that she accepted it without complaint.

"I know. That's why I did. Thought maybe you could call Adam and invite him and Zan to dinner."

"I'll do that." Merry Anna hitched the tote from her shoulder. "I brought you something." She took the wax-paper-wrapped tomato sandwich from her purse. "The first tomato. A sandwich, as promised."

Tara rose on her toes, then snagged the food from her. "I've been waiting so long for this!"

"Tell me about it. I was beginning to think I'd never get a tomato before the birds or bugs did."

"Ah, there are little tricks that I'm sure your Feed & Seed friend can teach you about gardening." Tara held the sandwich in her hand. "I'm having this right now. You better go, else Adam will have already fed that little one. Kids eat early. Remember, I raised three children. I know a thing or two about that."

"You? I had no idea. Well, I need pointers."

"Happy to help, my sweet neighbor. You just ask me anything. I've got experiences galore, and for what I don't have experience, I have an opinion."

Merry Anna knew that already. Tara gave the best unsolicited advice. "Okay, well, I'm going to text Adam right now, then get this in the oven." She picked up the pie and motioned toward the door.

"You have fun. Enjoy every moment this life tosses in front of you. It's the only way to really live."

"Thank you, Tara." She hugged her. "You are so special to me."

"Get out of here."

She texted Adam, inviting him and Zan over for dinner,

then drove home and preheated the oven. It didn't take long for the bunkhouse to start smelling like home cooking. She'd all but given up on Adam responding to the invite, when her phone rang.

Rather than text back, he had called, and that made her heart dance as she answered. "Hi. I thought maybe you didn't have your phone with you."

"Sorry. Just saw your message. We'd love to come, but we might have to eat and run. You could come with us, though."

"Where are you going?"

"I'll tell you over dinner. We're on our way." It wasn't but about fifteen minutes later when they showed up at her doorstep and knocked.

She'd already set the table and poured drinks. "Come on in," she called out. "It's ready, so you can sit right down after you wash your hands."

Merry Anna was so excited about how beautiful dinner looked. The crust had browned just right, and some of the gravy had bubbled up, leaving glistening, gooey sauce peeking through. She served it, and they all said the blessing before digging in.

"This is dee-lish-ish," Zan said. "You are a really good cook."

"Thank you, Zan." She turned to Adam. "You know I just heated it up, right?"

"Still counts. Thank you. It is very good," Adam said. "So, we're headed to the Farrell County Fair, just east of here."

"We're gonna watch the button busting." Zan scooped another spoonful into her mouth.

"Mutton bustin'," he corrected.

Merry Anna's heart flipped. It was one thing for Adam to ride. He was a grown man making his own decisions. But what if this sweet little girlie-girl decided to wear a helmet and cling to a dirty, oily, woolly, smelly sheep for dear life? It just didn't seem right.

"Are you coming?" Zan asked. "Please?"

"Definitely." But not for the reasons they thought. She was going to make sure that little girl didn't get hurt, because even though Ginger seemed convinced it was a harmless activity, Merry Anna couldn't imagine Zan riding a sheep.

Once Zan saw all the other kids lined up to ride the sheep, she was bouncing off the walls, wanting to do it. Merry Anna waited at the bleachers while Adam took her to sign up.

He stayed with her the whole time and even put her on the sheep.

Merry Anna held her breath. At least a dozen had already ridden, and most of them slipped right off the back before they got three feet past the open gate. Not a one of them cried. Maybe it wasn't as bad as it sounded.

She watched Adam and Zan drop down into the gate. At one point, Adam picked up the sheep with two hands and turned it around so he could get Zan positioned on top of it. The girl wore a big rodeo number on the back of her frilly cowgirl shirt.

Merry Anna took pictures. *Please don't let anything bad happen.*

Adam was yelling at Zan to nod so they'd pull the chute gate open. Finally, she did so, and, boy, did that sheep spring into the air. It looked more like a counting sheep than a rodeo sheep, but once it landed, it went running straight across the arena. That little blond girl was clutching the wool with white knuckles. Her legs were wrapped tight, and if Merry Anna hadn't just watched Adam put the kid on the sheep's back, she might wonder if Zan were Velcroed to the thing.

The girl's hat flew off, but she hung on. And when the buzzer rang, the rodeo clowns ran to intercept them, one stopping that leaping lamb, and the other lifting Zan up and raising her arm into the air like a champion!

All the spectators were on their feet cheering, and Zan was smiling and waving as though she'd just won a beauty pageant.

Adam retrieved Zan from the rodeo clown and shook hands with him, then scooped his daughter's pink hat up from the arena floor on the way out the gate.

Merry Anna ran over to them. "My goodness. Was it scary?"

"A little. I might not do that again."

"Well, you did real good," Adam said. "Once is enough, though, I think." His lips were pulled into a thin line.

"You okay?" Merry Anna asked him.

He nodded, but he had a strained look on his face. "I need to make a phone call. Can you take her for a minute?"

"Sure." Merry Anna took Zan's hand.

Adam took out his phone and punched in a number, rocking from boot to boot as he waited for an answer. "Hey, Mom, it's me, Adam. I owe you an apology. I never really watched any rodeo events with someone I loved in the ring. You're right. It's scary as all get out." He shook his head. "Yes ma'am. Well it's a long time overdue. I love you. Yeah, I gotta run. We'll catch up soon."

Merry Anna gave him a nod. That probably hadn't been an easy call to make.

"Seeing *that* as a parent is a whole different experience. And she was just on a little sheep."

"Exactly," Merry Anna said. "Maybe you should stick to letting her count them instead."

22

One day at a time was all Adam could take at the moment. It was the only way he knew to keep it all together, because there was a lot he didn't know about being a parent, and Carly wasn't well enough to offer any help.

The people of Antler Creek pulled together when necessary, and he was likely going to need them, if only for advice, for the unforeseeable future. He was glad he'd announced to the lead gossipers in town that he was now a father.

He and Zan packed peanut-butter-and-jelly sandwiches to take to work the next morning.

It was a superbusy day at the feedstore, but Zan entertained herself all day long. He'd had to round her up to eat lunch. By the end of the day, when he helped her gather all her things, she turned to him and said, "I'm so hungry my stomach could eat a whole pot of spaghetti."

"Oh, Zan. I'm sorry. Why didn't you tell me you were hungry? I'd have found you a snack."

"I guess I forgot."

"Come on. We'll run over to the café and get you some spaghetti. I love Maizey's spaghetti, and it will already be cooked. Way faster than me making it at home."

He hustled their departure, feeling terrible for not thinking to ask at some point if she needed a snack. Those were probably the things that real parents instinctively knew.

They walked into the café and sat in the same place as they had for their celebration.

Maizey walked over, wiping her hands on the towel that always hung from the waist of her apron. "You two having chocolate milk again?" She winked at Adam.

"No, that's just for special occasions. We'll have water today and two orders of spaghetti."

Maizey leaned her elbows on the counter, getting down to Zan's level and giving her a big smile. "How are you doing today?"

"I've been working all day. We are starving." She swept a hand across her forehead in such a dramatic way that Adam and Maizey both almost laughed.

"Well, I promise it won't take long for me to get that spaghetti out here to you. How old are you, young lady?"

"Five."

"Five? Wow! I guess you'll be starting school this fall."

"Yes ma'am. Daddy already bought me a lunch box with horses on it. I'm already practicing."

"Nice!" Maizey turned and put the order in. She made good on her promise, soon bringing the spaghetti out and scooching the plates in front of them. "One for Daddy, and one for daughter."

Hearing the words out loud was strange, but he felt pride. What would it have been like had he known about her all along? Would he have stepped up? He was a different guy back then. It was hard to say, but he was getting the chance now to make it right.

"Your folks know yet?" Maizey asked Adam.

"Magic question." He shook his head. Everyone knew his

parents weren't speaking to him, practically disowned him, because of the bull riding. "No, not yet. Don't know that it'll change anything, but they deserve to know they have a beautiful granddaughter."

Zan kicked her feet. "Me?"

"Yes ma'am. You."

"May I be excused to wash my hands? I have sauce everywhere." She spread her fingers.

"Yeah. Here." He mopped most of the spaghetti from her hands. "The bathroom is right over there."

"Okay."

She hopped down from the stool and went into the restroom.

"This whole thing is quite a surprise." Maizey blinked. "Hard to digest still."

"Well, like I said, I didn't know about her until recently."

"This wouldn't be the reason you've suddenly been seeing so much of Merry Anna, is it?"

"What do you mean?"

"I mean, you never really have been the settling-down kind, and now all of a sudden you find out you're a father and you're spending a lot of time with her. You're not using Merry Anna to watch Zan so you can keep being a rodeo hero, are you?"

He didn't appreciate what she was suggesting. "I'm not playing hero. I rodeo for a living. And as for Merry Anna, she's my neighbor and we enjoy each other's company. She knows everything that's going on."

"Sorry if that sounded harsh, but, Adam, you're a dreamer. Always have been. I love you, boy, but that little girl deserves a hero, and the kind of hero is you—her father—not some guy risking his fool neck every night."

He'd been prepared for looks, even gossip, but this was hard to take. Especially from Maizey.

"I'm doing the best I can. I've got to make the finals this year. My whole life plan depends on it. But after that—"

"That plan was all well and good when it was just you." Maizey sounded clipped. "It's not just you anymore."

"I do have to earn a living, though. I can't change that overnight," he said.

"You own the town's Feed & Seed. You have a college degree. There are other ways than rodeo for you to earn a living. You need to think about Zan, and in case you've been too busy with rodeo, making a living, and this little girl, you need to consider Merry Anna too. That's love in that woman's eyes, if you haven't noticed."

Love? "No. We—"

"I don't care what she's said or what you think. You two need to open your eyes and acknowledge what is growing between the two of you. I'm not the only one who's seen it." Maizey's jaw set.

Miss Vickie, sitting in the booth across the way, chimed in from over there. "It's true, Adam."

This wasn't going like he'd expected at all.

"Don't screw that up with her, Adam. She's a good lady," Maizey said.

Why is it that everyone is on her side, and she's not even from Antler Creek? He should've never sold that bunkhouse, and maybe none of this would've happened. Seemed like everything started sliding once he started selling things. He looked to heaven. *Grandpa, there's a better way to give me guidance. I'm listening, sir. I won't sell the Feed & Seed. I promise.*

Zan walked out of the bathroom, and the chatter stopped.

"Are you ready to go now, Daddy?"

Every time she called him that, it gave his heart a stutter.

"Yes. Are you going to pay the check?" he teased.

"I don't think I have enough money." She dug into her pocket and took out a penny, a nickel, and two dimes. She handed the coins to him. "Is this enough?"

Maizey took the coins from her hand. "It's the exact change. Y'all have a great day together."

"Yes ma'am." Zan waved her hand over her head in a whopping goodbye as they walked out of the Creekside Café. Ginger caught the door as it opened. "Hey, Adam. I heard you had a new little girl in your life." Her kids gathered around Zan.

"The rumors are true," he said.

"I was picking up dog food. Guys there mentioned it." She squatted to Zan's level, her hands on her knees. "I'm Ginger. I have children too. You'll have to come over and do crafts with us sometime."

"Thank you. I love to color."

Adam took Zan's hand. "Miss Ginger and I went to high school together. She makes the best Christmas cookies in the whole world."

"I like cookies."

"Don't we all. I hope we'll see you soon, honey. Adam, you holler if you need any pointers." Ginger gave him a wink. "You'll be fine. Can't be harder than riding a bull."

The landing might be softer, but he knew what to expect from a bull. He didn't have a clue about a five-year-old. If anyone had experience in this town, it was Ginger. Between her own children and the ones who gathered at their house, she always had a tribe underfoot.

He and Zan left. He had planned to ask Merry Anna to watch Zan so he could ride tomorrow night, but after all that with Maizey, he felt like he needed to prove to himself he wasn't using Merry Anna.

It was convenient, sure, but he wasn't dangling empty promises, was he?

He'd all but decided to call Ginger the next day to see if she could watch Zan. It would be the best thing to do. It would alleviate some of the rumors, and it would be good for Zan to get to know some of the other kids from Antler Creek.

It was bath night, and he and Zan had a routine, finally. He put a towel in the bottom of the tub so she wouldn't slip, then filled it with just a few inches of warm water and then tons of bubbles. She'd soak until she was pruney.

She changed into her sleep shirt and crawled onto the couch. "I'm so sleepy tonight."

"We've been busy. I'm going to try to do better to be sure you get into bed earlier. I'm sorry you're so tired."

"It's okay." She yawned, then folded her hands under her chin and started her prayers. She fell asleep before the amen.

Adam picked up where she left off. ". . . angels watch her through the night and wake her by the morning light. Amen." He kissed her on the forehead.

My little girl.

23

Adam let Shorty climb onto the couch with Zan, and he walked back to his bedroom. Next week he planned to clear out everything in the spare bedroom to turn it into something girlie for her. Merry Anna had offered to help.

Maizey's comment floated through his mind. *Love?*

He had more changes than he could handle already. Love was not in the cards. Best he knew, he hadn't ever been in love, except with the sport of rodeo. That was the only thing he'd ever felt he couldn't live without.

Maizey had said more than a mouthful, and he was kind of ticked about it.

She was right about one thing, though. He wasn't going to be able to risk his neck with Zan in his life.

He closed his eyes, wishing the answer would come to him. Did he really have to give up everything he loved to be a father? Some of the top riders had kids.

He named them off in his head.

The difference was, those guys had wives. They weren't single fathers raising a child. They had a partner to help shoulder the burden and care for things when they were hurt.

He grabbed his phone from the nightstand and texted Doc.

ADAM: Hey, Doc. Question for ya.

DOC: Shoot.

ADAM: You really think you could get me on the
       medical sports team?

DOC: I do. Let's talk.

ADAM: Okay. See you tomorrow night.

DOC: 👍

He let out a heavy sigh, then scrolled through the rest of the rodeo schedule for the year. It was July, but there were still so many rides to the finals.

He dialed Merry Anna's number, then hung up. It took him two more times before he actually pressed send and let the call connect.

"Hey, Adam. Everything okay over there?" she asked.

"Yeah. Can't a guy just call?"

She snickered. "Do you want to borrow a cup of sugar?"

"Maybe." He laughed. "No. I'm trying to come up with that backup plan I promised I'd be working on."

"I'm sure it's hard to sleep with all this on your mind. Word's whisking through town about Zan."

"Good. The sooner everyone knows, the sooner they can talk about something else. That's the good thing about small towns. Something else will happen tomorrow to replace yesterday's news."

"I guess that's a good thing."

"It is if you're the topic," he said. "I wanted to tell you that I really appreciate everything you've done for me lately."

"It's been my pleasure."

"Yeah, but no, I mean . . . look, I know some people have been speculating"—he gulped back his ego—"that maybe I was spending a lot of time with you just to have you help with Zan. Merry Anna, I'm a lot of things, but I'm not like that."

"I know that, Adam."

It wasn't as though he and Merry Anna had slept together or anything. She wasn't the kind of woman you treated like that. He knew that right off. She wasn't like most of the women he met—the ones who just wanted to tame a cowboy. He'd learned quickly that most girls who wanted to be with cowboys had no interest in what real cowboy life was like. They didn't want to deal with the farm, mucking stalls, and all the dirty work that went with it.

"I miss you when you're not around," he said. "I don't even know what I'm trying to say, and right now I'm out of promises, but I do want to spend time with you. I have to ride tomorrow night."

He heard her sigh.

"I know," he said before she could say anything. "I'm going to make a decision. I'm talking to someone tomorrow. I think I have a good option." *I hope it's a good one.* "Merry Anna, I was going to have someone else watch Zan here while I rode, but it might be my last ride."

"Really?"

There was no mistaking the surprise in her voice. Or maybe it was hope. "I don't know for sure, but if it is, I'd like for y'all to be there. You and Zan."

"I didn't know people were talking about us," she said. "That makes me feel a little foolish."

"Don't feel that way. It's all my fault. I'm sorry. I promise they are wrong. It's not like that. I'd never use you like that."

She hesitated. "I guess we prove them wrong, then."

"I'd like that chance."

"Yeah, I'll go. But I can't watch you do this over and over, not under these circumstances. You can't—"

"I know, I know. This is a one-night thing. One and done. I won't ask again."

"Okay, I'm holding you to it."

That was fair. "What time will you be home from work?"

"I'm opening tomorrow, so I'll be home around three thirty."

"Can Zan and I pick you up at the bunkhouse at four?"

"I'll be ready."

He hung up the phone. *Please let everything fall into place.*

Thursday-night rodeos were his least favorite, but he needed to talk to Doc, and this would be an easy points ride, so why not? Adam had planned to pick Merry Anna up early so he'd have enough time with Doc before the riders started coming in to get checked over and cleared to ride.

Unfortunately, things didn't go according to plan. Adam, Merry Anna, and Zan hadn't been on the road twenty minutes before they got hung up in traffic. They inched along for a while, and then nothing. Finally, Merry Anna found something on social media about an accident.

"A truckload of chickens turned over. All lanes are blocked."

He hissed under his breath. "How far until the next turn-off?"

She turned the phone this way and that. "I think it's about a mile ahead."

"We're just going to have to coast it out."

"What time do you ride?"

"Not for a while. I was trying to meet with someone beforehand." He regretted the tone in his voice. "Sorry. I'm not annoyed with you." He half grinned.

Finally, they got to the Archdale exit, and Adam sped down the ramp. Merry Anna grabbed for the door handle. "No hand brake over there, you know," he said with a wink.

"I know."

It didn't take long to get to the stadium once they got moving.

They went inside. The stands were already filling up. "We'll get seats while you go do what you need to do," Merry Anna said.

Adam watched them take seats in the center section just a couple of rows up.

He jogged to the back, where Doc was taping up a cowboy's ankle. Adam waved.

"Hey, Adam. You're riding tonight?" He pulled the purple adhesive wrap tight and sent the cowboy on his way. "I thought you were coming over to talk."

"Figured if I'm here, I better ride, you know, just in case. You got time after my ride?"

"Yeah, of course."

Adam nodded. *One last ride.* Nerves wrestled in his gut. He went to the arena office, checked in for his ride, and drew his bull—a new bull he'd never heard of out of a new contractor from Georgia—Rocket Fuel.

No one else had heard of him either.

He taped up his wrist and stretched before putting on his gear, then walked over to let Merry Anna and Zan know that he'd be riding third.

"We'll be right here watching," Merry Anna said with a smile. "I've got my prayer all planned."

"Last time you rode bulls, it scared me," Zan said.

"I won," Adam said, trying to comfort her. "Remember?"

She nodded. "But I was afraid."

"This time you'll be with Merry Anna. It'll be okay."

Zan's brows pulled together, but she didn't whine, didn't complain. "All right."

"Give me a hug for good luck?" he asked. She leaped into his arms and clung to him like a tree frog. He could feel her heart racing.

"Hold on tight, Daddy." She squeezed his neck.

"I always do, Princess."

24

Merry Anna fought back her tears when Zan told Adam to hold on tight. She thought about the night Zan clung to that sheep as though her life depended on it.

The difference was, Merry Anna knew that in this case, Adam's life could depend on it.

Her heart raced. At least he wasn't at the end of the lineup this time. She didn't know how many buckoffs she could take waiting to get through his ride.

He's a pro. He's going to be fine.

She took Zan's hand in hers and smiled gently, hoping to calm her.

The announcer opened the ceremonies. Everyone rose for the national anthem and Pledge of Allegiance, and every cowboy came out into the riding ring and held his hat to his heart for the whole thing.

Zan pointed to Adam. She'd been able to pick him out of the whole line of men in chaps.

Tonight's announcer sang out the announcements like he was calling the rounds in a boxing match.

"Are you ready to rumble?"

High-energy music cranked through the air, and the bulls were clanging through the gates into the chutes.

The first rider covered his bull, staying on the full eight-second ride. When the buzzer rang out, he came off so gracefully that it looked like a gymnastics dismount. Merry Anna clapped, and Zan did too.

The next rider was off the bull before its front feet hit the ground. He ran right back into the chute, making it look as if the bull got out and caged the cowboy for good measure. It was worth a chuckle, but the cowboy wasn't laughing as he stomped out of the ring.

Merry Anna was focused on the bucking chute. From her seat, she could see Adam rosin his rope. Zan didn't seem to realize he was getting ready to ride, so Merry Anna played it cool, hoping it would all be over, except the celebrating, before she realized it.

The other cowboys hung over the chute, helping Adam get set on the bull. With one boot on the fence, a cowboy gave Adam's rope a powerful tug.

Adam gave the nod, and the chute shot open with a bang that sent Zan to her feet.

Merry Anna helped Zan stand on the bleacher so she could see over the crowd. She held her close to keep her from wobbling off the boards that gave a little every time someone moved. Focused on Adam's ride, the red bull slung slobber as he spun in a compact circle. Merry Anna held Zan in one hand and her own heart in the other, wishing now she hadn't agreed to this one more time.

The seconds ticked off on the giant digital clock on the scoreboard.

Adam rocked and spun with the bull, his hand high in the air. It looked like easy money.

Thank You for giving him a safe ride.

Rocket Fuel looked so much smaller than the one she

watched him ride last time. The bull stumbled forward and turned in the opposite direction a half step, then back the other way.

Merry Anna watched Adam slide toward his hand, then spur the animal. The bull sprang into the air and lurched forward.

The buzzer sounded. She whooped a joyful holler, so thankful he'd made the eight seconds.

But Adam was in the air over that animal's back. The powerful thrust from the bull forced Adam's body forward, and in a single nasty nanosecond, Rocket Fuel lifted his head, catching Adam in the skull.

Blood flooded the right side of Adam's face.

Merry Anna couldn't tell for sure, but the way Adam seemed to fold over his own arm and hang from the side of the animal, he may have been unconscious.

Zan screamed.

Merry Anna spun her around and pulled the little girl into herself in a hug, hiding her face from the commotion and wishing she also could look away.

The bullfighters did a deadly dance with the bull, who wasn't showing any sign of slowing down. Clearly, this bull didn't understand that the buzzer meant it was the end of the ride.

One of the bullfighters teased the bull while the other finally worked Adam loose. Adam fell to the ground in a heap.

Emergency personnel rushed to the gate, but the bull wasn't exiting. He snorted and spun toward the crowd. He pounded his foot, then scraped it back, turning slowly toward Adam. Finally, after what seemed like an eternity, the cowboy on the pickup horse roped Rocket Fuel, his horse pulling the unwilling bull toward the gate.

Adam tried to get up, but the medics raced to him and wouldn't let him move.

Merry Anna held her breath as she watched the team lift him onto a stretcher and carry him out of the ring.

The crowd cheered, yet Merry Anna and Zan both just stood there, speechless.

Adam raised a hand in the air, but Merry Anna wasn't convinced he was okay.

What am I supposed to do? I can't sit here waiting. Please be okay.

The rodeo continued. Another rider was already on a bull, another rock song pumping into the arena.

Merry Anna gathered their things and guided Zan. "Come on. We're going to talk to some people and check on your dad, okay?"

Zan nodded, then ran her hand across her nose, sniffing back the tears. It broke Merry Anna's heart. "Honey, it's okay to cry when you're scared or sad. See, *I* cried too."

"My mommy said never cry." She gulped a sob. "She said to be a brave girl while she's gone."

"Oh, you are very brave." She squeezed her hand. "I promise that your mom would say it's okay. You are a very special little lady. Your mom and dad are very lucky to have you."

Merry Anna collected herself, then walked over to a guy holding a clipboard and asked for a report on Adam.

The guy lifted his gaze from the papers. "You his wife?"

She was tempted to lie, but surely all these guys knew each other. "I'm his friend, with his daughter."

Clipboard Cowboy disappeared behind a curtain and then came back out. "You can go back there."

Merry Anna tried to keep from dragging Zan, but she was anxious to see Adam for herself. Thank goodness that when they stepped inside the room, he was sitting on the edge of a medical table.

"I'm okay, baby girl. Come here. I'm sorry I scared you."

Zan ran to him, clinging to his leather chaps. With a handful of fringe in her fist, she stuck to him like glue.

Adam closed his eyes, then looked at Merry Anna. "Concussion. Stitches. I'm going to have one heck of a headache."

Relief allowed her to take her first real breath since the accident. "Adam." She shook her head.

"Knowing you saw that hurt me worse than the bull."

Doc walked over. "He's going to have to go over to the hospital. I want them to do an MRI and check for spinal damage."

"I could have walked off if they'd have let me. There's no spinal damage."

"Humor me." Doc turned his attention to Merry Anna. "I can let you take him, or we can have the ambulance take him over."

"I'm not getting in an ambulance," Adam interrupted. "Doc, this is Merry Anna. She'll take me."

"I can drive him." She'd never driven a truck as big as Adam's in her life, but she'd get him there.

"That's good, because he can't drive for forty-eight hours after that type of injury," Doc said. "Merry Anna, go ahead and pull the truck around here to the back. Zan can wait here with us."

Merry Anna went out to the parking lot and got in the truck, resetting the seat so she could reach the pedals. Then she started the engine and idled forward and around to the back entrance, where a guard rent-a-cop stopped her.

"Hi," she said. "I'm picking up Adam Locklear to take him to the hospital."

He waved her through.

She parked by the back door. It was already propped open, and from the truck, she could see Doc and Adam talking. Zan stood nearby, twirling. *Kids are so resilient.*

Merry Anna wished she were twirling too. Instead, her stomach spun like a washer off balance.

25

It was the early hours of morning by the time all the tests had been completed and Adam was released. The nurse wheeled him out, and Merry Anna jumped up from her seat in the waiting room. Zan slept curled up in the chair with Merry Anna's jacket under her head.

Merry Anna ran over to him. "I was getting worried."

"It's fine. Come on. Let's get home." He got up from the wheelchair.

She raised the keys in her hand. "I'll drive."

"No, let me. You're not comfortable with the truck. I promise I'll pull over if I start feeling bad. Really, this isn't my first concussion."

He thought she'd put up a bigger fight, but she didn't argue with him. He picked up Zan and sat her in the wheelchair in the otherwise empty emergency room. Then he pushed the wheelchair past the check-in desk. "I'll bring this right back."

Merry Anna was laughing. "I can't believe you just did that."

"They don't care. They wanted to send me out in it, and now they can say they did." He pushed Zan through the parking lot and then moved her to the truck. Merry Anna took the wheelchair and ran it back up to the building.

When she came back, she looked at him, worry in her eyes. "Are you sure you don't want me to drive? I can do it."

"I'd feel better if I drove."

She paused for a moment. "I don't like it, but you're the boss." She got in and took two bottles of water from her purse. She handed him one. "Here. Sip on this."

"Thank you." He chugged half of it. "And thank you for remaining so calm through all this."

"I wasn't." She twisted in the seat to face him. "It was horrible to watch. I never knew eight seconds was so long."

The left side of his mouth lifted. "It's longer than most people can imagine."

"I saw you talking to Doc when I picked you up. What was he saying? Was he telling you not to ride? How many concussions have you had?"

"He's been telling me to quit for years."

"Oh?"

"I'm older than a lot of these guys now." He pulled in a breath. "I was talking to Doc about joining the sports medicine team. He's mentioned it before. He knows I have a medical degree. I could come on as an apprentice until I got all my certifications done. I'd still be close to the sport."

She let out a sigh of relief. "It'll be hard for you to leave rodeo. I know how much you love it. But that sounds like a good option."

"Rodeo is all I've ever wanted." He sat there quietly for a moment. "When Rocket Fuel rolled me forward, I knew I was in trouble. A new bull that no one else had ridden before—you never know what's going to happen. I never see anything but the bull. But tonight something flashed in my mind. I imagined what it looked like from your vantage point." His gaze held hers.

"We shouldn't have come. We distracted you."

"No, putting that on y'all isn't fair. The course of my journey is changing. I could fight it. Lots of people do. They ride way longer than they should, and they get hurt. I think God's trying to get my attention."

"What are you going to do?"

"I think I know, but I'm going to get back to you on that. I'm not putting it off, though. I promise."

Merry Anna rested her hand on his arm. "You're a good man. Whatever it is you decide to do, I'm sure you'll have the best intentions."

He took her hand. This woman had no idea how much impact she had on him. He was so thankful she was here.

The roads were empty, and Zan was sleeping quietly in the back seat.

He saw Merry Anna nod off. She awoke with a start, then flipped through her phone.

A moment later, she sat straight up in her seat. "Wow, your ride is all over social media. It looks even worse on replay."

"People love to see us wreck. It's like the pileups in a car race, or bloody fights in hockey."

"When I was watching, it was like slow motion," she said. "It was the oddest thing, like suddenly everything was clicking off in frames." She replayed the video. "Crazy how fast it all happened in real life."

He pulled off to the side of the road.

Merry Anna snapped to attention. "Are you okay?"

"Yeah, I'm fine." He watched her let out a breath. "I just want to see that video. Can't do that and drive."

"Oh." She angled the phone so he could see the screen. The still showed his head just coming up from Rocket Fuel's horn. The unnatural angle of his body made him wince. He pressed play on the video. It started when the chute opened and ended with him on the ground in a heap.

"Terrifying," she whispered. "I'm so thankful you're okay."

"Over eight thousand likes already." As much as he'd hoped for that kind of lift in his brand when he was trying to buy in with that livestock contractor, this wasn't the way he'd meant to do it.

"That's just that one thread," she said. "I saw at least three other posts on my feed, and I don't even follow bull riding or cowboy stuff. I can imagine how many are popping up from the real fans."

"You're not my real fan?" He pouted. "You're only hanging around to get my gold buckles. That's it, isn't it?"

"Sure. Who wouldn't want to wear a gold salad plate around their waist?"

He pulled back, pretending to be totally offended, then pointed to his belt. "I'll have you know I work very hard for these salad plates."

She swatted him. "Stop. You know what I mean. I've seen the rows of them in your house. Doesn't that ever get old?"

"No, it really doesn't." Nostalgia rolled through his veins. Could he leave the sport and not become bitter about it? *I hope so. I need to find a way.* He tilted Merry Anna's phone away from him.

"That is hard to watch."

"I know. You could've been—"

"Not because of that. That bull was barely working at the beginning. I was spurring him to get a decent ride. If only I hadn't taken my attention off him that one millisecond." He pointed to the phone. "That shouldn't have happened. I'm blessed I made the buzzer." He pulled back onto the road.

Merry Anna sat quietly.

"Hey, did anyone post my score? I never did get my score."

She scrolled through the posts, then went over to the rodeo website. "86."

"Hmm."

She tucked her phone back into her purse. "That was the top score for the night, though."

"That was a gimme." He shook his head, unimpressed. "That wasn't a winning ride."

She let out a huff. "Can you just be thankful?"

He pressed his lips together. "Yes. I'm very thankful. Mostly that you two are okay and we are almost home. Sorry, mood changes are part of the concussion."

"How about I stay on the couch with Zan? That way if you need anything, I'll be right there. The doctor said you might have some blurred vision, nausea—"

"I've had more concussions than that doctor has probably ever diagnosed. Besides, I didn't mean to have you out all night. I know you have to work today."

"I sent Krissy a note from the hospital. I've got the day off."

"I'll be okay, but yeah, if you don't mind staying in case Zan wakes up and I'm asleep, that'd be really helpful." *Tell her you want her to stay. It's not about Zan.*

"Good. I'd feel better about that."

"I don't want you to stay for Zan." He swallowed, then let his heart set the story straight. "I like the thought of waking up and you being there."

"I'd like that too." Merry Anna smiled and put her phone in her lap. "Thank you for telling me that."

"It's overdue."

They pulled into the driveway at four fifty that morning. Zan was fast asleep. Adam carried her into the house and tucked her in while Merry Anna gathered a pillow and blanket from the hall closet and settled into the corner of the couch.

"Good night, Merry Anna. Thank you. For everything." He turned the lights down and went to his room. He swallowed a few ibuprofen and downed a bottle of water, then went and stood in the shower for as long as his legs would hold him before crawling into bed.

He looked at his phone. He had dozens of texts and voice mails, and it was barely daylight. There were always more messages over wrecks than the good rides. He set his alarm for every three hours until eight o'clock that night. He'd be up way before then, but he knew the routine. Get up and move around every three hours to make sure he could see straight.

When his alarm went off, he got up and drank some water. He put on a shirt and walked out into the living room. As soon as Zan saw him, she ran to him.

"Good morning to you too." He picked her up, making her scream at a pitch so high that it made him shut his eyes. "Boy, you are a squeaker." He lifted her again, sending her into a fit of giggles. Good thing she was so light. His shoulder resisted the reach, so he set her down before he dropped her. "Did y'all get something to eat?"

"Merry Anna made us peanut butter toast. It was really good."

"My secret recipe," Merry Anna teased, cleaning up some of the crayons they had spread out on the hardwood floors.

"Thanks for doing that," he said. "I meant to get up and make something for y'all."

"I think you should take it easy today, Cowboy."

"I don't know if you've noticed or not, but I'm not really good at that."

Merry Anna pointed a crayon at him. "You could try. We'll be fine playing together, won't we, Zan?"

"Yep. I'm making you a get-well card, and it's not done yet, so you can't see it."

"Oh. Well, I wouldn't want to interrupt that." How could there be so much good packed into one tiny child? "How about I make you two a deal. I'll go rest for a couple more hours, but then I'll make lunch. I'll barbecue some chicken on the grill. That'll get us outside for some fresh air too. Deal?"

Zan swung around to look at Merry Anna.

"He's a pretty good cook," Merry Anna said with a shrug. "What do you think?"

Zan reached for Adam's hand. "Time for you to rest, Daddy. We'll see you for lunch." Zan marched him all the way back to his room.

He got in bed, and when Zan pulled the covers up, tucking him in just like he'd done for her, he was about done in. She leaned forward and kissed him on the forehead.

He choked back emotion, not wanting to scare her by crying. *So this is what unconditional love is all about.*

26

Adam felt a lot better when he got up and started making lunch. He kept a bottle of water nearby, sure to stay hydrated and keeping ahead of the pain with ibuprofen every four hours.

The three of them were sitting at the picnic table, just finishing up lunch, when a blue sedan turned down the lane, past Tara's place, and onto his property.

"Were you expecting someone?" Merry Anna asked.

He shook his head, watching the car come up the road and into his driveway.

A pink Lyft sign was on the dashboard of the car.

The back door opened, and his mother stepped out of the car. "Mom?" He got up and walked over to her. "What are you doing here? Is Dad okay?"

"Really?" She put a hand on her hip. "Do you think I don't see the internet?" She threw her arms around him, crying.

"Mom, I'm okay."

"I saw you get tossed around. They showed you carried off on a stretcher. I couldn't get any information. I've left a hundred messages on your phone and texted too. Nothing!"

"I'm sorry. I had no idea you would see that. I wouldn't have wanted you to worry."

"I didn't tell your father. I knew he'd be mad as a box of frogs. I told him it was an emergency and I was going to see my sister. A half truth. This is an emergency."

"I'm so sorry I worried you."

"Let me look at you. You're too skinny. Look at that bandage." She pressed on the white bandage covering the stitches in his head.

"Ouch."

"Concussion?" She leaned in, looking at his eyes as though she'd be able to tell.

"Yes, but I'm going to be fine."

"Thank the Lord. I prayed all the way here." She let out a long breath, dabbing at her tears. "I didn't even notice you have company. How rude of me." She didn't hesitate, marching right over to the picnic table where Merry Anna and Zan sat. "Hi. I'm Adam's mother."

"Mrs. Locklear, so nice to meet you." Merry Anna stood. "I live over in the bunkhouse. I'm Merry Anna."

His mother's face lit up when she looked at Zan. "My goodness, aren't you a pretty thing."

"Thank you." Zan twisted back and forth.

Adam stood there, knowing what was about to happen with no way to soften the blow.

"And so polite," his mother said, reaching out to touch Merry Anna's arm. "You must be so proud."

Yep. Mom had just assumed Zan was Merry Anna's daughter, and as easy as that made things for the moment, this wasn't something he was going to be able to hide from her. Plus, everyone in town already knew the truth.

He placed his hand on his mother's arm. "So proud," he said. "Hey, Mom, I'm glad you're here. I need to tell you something."

Merry Anna looked at him with pleading eyes. He could tell she was searching for direction. "Merry Anna, do you and Zan want to run up to the house and see what kind of dessert we might have?"

"We're on it. So nice meeting you, Mrs. Locklear." Merry Anna swept Zan's hand and jogged up to the house.

"Thank goodness you're okay. Son, I just knew you were going to be in a hospital bed half-loopy. To see you here, outside, entertaining. I'm so thankful. It looked so much worse on that video." She sat down at the table. "When you called and apologized that night, your dad and I were stunned. I'm so glad you finally understand how we feel."

He sucked in a reluctant breath.

"So, why did you ride again after that?"

"It's what I do, Mom." He was trying to not get defensive. It was an old battle that had scarred their relationship for way too long. "It's how I make a living. I love the sport, but that's not what I need to tell you." He paused, not knowing how to start. "Zan."

"She's absolutely adorable. I had no idea about you and Merry Anna. Oh gosh, I'm missing everything."

That just made it harder. "Zan is my daughter."

She blinked, then dropped her head forward. "Your—"

"Hold on. I didn't even know she existed until a few weeks ago. A barrel racer I went out with a few times showed up with her out of the blue. We were together only a couple of times, and I was always careful." It sounded lame and irresponsible. "She later just quit showing up around the rodeo, and I all but forgot about her until she showed up on my doorstep one Saturday morning with Zan."

His mother clutched her heart. "Are you sure she's your daughter?"

"Yes. I took a paternity test, but before the results came back, I was already feeling that bond."

"This changes everything, Adam. Raising a child is serious, and that little girl is depending on you."

"Yes ma'am. I know. I'm working on a plan."

"I most certainly hope it includes quitting all this bull riding. You've been living a death wish, and you just can't do that with a child depending on you." Her jaw pulsed.

"I know, Mom. That's not how it is." He felt his defenses rise. "You could just as easily say that about Dad and his smoking. That's not fair."

She folded her arms across her chest.

"Mom, I don't want to argue. I'm well aware I need to make some changes. I'm figuring it all out."

She looked like she was about to cry. "When were you going to tell us?"

"I guess I was waiting until I knew what the plan was. To avoid *this*." Then he tried to soften his tone. "You're her grandparents. I was going to tell you."

"I know you don't want to hear it, but I think this rodeo stuff is an addiction, like the thrill someone gets on drugs. Can we get you rehab? What can we do to help you?"

"Nothing. I'll make the decisions that need to be made, and Zan is my priority."

"It sounds like you know it's time to be a father first."

Isn't that what I said? "I do."

"And what about this gal?"

"Merry Anna?" He looked up toward the house. "All this is new. I've only known her a couple of months." He smiled. "She's not like anyone I've ever known."

"My goodness. You have a lot going on."

"You can say that again." He felt like he was observing his

old life as a stranger. "I want to be the one to tell Dad about Zan."

"Oh, Adam. If he finds out I knew about it and didn't tell him, he will never forgive you or me, and I've already met her."

"I just need a couple of weeks. Please?" The last thing he needed was Dad adding to all this.

She looked worried.

"Besides, you didn't tell him you were coming here," he reminded her. "You'd have that to explain too."

"I shouldn't have done that. It was wrong, but I was afraid he'd stop me." She sat down. "Honey, I was so worried when I saw that video."

"I'll bring Zan to the house once I get it all figured out. It won't be long. It can't be." He wondered what Merry Anna must be thinking right about now.

His mother glanced over at the car still sitting in the driveway. "I told the driver we'd probably have to go to the hospital. I guess I'll have him take me back to the airport."

"That's a good idea."

"You're really going to come home? I want to know that little girl."

"Yes ma'am. I don't know how Dad's going to take it all, but I'll do my part."

"He's getting older, Adam. He's softening. He does miss you."

I'd never know it.

He waved as the car pulled out of the driveway. Merry Anna and Zan came back outside, but neither of them said a word. Questions hung in the air.

"If you're feeling okay, I'm going to head home," Merry Anna said. "I think you probably need some time to yourself."

Adam nodded. "I do."

"I'm a phone call away if either of you needs me."

He watched Merry Anna walk away.

Zan slipped her hand between his fingers. "She's really nice."

"So are you." He squeezed her hand, then made sure the grill was turned off and had Zan help him clear everything away.

Later that evening, Doc called. "Just checking to see how you're feeling tonight."

"Thank you for calling. I'm doing fine."

"I wanted to call to see how you were, but I also wanted to officially extend you a job opportunity. Adam, I'd love to have you come on board with me. I think you'd be a great part of the team."

"You're kidding."

"No. Now, it'll still mean a lot of travel, maybe more than you're doing now. We fly a lot to fit everything in, so it'll still be something to work out, but I can start you with a salary and insurance for you and Zan until you can get all the certifications straight. Then we'll renegotiate."

"That's mighty generous."

"Adam, a lot of these guys out here—they don't have any other skills. You have options they don't. You need to be smart about this."

"If I weren't so close to the title this year, it would be a way easier decision." But he knew he had to do the right thing. As much as he yearned for that win, there were bigger things at stake here.

"I get it. When I was bronc riding, I felt the same way. It's always going to be after the next ride, but you know it's true that sometimes there's not a next ride. You've been lucky so far."

"I have. I know it," Adam said. "Working with you would keep me close to the sport but eliminate that risk."

"I know your focus is on that little girl, but your friend Merry Anna—she was really tore up. You two serious?"

Adam cleared his throat. "Could be."

"She know that?"

"I haven't said it in so many words." *She's got to know.*

"You have to say the exact words, Adam. That's the only words they hear. If you care about her, include her in the decision."

Adam laughed. "I know what she'll say. Same thing you're saying."

"So, she's smart."

"Yeah, she's smart. I feel like I need to say yes, but I also wonder if being close to the sport is going to make it even harder."

"Wasn't for me," Doc offered. "But everyone is different. I'll also say this. You can't take another concussion. It would be hard to allow you to continue to ride anyway. I'm working the Archdale rodeo out by you again this weekend, but why don't you let me know by next Wednesday? That'll give you some time to think about it. If you say yes, I can have you start the next weekend. We'll be in Mesquite."

"I'll let you know." What were the odds that the first day on his new job, if he decided to take it, would be in the town where Carly's folks lived?

27

Merry Anna got up on Wednesday morning and set off on foot to work. Tara was standing out near the road, picking up her newspaper, when Merry Anna walked by.

"Good morning, Tara."

"Good morning. I was hoping I'd catch you."

"Do you need me to order some more things for you?"

"No, I was wondering if the two of us could have lunch today. What time is your lunch break?"

"Usually around one. That gives Krissy time to get to the bank and back before I leave."

"Let's meet at the coffee shop just two doors down. I love the chicken salad sandwich they have."

"Yeah, that'd be nice. I'll meet you there."

"Good. Thank you."

Merry Anna went on her way to work, but something about Tara's tone bothered her. She seemed a little perturbed about something. She'd know soon enough.

The walk to work was pleasant, the sun warm on her face. She swung her arms, enjoying the hint of sausage in the air. *Sage.* She wouldn't have known that smell a few months ago. She had some growing in her garden. Someone in one of the apartments above the stores on Main Street must be making breakfast.

An odd vibe forced her to stop and look behind her. There was nothing there, but she was unnerved enough to hug her purse close to her body as she walked the rest of the way to work. The feeling hung over her, weighting her with worry as she unlocked the front door and stepped inside.

She scanned the street as she flipped the sign to Open. Her heart pounding, she sat down in the chair by the register, trying to calm down. Crossing one foot over the other, she pulled her phone from her purse and called Adam to try to interrupt the worry.

"Hey, Adam. Everything good at the Locklear abode this morning?" She tried to sound cheerful, not wanting to worry him with some silly nothing. He had enough on his plate.

"We just had pancakes."

Hearing his voice helped. "Perhaps you should lay off the syrup a little. You may be able to handle a bucking bull, but I have a hunch a sugared-up five-year-old could be way more unpredictable."

"Hadn't really thought of that. Good point."

She didn't want to dote, but she had to ask, "How're you feeling?"

"Really good."

Whatever she was feeling didn't have anything to do with their relationship. That was a relief. "I was hoping y'all might want to do something tonight."

"That would be great. Count us in."

She looked up when a shopper walked through the front door. "I've got a customer, but I'll check in later."

"Stop by the store on your way home," he said.

"I'll do that." At least if she still had this feeling, she could hitch a ride with them back home.

The rest of the morning, there was a steady stream of customers.

Krissy had warned her that the weeks before and after Fourth of July were the most popular holiday weeks for Antler Creek.

Three out-of-towners came in, wanting to special-order barn quilts after having just driven the barn-quilt trail. That tour was good for business. The barn-quilt tile ornaments Krissy painted practically flew off the shelves. They had only a couple of the Angels Rest ornaments left in stock.

Krissy came in around noon, and before Merry Anna realized it, it was lunchtime.

"I was going to meet Tara down at the coffee shop for a quick lunch. Can I bring you something back?"

"A sandwich, and a cup of sweet tea, if you don't mind." Krissy took some money from her pocket.

"I've got it." Merry Anna rang up one more customer and then went to the coffee shop. Tara was already sitting at the table in the far corner, a half-empty cup of coffee in front of her.

"How long have you been here?"

"A while. I was anxious."

"Is something wrong?" Merry Anna sat down.

"Yes. Look, this isn't my business. I know that, and if this had happened a few weeks ago, before that woman dropped off that child to Adam, I'd have probably kept my opinions to myself, but I just can't stand by and let this happen."

"What has you so upset?" *And how does it pertain to me? Is this about the bull riding?*

"If you are not in a position to make a commitment to

Adam, you need to leave him alone. Not only is it wrong, a sin even, but that little girl shouldn't be exposed to that sort of thing."

"What are you talking about? My commitment?" *Sin?*

"I know."

"About what?" Merry Anna sat back in her chair. "You aren't making any sense."

The waitress came up. "Are you ready to order?"

"I'll have the chicken salad sandwich, same as Tara. And one to go." Merry Anna flipped the menu to the waitress. "Also some water, please." Her stomach churned.

"While you were at the rodeo with Adam, a man was at your house. Being a good neighbor, I walked over and asked him what he was doing snooping around."

"Snooping?"

"He went right inside your house. I saw him with my own two eyes."

That feeling from this morning was back. "Who?"

"Your husband."

"I told you I'm divorced." Merry Anna picked up her phone and scrolled through the pictures. "This guy?"

"Yes." Tara's lips pulled into a tight line. "He was quite convincing that you two are still married."

"He has no right to be here. I have receipts and final divorce papers to prove it." She hugged herself. "I don't know how he found me. I purposely didn't tell him where I was staying."

"He said your parents sent him to bring you back home."

That burned in her gut. "Not even my parents know where I am." A shiver ran up her arm, reminding her of the feeling she'd had this morning. "When did you see him?"

"Yesterday."

"I must've been at Adam's house when he showed up."

Anger bubbled inside her. "Tara, I promise you I'm not running around on a husband I left back in DC. I would never do that, and I know how precious this situation is with Adam and his daughter. I would never do anything to compromise that."

"Don't be mad at me," Tara said. "I was just acting on what I heard."

"Thank you for stopping him and caring enough about me to stop me if I were doing something foolish, but I promise you I am not."

Tara lifted her mug and took a sip of her coffee, then set it down. "Cold." She waved at the waitress, lifting the mug in the air to get her attention. "I'm so relieved. I was really disappointed. I know we've only just met, but you're kind of like a daughter to me. My children are spread out hither and yon. I don't see them much anymore. I've loved spending time with you."

The waitress came over and topped off Tara's coffee and put a glass of water in front of Merry Anna.

"I'm sorry I jumped to conclusions," Tara said. "It didn't seem right, but he was very convincing."

"It's fine. I'm glad you let me know. It gives me the creeps that he was in my house. I've always felt so safe here in Antler Creek. Kevin can be very manipulative."

"It is odd. You know, it's funny, because the whole town is abuzz thinking Adam is using you just to help with that little girl, and here I was thinking the opposite."

"The whole town thinks that?" If it was one thing she hated, it was being made a fool of.

Tara's mouth dropped open, as if she realized what she'd said was probably out of line. "Sorry. Not everyone. I don't even know . . . everyone." She waved it off.

"I haven't even told Adam I used to be married. I need to tell him about this before Kevin tries to convince someone else we're still married. No telling what other snooping and lying he's been doing around here."

The waitress brought lunch to the table and set the sandwich-to-go in the empty chair next to them.

"I think I'm going to need mine to go too," Merry Anna said. "I'm sorry, Tara. I can't eat right now. My stomach is in knots over this."

"I understand. I'll keep an eye on your place. If he shows up again, do you want me to call the sheriff?"

"Yes, please do." She'd be sure to tell Krissy about the incident as soon as she got back to the store. Maybe Grady could be on the lookout for Kevin and find out what he was doing in town.

The waitress brought a box. Merry Anna put the box in the bag with the other sandwich and laid a twenty-dollar bill on the table. "That should cover it. I'm going to get back to work."

She left the coffee shop, her head on a swivel. Did Kevin know where she worked too? She walked back to Hardy House and stepped behind the counter. She busied herself while Krissy helped a customer, which seemed to be taking forever.

Once the customer left, Merry Anna pulled her aside. "Krissy, I just found out my ex-husband has been here looking for me. I have no idea why, but Tara saw him coming out of my house yesterday when I wasn't there."

"That's odd."

"Has anyone been in here asking about me?"

"No. I'd have told you if anyone had, and I certainly wouldn't have given out any information." Krissy raised a finger and made a call on her cell phone. "Hey, Grady, when you're out this way, would you stop in?" She nodded. "Thanks, darlin'."

"Thank you." Merry Anna swallowed hard.

"We'll let Grady handle this. He'll know what to do." She led Merry Anna to a chair. "Honey, you're shaking."

"I had this weird feeling this morning when I was walking to work. Then Tara told me that Kevin had been in my house. Oh, and he told her we're still married and that he was here to take me back home. I almost forgot about that part. I'm livid. Freaked out. Confused. Something."

"You have every right to be hopping mad over that. Take a breath."

Merry Anna inhaled deeply, trying to calm down. "When I left DC, the divorce was final. He was fighting for more alimony, so I told him that if I couldn't live on what I was paying him, then I'd pay him more. Well, of course I've done it just fine. I was more than generous with him in the settlement, but he'd almost had me convinced it wasn't enough. I've learned a lot about myself through that wager too."

"I knew you were going through something."

"I should have been completely up front with you, but I had no idea I was going to stick around. I thought I'd work here a couple of weeks and move on. Then I fell in love with this town, and you, and started going back to church. Everything changed."

"So you moved after the divorce?" Krissy asked.

"We had to sell the house and split the profits. I'd gotten a condo, but then I decided to take a sabbatical to discover who I really am. I was married to my high school sweetheart, and I've worked in my family's business my whole life. I didn't even know myself anymore."

"That sounds rather isolating."

"I guess it was. I knew divorcing Kevin was the right thing, but I had this need to be away and unbraid myself from my past to figure out my future. I packed one bag, locked up the condo, and tried to tender my resignation, but my family wouldn't accept it. So I took the leave of absence, and here I am."

"If you don't mind me asking, what did you do back in DC?"

Merry Anna felt ashamed to tell her. She knew most of the people around here had thought she was going through a rough patch of the financial variety, and she had just let them believe it. "I'm the COO of the Supply Cabinet."

"C . . . Oh? You mean the biggest chain of office supplies in, like, the whole United States?"

"Yeah, pretty much."

"No wonder you're such a powerhouse here." Krissy put her hands over her eyes. "You must have thought I was nuts to offer you this little job. I feel like such a fool."

"No!" Merry Anna's eyes teared up. "Please don't feel like that. You rescued me. I love this job. I can't even begin to tell you what this job and your friendship mean to me."

"I rented you a *bunkhouse* to live in." Krissy sounded embarrassed.

"I love that place. I believe it's where I was supposed to be. You and I becoming friends—meeting Adam, Tara—all of it. I'm so grateful I landed here. Please, please, forgive me."

"Oh, Merry Anna. We're friends," Krissy said. "I felt that from the first moment we said hello in this store. There's nothing you could do or say to change what I think of you."

"Thank goodness. I felt the same way." She bit down on her lip. "I only hope Adam won't feel like I deceived him. I wasn't truthful with him about my divorce, my job, my financial status. I just never thought I'd stay here. I never intended to be secretive. It all just sort of happened, and I loved being anonymous. I was trying on new things to see what felt right. I finally know what it feels like to be me."

"Adam will understand." Krissy rubbed her hand across Merry Anna's back. "I hate that you're so upset. Why don't you go on home and talk to Adam? You'll see. It will be fine. I'll tell Grady everything when he gets here. Send that picture of Kevin over to me. I'll give it to him."

Merry Anna pulled out her phone and sent Krissy the photograph.

"Will you be okay to walk home? I can close up and take you, or, hey, you can take my car. I'll catch a ride with Grady."

"No, the fresh air will do me good," Merry Anna insisted. "I love this town and everyone in it. I'm not going anywhere." *He's not going to steal my joy.* "I'm feeling better. I'm going to call Kevin on my way home and let him know that I will have him arrested if he comes back around." *I don't care what my folks have to say about it either. This is my life now, and I'm taking charge of it.*

28

Merry Anna walked down the block, trying to shake the heebie-jeebies all this mess with Kevin was giving her. This town and her choice to go simple for a little while had become complex, and it weighed on her heart. She'd never intended to deceive anyone.

Dialing Kevin, she wasn't surprised when he didn't answer. Controlling her voice, she left a message. "You could at least have the decency to answer. I know you've been skulking around, and you going into my house is trespassing. Don't you think for one minute that I won't have you arrested. We are not married, and we are not ever going to be anything again. I protected your reputation when we were married, but I'm going to fill in my folks on every bad habit and stupid thing you've done over the years. Your free ride is over, Kevin. Stay away from me."

She ended the call. She wasn't going to take this from him. For the first time in her life, she knew what happiness was. She knew what it felt like to do something because it was the right thing to do and not just for the money.

She scanned the lot of the Feed & Seed for Adam's truck. He was parked in a different spot this morning. One near the stairs. *Probably for Zan.* So much joy flooded her at the thought of them. *Kevin, you will not ruin this for me.*

Nervous to tell Adam the whole story, she knew that the longer she waited, the harder it would be. She veered from the sidewalk to the parking lot. While walking through the racks of summer flowers and garden tools, she said hello to a woman she recognized as a customer of Hardy House. "How are you today?"

"Doing great. Don't they have the best plants here?" the woman said.

"I totally agree." The cowbell on the door clanked as she stepped inside.

A little blond head popped up from the other side of a stack of horse feed. "Hi, Miss Merry Anna! Boo!"

"Did you see me coming?" Merry Anna teased.

"Mm-hmm. I was sitting on top of these bags and saw you walking down the street. I was crossing my fingers and hoping you would come here, and then you did!"

"Well, it sure is good to see you. How has your day been?"

"Very good. I've been making some new signs for the store." She scrambled from behind the feed bags and grabbed a stack of papers. "See, I drew this one for the horses, this one for the dogs, and one for the cats. I tried to do one for birds, but I don't really know how to draw those very good. They look like bubbles. Now people don't have to read, and they'll know what to buy."

"You are a thinker," Merry Anna said. "And that is very good marketing. You know, I've been painting something lately too."

"You have?"

"Yes. I've been painting a barn quilt. I'll show it to you sometime."

"What's it look like?"

Merry Anna smiled. "At first it was just going to look like blocks of pretty colors. But then I decided to add hearts and birds in the blocks, because this place makes me so happy, and the birds are so beautiful."

"I think I would like that."

"I'll show it to you. I'm almost done with it, and I can't wait to hang it on my house."

"Maybe we can make one for *my* house. Will you help me?"

"I most surely will," Merry Anna said.

"I thought I heard your voice. Hey there." Adam walked over and slung a casual arm around her waist. "I see my marketing department is catching you up on the new promotion."

"Yes." Merry Anna gave Zan a nod. "I see great things for the future of this place."

"That's good, because changes are coming." He slapped his hands together. "In fact, you walked in at just the right time. Could you do me a big favor?"

"Sure, what do you need?"

"I've got to get somewhere. It was a last-minute thing. Could you watch Zan tonight? I promise it won't be too late."

Zan jumped in the air. "Girls' night! Hooray! Can we play makeup?"

Merry Anna loved how this little girl was so comfortable with her already. "Makeup? Heck yeah. I've got tons of fun makeup. We can even do our nails."

Zan's lips formed an O. "This is going to be so much fun!"

"Would you mind if y'all did your makeovers at my house?" He leaned in, lowering his voice. "I'm trying to do better about keeping her to a routine."

Sounded like he'd been doing some reading. How sweet.

"No, that's fine. We'll stop by my house first and get some things."

"You're sure you don't mind?" Adam asked.

"Not at all. I had no plans, and it'll be fun spending some time with my new bestie." Merry Anna raised her hand, and Zan gave her a high five and then hugged her around the waist. That warmed her.

"Can we go right now?" Zan asked.

"I need to talk to you about something as soon as you have the chance, Adam," Merry Anna said.

"Can it wait until this evening?"

"Yeah, yeah. That's fine. I was heading home anyway. I'll take Zan with me."

"That'll be great," he said. "Then I can get out of here early too."

Merry Anna and Zan started walking home. It wasn't until they were almost there that Zan remembered she'd left her lunch box and all her crayons at the store. She looked so sad about it that Merry Anna felt bad.

"Do you want to go back and get them?" Merry Anna asked. "It's kind of a long walk for little legs like yours, but we can if you want to."

Zan pressed a thoughtful finger to her lips. "I think so. We'll miss out on so much fun if we don't get them."

They retraced their steps back to the Feed & Seed.

Adam's truck was already gone, and that hit her kind of wrong. They walked inside, and Zan ran to the back to get her things.

Jim walked over. "Oh, hey, Merry Anna. I thought you were another last-minute customer."

"No, Zan forgot some things, so we came back to get them."

"No problem. I'm just going to finish getting things inside so we can close up on time tonight."

"Adam sure got out of here in a hurry," she said, trying to make it sound like idle chitchat. "I can't believe we didn't pass him."

"Yeah," Jim said. "He wanted to beat the traffic so he could make good time out to Archdale."

Archdale? The Rodeo? It hit her like a punch. That's where he rode the other night when he landed in the emergency room. He'd led her to believe he was making changes, or maybe that's just what she'd wanted to hear.

Tara's words came rumbling back to her. An ugly truth. He *was* using her to take care of Zan. He wasn't making new plans at all. *I'm such an idiot. Again!* She couldn't trust herself with decisions about the men in her life.

"Got 'em," Zan said, running toward her.

"That's great." Merry Anna flashed a forced smile to Jim. "We're out of your hair now. Have a good afternoon."

She walked toward home with Zan in tow, trying not to let her anger show. Her insides were boiling.

"You're walking too fast for my legs," Zan said.

"I'm sorry." She slowed.

Zan's face was pink from running alongside.

He tricked me. Why didn't I ask for specifics? I'm just too nice. Everyone in town is already speculating that he's using me. And here I practically rolled out the welcome mat for him to do it.

But then she looked at the little girl clutching her hand. *It's not her fault. She hasn't had the best start in life. She's not the one using me.* She wouldn't let her irritation with Adam affect how she treated Zan.

"We're going to have the best time," she said to Zan.

"I'm so excited!"

They picked up the makeup kit and a few other things from her house and then walked down to Adam's. Shorty greeted them at the gate.

Zan hit her knees and hugged the little dog. "He loves me so much. It makes my heart have the hiccups."

"That's a lot of love." Merry Anna gave the dog a little scratch on the ears, then walked up the steps and went in the house. "Why don't you bring Shorty inside. I bet he's ready for food."

"I am too. I only had half of my sandwich at lunchtime today."

"Well, I'm sure there's plenty in here to eat. Let's see what we can find."

She let Zan feed Shorty while she sliced an apple and cheese. "This should hold you over until I can heat up the meat loaf. Go wash your hands."

Zan washed up, then wiggled into the chair at the table and began nibbling. Merry Anna hadn't noticed until now that Zan was covered in dirt, probably from crawling around that old warehouse all day.

"I think you're going to need a bath."

"I'm a mess. When I washed my hands, it made mud."

Merry Anna laughed, finally able to relax a little. She sat with Zan while she finished her snack, and then she ran the water in the tub for her.

"I'll be right in the kitchen. Just call for me if you need help." She had no idea how much assistance a five-year-old was supposed to need, but this little girl didn't seem to require much help with anything. *I should be so lucky to be as smart as she is.*

Merry Anna was going to have a very different chat with

Adam than she'd originally planned. She didn't even know if she would explain Kevin or not at this point. How could Adam do this? *Here I've been all say-yes-to-new opportunities, and look where it got me.*

A bitter taste hung in the back of her throat.

Anger kept her from crying, because she'd almost believed she had a fairy tale with Adam and Zan.

29

Merry Anna checked to see if Zan needed help getting out of the tub.

"No ma'am. I'm almost dry."

A few moments later, she heard a cheerful "Ta-da!" Dressed in a white nightgown with little blue flowers on it, Zan came out of the bathroom and twirled. "This is new. Isn't it pretty?"

"It is, but you looked pretty cute in those rodeo T-shirts you used to sleep in too."

Zan pulled the edges of the nightgown out to the side. "I like this way better."

"Me too. Come on, let's fix you up all pretty. I brought my supplies with me." Merry Anna spread her makeup across the vanity, an array of eye shadow, blush, mascara, and eyeliner, alongside expensive creams and makeup remover, which they'd no doubt be needing later. Then she took a leather cup from the bag and began setting each of the makeup brushes in it like a bouquet.

Zan gasped, touching each of the colorful jars and compacts. "What are these for?" She waved a fluffy makeup brush in the air.

"To make your makeup look flawless." She took the brush from her hand and moved it softly across Zan's nose and cheeks. She remembered how special those moments were with Mom in front of her big lighted makeup mirror. There wasn't anything frilly here in Adam's house, but hopefully it would be just as special. She swept the brush over Zan's eyes.

Zan giggled every time Merry Anna used the soft big brushes on her face with nothing on them at all.

The sweet little girl looked like a miniature Miss Texas when she was done—blond, fresh, and beautiful. Her lips were bright magenta. The eye shadow and mascara made her blue eyes sparkle. Merry Anna ran her hands through Zan's fine hair. The waves wrapped around her fingers as she smoothed the tangles without pulling.

"Do you know how to braid?" Zan asked. "My mom used to braid my hair."

Her heart skipped. "I sure do. Would you like me to braid your hair?"

"Yes, please. I'd like that a lot."

Merry Anna worked a french braid in the back and finished it off with a ponytail holder. Small curls fell across Zan's forehead and cheeks. "You look beautiful," Merry Anna said.

"Thank you." The little Miss Texas hugged Merry Anna's neck tightly. "You're the nicest lady ever."

"It's about your bedtime. Let's wash that makeup off your face and get you ready for bed. Okay?"

Zan enjoyed taking off the makeup as much as wearing it. She loved the sudsy cleanser.

"Ready for bed now?" Merry Anna dabbed a soft towel to dry Zan's skin.

"Yes." Zan took Merry Anna's hand, and they walked back into the living room. She crawled up onto the couch. Merry Anna was sorry that Adam hadn't gotten the bedroom ready yet. He'd made it sound like a simple project. *Guess he was too busy running off doing his own thing to fix up the room. He probably figured if he waited long enough, I'd offer to do it.*

Still, Merry Anna wasn't going to take it out on Zan. She tucked her in and they said prayers, ending with Zan's sweet amen.

Merry Anna sat down on the couch, draping her hand over Zan's feet. She didn't even bother to turn the television on. She waited for Zan's breathing to level, signaling she was already asleep.

Then Merry Anna closed her eyes.

The sound of Adam's diesel truck woke her. She sat up just as he walked through the door.

"Hey," he whispered. "Thanks."

She stood. "She's fast asleep." She nodded to Zan as she picked up her tote bag of things.

"What did you want to talk about?"

She was so tired and frankly didn't know where to begin. "People in this town think you're using me as a babysitter for Zan. At first, I thought they just didn't see the Adam that I know and let them think what they want. But you duped me into sitting with Zan tonight so you could rodeo? Really? That's a whole different level of bull." Her jaw clamped shut. The more she said, the madder it made her.

"Wait, it's not what you think."

"Isn't it? You didn't tell me you were rushing off to get to Archdale."

"No," he said, "you're right. I didn't tell you where I was going."

"I'm not an idiot." The words caught in her throat. "I may have been blind to some things, may have let myself get a little too close too fast, but I won't make that mistake again. I'm exhausted. I'm going home. I'm beat."

He followed her to the door. "Get some rest. I can explain, and I will."

She walked out, and he followed behind her. "How about I get the horses ready in the morning. We can all go for a ride. We can talk then."

She wasn't going to allow herself to get sucked into this any further.

"How's that sound?" he asked again.

"Like you have more energy than I do right now." She waved and walked home, promising herself she'd do what she could for Zan but that's where it would stop. Adam had flat out told her in the beginning he didn't have time for a relationship. What had made her think anything had changed? She'd let herself get swept away by a kiss that had clearly meant more to her than him.

She crawled into bed, exhausted and a little sad despite her efforts to look at the whole situation from another perspective.

On this journey, help me resist judgment and find kindness and understanding for others.

The next morning, Merry Anna awoke in better spirits. She enjoyed spending time with Zan, and if Adam needed her to babysit, she could do that. He could use her only if *she* allowed it. She washed her face and brushed out her hair, wondering if Zan's braid made it through the night.

She unpacked the makeup kit she'd taken to Adam's, putting everything back in the vanity where it belonged. As she placed the fluffy brushes in the crystal glass on the counter, she reveled in the memory of the twinkle in Zan's eyes when she'd moved them across her soft skin. Such a simple act.

A series of tweets and whistles followed by a myriad of notes came through the window. Her favorite bird was singing a tune. She'd come to expect it each morning. She could picture his feathers fluffed out and cheeks puffed, too, as he sang an original melody just for her. Sometimes she found herself putting words to the song.

She changed out of her pajamas. It was supposed to be in the high nineties today with humidity to match. After opting for a soft-yellow pair of shorts and white T-shirt, she slipped her feet into a pair of sandals and pulled her hair into a ponytail to go outside and reward her bird friend with a little treat.

In the kitchen, she grabbed one of the old pine cones she'd collected for decoration. One of her customers at the store had told her about spreading peanut butter into the open crevices and sprinkling sunflower or thistle seeds over it. It didn't take but a minute to make. She took a couple of twist ties from the box of trash bags and made a hanger for the top of the pine cone, then walked outside to hang it on a limb near the fence post where the bird liked to be.

The heat washed over her as soon as she stepped onto the porch. The robin sang out.

"Good morning." That little bird stretched even taller and louder to tweet a greeting back to her. "I brought you—"

"Hey, Merry Anna."

Startled, she spun around, dropping the pine cone on the ground. "You scared me." And then it registered. "Kevin?" Even being warned that he'd been around, she hadn't expected him to surprise her like this. "What are you doing here?"

"I came to bring you back home." He smiled, as if she should be happy to see him, which she absolutely was not.

His smile ticked her off. She didn't like it one bit that he'd crossed into her sanctuary, a place she'd for the first time truly understood what it was like to feel peace within.

"I don't know why it took me so long to figure it out," he said with a snicker. "I was talking to your folks, and I realized what I should've done long ago. If you wanted me to chase you down and beg you to come back, you should have just stuck around rather than force me to go to pretty great lengths to track you down."

"You shouldn't have. If I'd wanted you to know where I was, I'd have given you that information myself. How *did* you find me?"

"I had the collections team do some digging. They tracked down credit card charges."

"You are not on those cards. You never were." She'd closed every account they'd ever held jointly, not wanting to take any chances that he might be able to access her credit or information.

"Wasn't that hard." He swept his arm toward the fields. "You really did come out to the middle of nowhere. No wonder you could live on that little bit of money. Look at this place. Our garage was bigger than this. Is this really where you've been living?"

She didn't want to get into it with him. She stopped owing him answers when they'd filed for divorce.

"You need to leave. Clearly, you don't understand what divorce means. I've already told the sheriff about you." Angry heat flushed her cheeks. "I know you broke into my house. Neighbors look out for each other around here."

"I didn't break in. It wasn't locked."

"That's really your word against mine, isn't it?"

"Okay, you've made your point. It was hot out here waiting for you, and honestly I couldn't believe you were actually living in that place. I had to see for myself." He touched her arm. "You do know I would never be able to live in a place like this. That wager means nothing if this is the manner in which you expect me to live."

She pulled away from him.

"Let's just roll back time. I screwed up. Your folks aren't too happy about all this, so it's time you got back to work." He lifted his hand. "I'll do whatever it is you want me to do."

"I want you to leave right this minute—that's what I want you to do. I'm going to march right into that house and call the sheriff to come haul you away."

"You wouldn't." He laughed.

"Don't try me. I'm no longer the person you were married to. I'm quite sure I'll surprise you with how certain I am that I will call, and I *will* press charges." Her heart was in her throat. "I know you've been schmoozing my parents, trying to wriggle your way into their good graces, or, more importantly, their pocket now that you're not living off me."

"You've played your little game long enough. I get it. You're still mad."

"No, honestly, I'm not. I'm happy to be rid of you. My life has never been better." She didn't know why she was bothering to go into this with him, but she couldn't stop herself. "What's the matter, Kevin? Have they finally figured out you can't do that job you talked them into?"

His lips twitched.

"I told them you're not qualified for that job," Merry Anna said. "You can't fake your way for long."

"So, *you're* the reason they're suddenly pushing me so hard?"

"No, that's part of the job. Of course, you wouldn't know

that, because you never have been able to stick it out long enough to really commit to one."

This time that twitch turned into a snarl, and he grabbed her arm. "Come on. We're leaving."

"Stop it!" she yelled at him. "I'm not going anywhere with you."

"I saw you come back from next door in the middle of the night. I guess that's what or *who* has you all tangled up in this little town."

"That is none of your business."

"I miss you. I've never loved anyone like I love you, Merry Anna. My life is just . . . I need you to give me another chance. I'm a changed man. No more running around. I promise I won't ever do that again. That was a mistake."

She started laughing. Everything he said, she'd wanted so badly to hear right after she'd caught him. If only he'd said those things then, she'd have been wrapped up in their relationship forever.

Even throughout the divorce, it probably would've swayed her. After all, she'd never known a relationship with anyone else.

But now she knew she didn't need someone to be complete. She knew she was more than her work. All those investments and properties she'd fought for in the divorce—she hadn't missed them at all.

"It's not going to happen." She started for the house. He was hot on her heels, but she didn't let it stop her. She didn't even turn around.

He called out from behind her, "You can't be married to someone since high school and just flip a switch. You can't run away and pretend none of it ever happened."

She raised her hand, shaking her head as she walked inside and slammed the door.

"Who are you to judge me? I made one little mistake. You won't even listen."

Her breath coming out in short puffs, she ran to where her phone was plugged in next to her bed. She fumbled, wishing she'd locked the door behind her, hoping he'd already left. Finally, she pressed send on Krissy's number.

"Krissy, it's Merry Anna. Kevin is out front. Can you call Grady for me? Please hurry." She dropped the phone on her bed and ran to lock the front door.

She was able to twist the dead bolt just as he grabbed the handle. She let out a breath.

He banged on the door.

"Get out here and talk to me." He slapped the door three times. "It was you that broke our commitment, never having time for me. You forced me to find others to fill that void. All you did was work. You—"

"Stop it. Just stop right now!" she shouted. "I'm not perfect, but I never said I was. I realize I am partly to blame for our marriage ending, too, but you know what? It was a blessing. Yes, a blessing, Kevin. I love my new life. I'm helping people, and I'm doing things other than work. After all these years, I'm trying things that I'd never tried, and—"

"A blessing?" he sputtered.

She heard the gravel before she saw Grady's car out the sidelight next to the door. "I think your ride just showed up," she said.

Peering through the glass, she caught a glimpse of Adam and Zan over by the fence. Grady got out of his car with his hand on his hip.

Grady's voice carried. "We have a problem?"

She ran and lifted the living room window, not wanting to open the door to where Kevin was still standing. "A trespasser." She held her voice steady, determined to stand her ground with him. She glanced toward where Adam and Zan had been standing, but they weren't there now.

Kevin came over to the window, throwing his chest out to her. "Really. We're doing this?" He looked at her as if daring her.

"Yes. And if you go back to that job at the Supply Cabinet, I suggest you put in your whole eight hours a day and dot every *i* and cross every *t.* I'm not going back, but I *am* still on the board."

"Let's go, sir." Grady had come up on the porch and was towering over Kevin.

Kevin stared at her.

"Now, sir."

Kevin turned and looked at Grady, apparently not realizing until just then how big the man was.

Kevin's shoulders drooped.

She watched as Grady led Keven away to the edge of the yard. They stood talking for a minute, and then Kevin got in his car and drove off.

Once he cleared the driveway, Merry Anna stepped back outside to talk to Grady. "Thank you so much."

"So, that's your ex?"

"Yeah."

"Told him if he came back, I'd arrest him and that you would press charges. I don't think he'll bother you again, by the string of expletives he mumbled on his way out."

"I don't think he'd hurt me, but he's not welcome in my life anymore."

"You call me if he shows up again."

"I will." She sat on her stoop, catching her breath. After her heart rate slowed to normal, she walked over and picked up the pine cone and reattached the hanger. Her bird had taken refuge during the ruckus. Couldn't blame him.

She went to where Adam and Zan had been standing near the fence. They must have left when she was arguing with Kevin. *What did Adam hear?*

Chips was still saddled up at the hitching post across the way.

Adam must've come to get her for the ride. She hadn't planned on going. She was hoping to distance herself from him and ratchet down her feelings to where they all began. Friends. A much safer place if she wanted to keep her heart from getting broken.

She wanted to explain that scene, though. *Out of context, that conversation sounded awful. I have to get to Adam.*

She knew where he'd have ridden with Zan. She went inside and put on jeans and boots, then climbed the fence and ran over to Chips. "Hey, boy. I know we've only done this once, but I need you to help me out." She touched her hand to his face. "This is crazy." Her heart spun, but she didn't give herself a moment too long to think about it. If Adam could ride a wild bull, then she could certainly manage a trail horse. She lifted the reins that were loosely hooped over the post and tossed them over the saddle horn.

"Stay right there for me." She put her foot in the stirrup like Adam had shown her, and she bounced to get a leg up over the saddle. It took her a couple of tries, but then she finally pulled herself high enough to shimmy up and get her leg over with a grunt. It couldn't have been pretty. This was so much easier with his help. "Come on, Chips."

She pressed her legs tight against his body, then used her

stirrups to flap them, but with no spurs, it didn't do much. "I have no idea what I'm doing here, Chips. Take me to Adam."

Chips let out a fluttering breath and began walking. She wobbled in the saddle, then finally tried to relax. "I'm trusting you to get me there in one piece."

30

Adam heard twigs snap from over in the tree line. He and Zan sat at the old picnic table next to the trailer, making a wreath out of dried leaves, acorns, and pine cones they'd gathered in the woods.

The pile of those items was just a reminder of how hot and dry it had been. The mess of foliage looked more like fall than the middle of summer. Sometimes when the days were hot like this, severe storms popped up in an instant.

Zan tucked twigs into the twisted circle Adam had fashioned out of vines and an old hay string he had in his saddlebag. There wasn't much you couldn't fix with string.

He kept his eye on the tree line. The leaves began to curl upward in want of moisture that was sure to come. A moment later, thunder rolled in the distance.

He was getting ready to move Zan inside, when the unmistakable sound of a horse sighing from the mountain path alerted his nerves. Had Chips backed off the hitching post? Adam hadn't tied him but had just tossed the reins over top of the post. Normally, Chips would stand there until dark if no one came and put him away.

The horse whinnied from behind him and shifted from foot to foot.

On alert for Zan's safety, Adam stood.

Another whinny came from the woods path, and Chips cleared the trees. Merry Anna was riding.

"Merry Anna!" Zan yelled. "We're making crafts!" She scrambled to her feet from the picnic table.

"You wait here," he said to Zan. She sat back down, and he took off toward Merry Anna.

He walked in long strides right up to Chips and put a possessive hand on the horse's bridle. "What, now you're a horse thief too?"

"I just borrowed him." She patted him on the neck, and Adam wished Chips hadn't responded to her so gently. "I needed to get to you to explain . . . and I thought this would be the fastest way. Plus, he knew the way. I didn't. You invited me."

"Then you're now uninvited." There wasn't even the tiniest hint of teasing in the statement.

"I don't know what all you heard, but—"

"But what does it matter?" He looked away.

"Let me explain." Her brows lifted, concerned he'd misunderstood something he'd overheard. "Please, Adam."

His lips were pressed tight, his head shaking in disbelief that she was even sitting there on his horse. "Probably wasn't your first time riding a horse either, was it?"

"What?" She seemed to process his comment. "Yes, it was. What did you hear?"

"I heard enough. You've been married half your life. I'm not the kind of guy that spends his time with another man's wife, Merry Anna. I thought more of you." Disgust hung in the back of his throat. "I trusted you, confided in you."

Adam looked at Chips and mumbled the word *traitor* under his breath.

"Why couldn't you have just been straight with me?" he asked. "Was that too much to expect? Really?"

"I didn't mislead you. I'm not married."

"I heard him." He looked at her, wondering why part of him wanted to believe her. But he'd heard it with his own ears.

"I'm going through a lot of changes. You're a big part of that. I've learned so much about myself since I've been in Antler Creek. Look at me. I'm on a horse." She raised her hands in the air. "Look, no hands." She waved them, a little smile playing on her lips. "Okay, not funny."

Zan took the gesture as a friendly cue she could join in. Adam spun around but kept his tone in check. "Zan, you keep working on that wreath. I'm going to talk to Merry Anna for a minute, okay?"

"Yes sir." She sat back down, pressing pine needles into the wreath.

"Adam, I'm divorced. I was divorced, papers in hand, well before I ever rolled into this town."

He didn't comment.

"Before I came to Antler Creek, I believed the breakup was all Kevin's fault. He cheated on me, and I caught him red handed. The divorce wasn't pretty, and I ended up having to pay him alimony. He wants more. Now I do think I'm part to blame for that failed relationship. I didn't break the marriage contract like he did, but I did have my priorities wrong. I put my job first, before everything. I was so dedicated to that job that I didn't even know who I was anymore."

"Married to that guy since high school? That's a long time. How could you have not told me you'd been married?"

"At first, I didn't think I'd be in Antler Creek long enough for it to matter, and you know what? I wasn't proud of it. I was hurt and embarrassed, and I was searching for something inside myself."

"You were playing a game. You were just a character in a movie or in a book, letting us be the backdrop for whatever it was you had going on in your head. People around here don't do things like that. They are sincere. This is real life. Real responsibility."

"You're going to tell *me* about responsibility?"

"I may not be doing everything right, but at least I'm trying," he said. "You made a fool of me."

"Don't pass judgment on me for not being completely transparent," said Merry Anna. "You weren't so transparent either."

He was tempted to tell her why he was in Archdale last night, but what was the point? "I'm not having this conversation."

"Adam, I was faithful to Kevin the whole time I was married and even through our divorce. I never made light of our marriage contract. I wasn't perfect, but I didn't just run off. Look, he was here to cause trouble. Tara caught him poking around my house. He's grasping at straws. I was his meal ticket for a long time."

"He took advantage of you." Adam's words were steady. "It's why you were worried I was doing the same thing."

"And that wasn't fair. I know it." Her words sounded sincere. "I've wasted a lot of precious time doing things that didn't matter. I want my life to be different. I'm different now."

He wanted to believe her.

"I was so embarrassed that Kevin wouldn't keep a job that I never even told my parents. They were completely unsupportive of the divorce. They think once you get married, you stay married at all costs. But I couldn't live with the cheating. I carried the burden of that broken heart and disrespect. It hurt." She swept a tear from her cheek. "No journey is perfect. I know that, and I'm not looking for you to feel sorry for me."

If she weren't on that horse, if she were standing right here in front of him, he'd hold her. "I *am* sorry that happened to you." He put his hand out to help her get down.

She placed her hand in his and turned in the saddle, placing her other hand on his shoulder, then swinging her leg over and sliding down.

"I'm sorry I didn't tell you sooner. I didn't know he'd tracked me down. He had no right to do that. I promise I'll be here for you. For Zan. I know we could do this. I *really* like you, reckless ways and all, but if that's not what you want, if you just need a friend, I'll be here for that too."

"He said you needed to go back to your old job."

"There's more that I should've told you, but I can explain. I worked in the family business. I never knew anything else. When I stopped here, it was not my plan to meet someone. I didn't plan to stay but a week or two, but this place, you . . . you captured my heart."

"Merry Anna, I can't deal with all the secrets and half truths. I'm on shaky ground here. I have no idea what I'm doing. I'm the father of a five-year-old, and I just turned my whole life's path on its head. I can't suffer a speed bump. There's too much at risk. The only thing I do know is that I have to put Zan first."

"I agree completely. I can help with that."

"You accused me of using you to do that very thing." He didn't know what to think. "No, I can't deal with all this right now. I need time." He shrugged and turned away. It wasn't easy doing the right thing.

She walked Chips over to the hitching post and laid the reins over it. For a moment, he thought she might go sit at the table with Zan and stay, and part of him wanted her to.

"Hi, Merry Anna," Zan called out.

"Hi, Zan." Merry Anna made her way back over to where he stood. "I'm going to walk home." She took a long steadying breath. "Adam, you're really special to me. I can't imagine you not being in my day-to-day. This town is important to me too. I plan to make my life here. I hope you can find it in your heart to forgive me." She pressed her hand to his forearm. "You don't have to believe me or even be my friend, but please, please forgive me."

He lowered his gaze and swallowed.

"The truth, no matter what you heard, is that you and I have been there for each other. Both of us are going through big changes in our lives. I don't know if our paths intersected just to force us in new directions or if we are meant to be together, but something happened here." She patted her hand to her heart.

He nodded, knowing exactly what that meant.

He felt it too, but he let her go.

31

Merry Anna walked through the woods, feeling hurt and questioning her actions.

Had she just been playing a part? Had she been searching for herself so badly that she'd made this cowboy her hero?

She reached out and pulled a leaf from a low tree branch. Twisting it between her fingers, she questioned her heart.

Her phone dinged. She was reluctant to even look, but when she did, it was a message from her mother:

> Kevin told us he showed up on your doorstep. We were wrong about him. He's fired. Forget that stupid wager with him. He's bamboozling money wherever he can. We're sorry. Please come home.

She knew what her mother wanted to hear, but she couldn't do it. She couldn't leave Antler Creek.

What I feel is real, isn't it? This isn't just about the town. It's Adam. I love him, and I love this town, and I love Zan. This is real love.

She'd never loved like this before. She'd never felt this strong pull that touched her soul. *I love you, Adam.* Just as Tara had said, she was more when she was with him. *This is special, and I want to be a part of it.*

Tears streamed down her cheeks.

She sucked in a gulp of air, sniffing back the waves of emotion.

Her eyes ached, tears blurring the path. She wasn't even sure if she was going the right way.

She hadn't spent her time with Adam and Zan to fill a void or try them on for size. She loved sharing with them. When he sat with her in church, she felt different. When Zan reached up and held her hand, she changed inside. Things she never knew she'd yearned for became so clear.

She went home and put a wet cloth on her face. Lying on the couch, she cried herself to sleep and didn't wake until it was dark.

She got up and walked outside. A lunar halo circled the moon. She'd grown to love the way every day brought her something new to appreciate. As she gazed into the sky, heat lightning flashed in the distance.

Lowering herself to the steps, she thought about all the things that had happened since she arrived in Antler Creek.

Frogs croaked, sending out banjo-like twangs even longer than normal, pulling her into a trance until a clap of thunder startled her back. She jumped up and went inside to close the windows. A storm was brewing, inside and out.

The next morning, Tara called and woke Merry Anna.

"Hello?" Merry Anna answered without even opening her eyes.

"Did I wake you?" Tara asked.

"Yes." Merry Anna felt like she had cotton in her mouth. "It's okay."

"I can't believe you're sleeping through this storm. That

thunder shook my house so hard it made the glasses clink together to the tune of 'Jingle Bells.' I wanted to check on you."

"I didn't hear a thing." But she heard it now. Merry Anna turned on her bedside lamp.

"Thought I'd come up and have you help me search for the perfect bathroom hardware," Tara said.

"I'm not going to be able to do that today."

"Are you okay?" Tara asked. "I really didn't call about hardware. I'm worried about you."

Merry Anna felt herself choke on a tear. She didn't want to worry Tara, but she also couldn't make herself get up this morning. Funny how she never felt this low when her marriage ended but that today it was hard to even breathe. "I'm fine. Yesterday was a long day."

"I saw the sheriff. Figured that good-for-nothing ex of yours had shown back up."

"He did, but I'm okay."

"Want me to bring you some lunch? Or ice cream? A good pint of chocolate always does me good."

"No, it's a messy day. You don't need to be out there in it. Thank you, though. That's really sweet of you."

She moved from the bed to the couch, but that was about as far as she got all morning. Krissy texted her.

KRISSY: Weather is going to be crazy tomorrow.
We won't have many customers.
MERRY ANNA: Thank you.
KRISSY: You let us know if you need anything.
MERRY ANNA: I'll see you Monday.

It rained through the afternoon, gusts making the bunkhouse walls creak. The weather seemed fitting for what she was going through. The words from last week's sermon popped into her mind.

"The Father is with you and will keep you anchored until this storm passes."

And although the wind battered the side of the building and the thunder crashed almost in time with the lightning, meaning the storm was right over her, she wasn't afraid.

The lights flickered. She gathered the candles she'd bought and put them together on the coffee table. All were decorative, not likely to cast much light. The sky was dark, clouds so close she felt as if she could stand on the roof and grab one or, better yet, shoo it away.

She brought up the weather report on her phone. She'd never even thought about getting a little emergency radio. Flash flooding and more rain. Several counties were under weather alerts, and Wiles County was right in the crosshairs.

Something crashed against the back door. She ran to check. Thank goodness it hadn't broken the window, but her plants, even though they were on the porch, were getting pummeled. All her perfect tomatoes were scattered in the bottom of the boat, some out on the patio decking.

She ran outside, grabbing a plant or two at a time and setting them inside until she'd rescued them all from her boat garden. They were heavy from the water and dripping everywhere, so she grabbed towels and transferred the plants to the bathtub and the sink, carefully draining the water and propping up the waterlogged stems.

She pushed towels against the back door where the water had blown in. Chilly from the cold rain, she changed clothes and blew her damp hair dry.

Not a second after she put her hair dryer down, a loud bang made her scream, and the lights went out.

She opened the drapes, hoping to get a little of the afternoon light, but the clouds were so thick that it was like dusk.

She saw her bird feeder half-submerged near the fence. Water rushed like a rocky creek down the driveway and past Tara's, almost circling her house like a moat.

I hope this rain slows down soon.

It was too dark to read, so she grabbed a pillow and blanket from her bedroom and settled in on the couch. The sound of the rain was soothing in a strange way, so loud that no other thoughts were able to settle on her brain. She grabbed her phone to call and check on Tara, but the battery was dead. She wished she'd thought to charge it this morning.

Night came, and there wasn't light for as far as she could see. The lightning and thunder had finally subsided, but the rain still fell in a steady, drenching hurry.

32

On Saturday morning, the sky was brighter, and the rain had slowed to more of a menacing drizzle. She got up, put her raincoat on, and walked outside to survey the damage. A tree had fallen on the fence, and the water was so deep that it covered Tara's porch.

Leaves and debris were scattered everywhere.

From there, she could see the lower pasture at Adam's. Usually, there weren't any horses down there, but today there were three, and they were up to their bellies in water in the gully. A huge tree had fallen across the paddock, blocking them in.

The horses were pushing through the water, trying to find high ground. They seemed afraid and frantic, and she tried to think of a way to help. She put on her swimsuit, knowing she'd be sopping wet, then put on a pair of yoga pants and her rain jacket. She glanced around, wondering what she might take with her to get down to them. She headed outside.

The ground was soft, and in some places, the water hit past her knees. She fell in the slippery mud.

She went back up to the house, but her heart ached for those horses struggling below. If she could just get down the hill, she could open that gate, and the horses could come up the hill. It was better for them to be loose in her yard than in that deep water.

This wasn't oceanfront property when I moved in.

That thought triggered an answer. She ran through the house, almost slipping on the glossy wooden floors before she grabbed the back door and started dragging the boat down the steps.

I hope this thing is seaworthy. At least if it tipped over, the water wouldn't be over her head. As long as she kept her cool, she'd be fine.

The boat was easier to drag once it hit the water. She took off her belt and hooked the boat to the fence pole, then waded over to her driveway gate and closed it.

She unhooked the boat, then lifted one leg and put it inside and threw herself headlong into it. The boat slid forward, and she felt like one of those bobsledders in the Olympics as she floated downhill.

Except I don't have a clue what I'm doing.

The boat skimmed through the water, and she didn't really have any way to steer except to lean, which she wasn't entirely sure was even working. It could have just been the luck of the terrain, but she made it almost all the way down the hill before the boat came to a stop on a flat ledge. She got out and dragged it over right in front of the red pole gate. The horses whinnied and threw their heads.

I'm coming.

She didn't take a running start, instead setting the boat close to the edge and stepping into it. Cherry tomatoes and leaves and stems were squished into a messy gazpacho at the bottom that looked like a bloody mess. She sat and scooched her weight forward until she was moving again. It took a while to make it the rest of the way down. By the time she was within fifty feet of the gate, her legs were burning.

She climbed out of the boat and walked the rest of the way. "It's okay. I'm coming."

Unlatching the gate was almost impossible. Her hands were cold and soaked.

Come on! I didn't come all this way not to be able to do this. She switched hands and then pressed as hard as she could to get the clasp to open and slide over the link. The gate finally swayed. She walked it open, having to push it past all the debris that had been swept in its path.

She called as she'd heard Adam do that day, "Hee-yah! Over here. Yah! Yah!"

She waved her hands in the air. "Horses, this way! There's drier ground up here. Please!"

Tara called from across the way, "Merry Anna! What are you doing?"

"Are you okay?" she yelled back.

"Yes." Tara stood there in water up to her calves where the porch was. "Power's out and the house is on spin cycle, I think, but I'm fine."

Merry Anna hated to hear that. Tara had been working so hard on that place. She hoped it was insured for this act of God.

"I tried to call," Tara shouted. "You didn't answer. I was worried."

"Sorry!" *I was having a pity party* wasn't something she was going to yell across the field.

Finally, one of the horses pulled through the muck and water, his head bouncing up and down to pull himself forward, and came through the gate. The others followed along.

Yes!

The horses galloped up the hill, their hooves splashing against the drenched ground. Merry Anna grabbed a branch and shoved it through the gate and fence to lodge it open. She got back over to the boat and pushed it through the water, holding on to it for balance until she got to Tara's.

"Can you believe this?" Merry Anna said.

"Never seen anything like it." Tara walked over to her. "Crazy!"

"It's not going to be an easy walk, but I think we can make it back up to my place if we can just get up to the road from here. We can steady ourselves with the boat. I don't have electricity either, but you can't stay here up to your ankles in water."

"You got that right. My toes are numb already."

"Put a few things in a garbage bag and tie it up tight. Your insurance information, for one."

"Gotcha. I'll be right back."

Merry Anna hoped Adam and Zan were okay.

Tara came out and tossed two small bags into the boat. "Let's get this one-boat regatta going." She sat on the porch and slid to the ground, one hand on the side of the boat.

They made it a good ways from Tara's house, but as they tried to get their footing to climb back up to the roadbed, the wind shifted. It seemed as if in a single gust, the sky opened again, and the rain fell in buckets. Each drop stung Merry Anna's skin. "I'm sorry. Oh gosh. I don't think you're any better off now," she yelled over the rain.

"I'm cold." Tara's chin quivered.

Merry Anna knew they couldn't do much, and they were both tiring quickly. Progress up the hill was almost impossible.

"I think we're going to have to wait until the rain stops," Merry Anna said. She could see how hard this was on Tara. "I'm going to tip the boat up on its side against the board fence right here, and we're just going to hunker down."

"I can help you."

Merry Anna let Tara do what she could, but she took the brunt of the effort to get the boat in place. They huddled together. At least they were out of the rain and wind. She held Tara's freezing hands in her own. "We're going to be okay." *We are safe in Your arms.*

Tara said a prayer and squeezed Merry Anna's fingers.

33

Merry Anna was under warm blankets in the
hospital bed, still shaking. Thank goodness Grady had come
to check on her and found her and Tara huddled under the
boat, clinging to those bags that Tara had packed. He'd driven
them straight to the hospital.

She'd been falling in and out of sleep the past couple of
hours, and Krissy had been right there with her the whole
time.

"You are a true friend," Merry Anna said.

"You better believe it. I know a special person when I spot
one. I'm not about to lose you."

"I was so worried about Tara."

"I know, but she's doing fine. I'm pretty sure they're going
to keep her in here a couple of days just as a precaution because of her age. Besides, with her house flooded, this really is
the best place for her."

"She's worked so hard on that place. We're going to have to
pull folks together to help her."

"That won't be a problem."

Merry Anna closed her eyes.

"You're crazier than I am!" Adam's voice woke her.

Am I dreaming? She opened her eyes.

Adam and Zan stood at the foot of her bed. "I'd have brought flowers, but as soon as I heard, I came straight over. Thanks for calling me, Krissy."

Krissy leaned over and whispered in Merry Anna's ear, "Don't let this guy go. There's nothing that is going to break the bond you two have." She walked around the bed and gave Adam a quick hug. "I'm going to go check on Tara. I'll leave y'all. Zan, you want to come with me?"

"Can I?" She looked up at Adam.

"Yeah, go on."

Zan skipped off at Krissy's side.

"I didn't know you had that kind of thing in you," Adam said. "City girls don't do what you did back there."

"I didn't know either, but when I saw your horses struggling, I just had this need to help them."

"Thank you. What you did was crazy, but it was definitely helpful. I'd like to ask that you don't do it again, though."

"I think I can agree to that," she said.

"Remember when you asked me to forgive you?"

She squinted and nodded.

"I do forgive you. How could I not?" He placed his palm on her chin.

She reached up and placed her hand on top of his.

"Merry Anna, I never meant to take advantage of you with taking care of Zan. I'm really sorry if it looked that way." He kissed her on the cheek. "I have strong feelings for you. I'd do anything for you. Anything."

"My own baggage may have gotten in the way. My self-confidence took a real hit after all that with Kevin. I was broken. You've been so good for me."

"It works both ways." He sat on the edge of the bed. "For two people who vowed they didn't have time for relationships, didn't need them, we both sure did flunk that test."

She still felt icy cold to the bone, but somewhere inside, her heart was warming. "I really want to stay here in Antler Creek. When I realized how bad the storm was, all I could think about was you and Zan. I've fallen in love with you. There you were with all your cowboy bravado, like no one I'd ever known before. You didn't want anything. You didn't pressure me. It was safe, I thought. I don't even know how this happened. I want to be here." *Please give me a reason to stay.*

"I want you here too. They say God has our paths all planned out before we're even on this earth. He knows what He's doing. Who are we to fight it? I'm done fighting it. I feel my path leading me in a whole new direction, and you're right in the middle of that road. I'm scared—I won't lie—but I know it's going to be okay."

"Adam, I'll love you forever, and I don't even care if that means I have to hold my breath for eight seconds while you try to win a saucer-sized gold belt buckle." She sucked in a stuttering breath. "I'll be there for you. For Zan. Forever."

"Well, I think I can make that choice easier for you."

"What do you mean?"

"I made my decision. That's why I went down to Archdale the other night. I didn't ride. I took the offer from Doc to join his sports medicine team on the rodeo circuit."

"You didn't ride?"

"No. I'll be honest—when I got there, I thought about it, but I'm pretty sure if I'd tried to, Doc wouldn't have approved me to ride after that last incident."

"You had already decided?"

"Yes. I'll be switching gears. All that money I've been putting aside for bucking bulls—it was a risky plan anyway. Everyone knows it's hard work and genetics, but it's also a heck of a lot of luck to come up with rank bulls that pay out big. I'm going to be investing that money differently. Might even send my daughter to med school and work in some vacations. Do you know I've never been on a vacation?"

"Never?"

"No. I've traveled, but always for rodeo." He gripped her hand.

"That feels good. Your hand is so warm." She squeezed it. "We have some planning to do."

"Well, the first thing we need to plan is for you to be well enough to go to Texas with Zan and me on Friday. It's my first day on my new job, and Zan's grandparents live just outside of Mesquite. Carly is staying with them. She's doing better and ready to see Zan. I think Zan should get the chance to visit with them and for us to have a little alone time."

"Are you sure?"

"I already called them. They are so excited to see her, and she's ready for it too. It'll be her first plane ride."

"So many firsts are yet to come," she said.

"I want you to be with me when I go to my folks' house. I've got to set some years of mistakes straight with them."

"Anything. Yes. I'm ready."

"Oh, but one thing. It might be better if we don't mention this little storm-rescue deal here. I don't want them to think you're more reckless than I am."

"That would have been hard to beat. I'm no cowboy, after all."

He kissed her on the nose. "Rodeo and a cowboy lifestyle are part of my history. I used to believe that was my destiny. Now I know that Zan is my priority and you were sent to be on this journey with me. What remains true is that the day I heard your ex say you were his, my heart twisted and I knew I could never live without you. I'm so thankful for you."

Krissy walked back into the room with Zan, whose mouth was downturned. "Miss Tara is very sad about her house," Zan said. "We're going to have to help her."

"We sure will," Adam said. He stretched out his arms from his spot sitting on the edge of Merry Anna's hospital bed.

"Can I get up there with you too?" Zan asked.

"You sure can." Merry Anna scooted over as much as she could.

Zan climbed up with a little help from Adam and sat between them.

"The important thing," Zan said, "is everyone is okay."

Merry Anna felt the hot tears coming down her face. "Better than okay." She turned to Adam. "I'm so thankful I said yes to new opportunities, else I'd never have met you or Zan or felt all this."

"I have a feeling Zan is going to keep us in line," he said to Merry Anna. He looked at Zan and then back at Merry Anna. "If they gave gold buckles for the cowboy luckiest in love, mine would be as big as a Thanksgiving platter. You two are my best girls," Adam said. "Forever."

Merry Anna thought for a moment. "I just got an idea for the perfect barn quilt to represent the three of us, and I'm going to need a lot of gold paint."

Acknowledgments

A special thank you to the Ogburn family of Tobaccoville, North Carolina, who so kindly welcomed my family over the holidays and into the New Year. I'm grateful for their hospitality as we searched for a new home and the inspiration they provided of the authentic cowboy lifestyle while I worked to get this book done.

The funny thing is, I'd pitched this story long before we landed in the bunkhouse at the Ogburn family farm. Yes, a real bunkhouse, just like the one in this book. My family says if what I'm writing is going to come true, they'd like me to set the next book in a mansion or on a beautiful island. I thank my family for their support and patience, allowing me to have the best job in the world.

Thank you to my agent, Steve Laube, for always being available and helping me navigate the ever-changing publishing business with grace—and for always having a kind and motivating word and a few good jokes too. Smiles are priceless.

I'm so grateful to write with the amazing WaterBrook team. Each member brings a special touch to the package. Heartfelt thanks to my editor, Becky Nesbitt, for helping me dig deeper and dream bigger to create a memorable story. Leslie Calhoun is a champion and always goes the extra mile to help my stories gain visibility in this crowded marketplace. I appreciate you all.